*Allises*

*Happy Reading*

*♡ Kristy*

# *Beyond the Fortuneteller's Tent*

*Kristy Tate*

*It was lovely to meet you!*

# Other Books by Kristy Tate

The Witching Well series
*The Highwayman Incident*
*The Cowboy Encounter*
The Beyond series
*Beyond the Fortuneteller's Tent*
*Beyond the Hollow*
*Beyond the Pale*
The Rose Arbor Series
*A Ghost of a Second Chance*
*The Rhyme's Library*
*Losing Penny*
*Love at the Apple Blossom Inn*
Seattle Fire
*Stealing Mercy*
*Rescuing Rita*
Other
*Hailey's Comments*
*Stuck With You*
*A Light in the Christmas Cafe*

# Beyond the Fortuneteller's Tent
## Copyright 2013 Kristy Tate

# Beyond the Fortuneteller's Tent

# Chapter One

*The Royal Oaks Renaissance Faire is the brain baby of Mrs. Brighton, part-time English teacher and full time witch. Glass blowers, potters, and herbalists mingle with students, teachers and parents on sawdust strewn paths lined with wooden stalls. Axe throwing is not only allowed but encouraged. Games include Drench-a-Wench (Mrs. Brighton) and Soak-a-Bloke (Principal Olsen). Wizards, elves, beer and barely covered booties are all welcome as long as they help raise thousands of dollars for the high school drama department.*
*—Petra's notes*

Petra stared at the fortuneteller's tent -- silky curtains, beaded strings, the faint aroma of vanilla, a gaudy riot of color. She'd been waiting forever, but now that she was here, she took a breath and then another.

Robyn squeezed her hand. "It's so romantic," she whispered. "This is the perfect place for him to ask you."

"It's so him, right?" Petra returned Robyn's squeeze, but her gaze never left the tent. She thought it ugly, garish in a more-is-less way. She sighed and wished that Kyle had asked without hoopla. Maybe she should have asked him. Maybe they shouldn't go. Prom was so yesterday, dated like a debutant ball… *Or a jousting competition,* she thought, her gaze going to the nearby stadium.

The frustration of denial settled between her shoulder blades like an unreachable itch. Why did she even care about prom? She'd been with Kyle for months; a silly dance didn't define their relationship.

Or did it? Some of her friends already had their dresses. Petra hadn't bought one, that would have been presumptuous but she knew which one she wanted. She'd found the perfect shoes. She hoped Kyle would be okay with the coral-colored vest she'd picked out for him.

"It's so who?" Zoe demanded.

Petra put her hand on top of Zoe's orange curls. Zoe was the pooper at the party, the stepsister that never should have come to the fair.

Petra could understand why her stepmother, Laurel, didn't want to take Zoe to a hospital to visit her Aunt Ida. No one sane would ever want to take Zoe anywhere, especially a place where people needed quiet and rest.

Robyn rolled her eyes at Petra. Robyn and Petra called themselves tele-friends, because they could read each other like open books. Now Robyn nodded at the tent, *just go.*

"Do you think he's in there?" Petra whispered.

Robyn widened her eyes. "He said he would be, didn't he?"

"Who's he?" Zoe demanded. "Are you talking about Kyle?"

Petra swallowed and tried to forget Zoe's existence. "He didn't *say* anything, but his note said to meet at the fortuneteller's tent. What if he didn't send the note? What if this is a joke?"

"Then it's not a funny one." Robyn shook her head and her curls bounced around her shoulders. "It was Kyle." She sounded way more confident than Petra felt. Robyn cut her a sideways glance, and another flicker of doubt tickled Petra's thoughts. Why did she suspect the fortuneteller's tent was more Robyn's idea than Kyle's? Petra squelched the thought. Kyle was her fortune. Nothing else mattered.

"Kyle has *hotitude* that sadly so often accompanies physical beauty," Zoe sighed, parroting her mom.

Petra groaned. Did her parents dislike Kyle because he was rock-star gorgeous? She shook away the other more legitimate reasons why her parents might not like Kyle.

"Ignore her," Robyn mouthed over Zoe's head.

"And just go already." She gave Petra a push toward the tent.

Petra dug in her silky flats. "Wait. How do I look?"

"As always, you're beautiful." Robyn straightened Petra's tiara, gave her a small hug, and then turned Petra tent-ward.

"Pretty as a Petra poopy picture," Zoe muttered.

Petra frowned at Zoe and then glanced at her dress, last year's prom gown. She and Robyn were the only two at the fair dressed as princesses. All around her she saw women in laced up bodices, men in tights and knee-high boots, horses in bright cloths and even a snowy white owl on a perch. Zoe in her pink flip-flops, cut-up pillowcase and drapery tassel looked more in place than Petra and Robyn. Petra sniffed. She loved the silky fabric, the seed pearls, and poufy skirt and didn't care that she was overdressed. She put a finger on the tiara; maybe the faux diamonds were too much. Too late now.

Straightening her shoulders, clutching her beaded purse, she headed to the tent. Her steps faltered, and she turned back. "Come with me," she said to Robyn, taking and tugging her friend's hand.

Zoe's mouth dropped open. "You can't leave

me alone!"

Robyn motioned to the fair-goers: teachers, fellow students, neighbors. "Alone?"

Zoe's eyes, for a moment, looked almost as crazy as her hair. "There are witches, people with swords, wild animals!"

Petra saw several people she knew, but Zoe had only just moved to Royal Oaks. Petra knelt so she could look in Zoe's crazy eyes. "And not one of them will hurt you, I promise. It's a petting zoo— no wild animals! But if anyone bugs you, *which they won't,* call a yellow jacket," Petra said, referring to the Royal Oaks security guards who patrolled the school grounds and used blow horns to keep peace. "Please, just sit."

Petra stood and pointed at a convenient stump, wishing for the zillionth time that Zoe would take lessons from their dog, Frosty, who greeted all instructions with lolling tongue and wagging tail. Zoe didn't receive instructions; she counterattacked them. Poodles and stepsisters had very little in common, except for in Zoe's case, the hair-do.

"If you leave me here—" Zoe began.

Petra silenced her by holding up a finger. "If you can be quiet, sit and not say a word, I'll buy you a funnel cake." She raised her eyebrows to see if Zoe would take the bribe, or if she needed to toss in a caramel apple. Health-foodie Laurel wouldn't pony up for brand-name peanut butter, let alone treats fried in oil and covered with sugary powder.

Zoe humphed, then sat and picked at the hem of her pillowcase tunic. Petra followed her gaze to the corral across the path. Zoe's expression lit up. "I want a funnel cake and to ride *that* horse."

Petra and Robyn both turned to watch a guy lead a stallion through a wooden gate.

"Giddy-up," Robyn said, staring.

The guy had brown, shoulder length hair tied back with a leather thong and wore soft, fawn-colored breeches and matching knee-high boots. His white shirt billowed around a wide leather belt that hung about his hips. Three simultaneous thoughts struck Petra. First: Everyone else, including herself, wore costumes, but this guy looked at ease in his breeches and boots, as if they were his everyday clothes. Second: His eyes and the small smile curving his lips sent a jolt of recognition up her spine although she knew they'd never met. She would have remembered. Third: This guy would never wear a coral colored vest.

"Isn't he awesome?" Zoe breathed, her eyes large and round. "He's so huge."

Robyn gave Zoe a look, and Petra laughed. "You can't ride him," she said, watching the

Arabian toss his mane and pull at the reins held by the guy. The stallion fought the bit, rose up on his hind legs and scissored the air with his hooves. "He's not one of the ponies they lead through the rink."

Zoe frowned, sending her freckles south. "I'm sure he'd rather be with me on the trail than in that horrible jousting place." Earlier, they had tried watching the knights' competitions. Zoe, unconcerned for the men being thwacked about by lances, had wailed for the sweat-dripping horses.

"I'm sure you're right, Zoe, but I'm pretty sure I'm right too," Petra said. "They'd never let you take him out of their sight. Besides, he looks fast and barely tamed."

"I like them fast and barely tamed," Robyn said under her breath, smoothing her pink chiffon skirt.

From the jousting arena came cheering and huzzahs. Petra heard the horses' hooves thundering and the clanging of lances hitting shields and armor. She smelled roasted turkey legs, the fires from the pottery kilns and dung. Her senses careened on overload, and when the guy with the horse caught her eye and winked, dizziness and a skin-pricking sensation of déjà vu washed over her.

Zoe looked up at Petra, smiled and said in a

voice as sweet as funnel cake, "If you let me ride that horse I won't tell about you face-sucking Kyle."

"There's been no face-sucking!" At least not in front of Zoe.

Zoe put her fists on her hips and jutted out her chin. "Who says?"

Petra blew at a loose strand of hair in front of her eyes. "You can't ride that horse!"

Zoe's gaze cut to the corral and lingered on the stallion. "But you can ask if I can."

Robyn nodded, a flirty smile on her lips. "We can ask."

Petra shot her a look that said, *Traitor*.

"Hot Horse Guy," Robyn murmured, flipping her brown curls over her shoulder.

"And offer him money," Zoe put in.

"How much money?" Petra nearly growled. Since her dad's marriage she'd been given an allowance 'to help you find your own financial feet in the real world,' Laurel's words. Petra's feet wanted a pair of coral-colored heels for prom.

"I saw him wink at you." Zoe's tone turned calculating. "Maybe you wouldn't need to pay him."

Petra frowned at Zoe; eight years old seemed too young to know the art of female bartering.

"We'll ask him right after we visit the fortuneteller," Robyn promised Zoe, sending a let's-get-together-soon smile at Horse Guy.

He smiled back and ducked his head.

Zoe scowled, folded her arms and watched the horses parading in the corral.

Petra turned to the fortuneteller's tent and forced herself to not look at hot Horse Guy, although she imagined she felt his gaze on her back. She towed Robyn by one wrist.

Held up by large wooden poles, the tent had brightly woven damask walls. A barrel-chested man wearing nothing but gold chains, large rings and red bloomerish pants guarded a money jar. A hand-printed sign propped by the jar read *Fester Foretells your Fate.*

"Fester?" Petra stopped short of the tent. "He sounds like he needs a squirt of Neosporin."

"You're stalling," Robyn pulled on Petra's hand.

"What if he's not in there?" Petra flashed the guy in bloomers a nervous glance but he remained motionless and expressionless, as if she and Robyn didn't even exist. What would happen if she poked him? Would he do more than flinch? Would he do even that?

"Then we'll have our fortunes read." Robyn gave the bloomer guy a sideways look, but he stared straight ahead not even looking at Robyn, which Petra found impressive. Most guys couldn't resist looking at Robyn.

"I'm telling Daddy that you ditched me," Zoe kicked her flip-flops heels against the stump.

Petra scowled at Zoe. Her parents had only been married a few months, and it stung to hear Zoe call *her* dad 'Daddy.' "We're not ditching you. It's more like we're parking you in a five-minute loading zone." Petra made a lever pulling motion. "There, I put on the emergency brake. You're stuck."

Petra turned her back on Zoe and faced Robyn. "What if Kyle doesn't think to come inside? He could stand out here forever while some hag predicts that I don't get into a good school and will end up selling shoes for the rest of my life."

"You love shoes," Robyn said. "Besides, I'm sure he's already inside."

"And, just like me, listening to every word you say!" Zoe added.

Petra gave Zoe another be-quiet-or-be-dead look, but then realized Zoe could be right. What if Kyle was on the other side of the curtain, waiting and listening? Fighting the flush creeping up her neck, Petra dropped money into Fester's jar and pushed back the curtain of crystal beads.

When the curtain fell back into place behind them, it carried the sound of breaking glass. Heavy incense hung in the air. Petra blinked, waiting for her eyes to adjust to the gloom. She scanned the tiny space, searching for Kyle. A crystal ball on a table draped in silks glowed and sent a shivery light that didn't reach the corners of the tent. Large pillows dotted tapestry rugs covering the ground.

Petra wondered if she should sit and wait. Could Kyle be hiding behind a curtain? No. He probably wasn't here yet, meaning that he hadn't heard her and Zoe. That was good. Wasn't it?

"Petra, welcome," a voice in the semi-darkness cackled.

Behind Petra, Robyn jumped. It took Petra a moment to find the owner of the voice, a hunched man on a pillow in a dark corner. Before him lay a pair of tarot cards, face up: a fool dancing, tossing stars into a purple sky and a magician holding a wand, scattering glitter.

"I'm afraid you must come alone," Fester said, leaving his gaze on Petra's face as his twisted hands gathered the cards, and tapped them into a deck.

Robyn's eyes flashed a question at Petra. Petra squeezed Robyn's hand.

"I'll wait with your sister," Robyn said.

Still expecting Kyle to show, Petra didn't watch

her friend leave, but she knew when Robyn had gone by the flash of daylight that came and then left with the rise and fall of the curtain and the tinkle of the beads.

"There are journeys some must undertake on their own," Fester the fortuneteller said, staring up at Petra.

# Chapter Two

*"No prosecution should thereafter be made on a
charge of witchcraft and that all persons professing to
occult skill or undertaking to tell fortunes might be
sentenced to imprisonment for one year, made to stand
pillory, and pledge future good behavior." George II*
*"Every person pretending or professing to tell
fortunes or using any subtle craft, means, or device, by
palmistry or otherwise to deceive, and impose on any of
His Majesty's Subjects will be deemed a vagabond and
rogue and be punished accordingly." George IV*
*So, why did they have a fortuneteller at the Royal
Oaks Renaissance Faire and not a pillory?*
*—Petra's notes*

Fester had riotous curls the same color as his
silver hooped earrings. Lined and crisscrossed, his
skin looked like aged leather. Struck by his dark
eyes, Petra stepped closer. The iris, so dark,
swallowed the pupil and appeared bottomless.
Endless.

Petra shook herself. Eyes weren't endless. She'd
learned about eyes in biology, had even studied a
cow's eye trapped in a jar of formaldehyde. Large,
yellowish and with a brown iris, the cow's eyeball

had given her a sick feeling. Her lab partner, Lloyd of the big glasses, had laughed and refused to take it from her so she'd quickly passed it to the girl behind her. Petra felt that same queasiness now, staring into the fortuneteller's eyes, but she found herself unable to look away. She cleared her throat. "I'm expecting someone. He asked me to meet him here."

Fester laughed, and the sound surprised Petra. Not an old person hoot or an evil cackle, but a laugh that sounded like church bells, the type that ring at funerals. A Dickinson poem sprang to Petra's memory: *oppresses like the heft of Cathedral tunes.* Shivers shot up her arms and she took a step back, nearly tripping on a pillow. "If Kyle isn't here, I'll just go…"

The laughter stopped. "You paid the price, did you not?"

"Well, yes, but so did Robyn." Petra reached behind her for the curtain. Her hand bumped against the beads which rattled but suddenly hushed as the man spoke.

"Then you must listen." Fester drew the fool card from the deck with a knobby finger, laid it on the rug and tapped it with a pointy fingernail. "Carrying all his possessions wrapped in a scarf, the Fool travels to destinations unknown. So filled with visions and daydreams he cannot see the dangers lying in wait. In his path, a small dog harries him, sending a warning."

Fester lifted his finger at Petra. The nail seemed almost as long as the finger, curling under as if it bent beneath its own weight. The finger and nail were both gray, the color of dead flesh. "You, my dear, are the fool. I am your warning."

*Kyle's the fool*, Petra thought, fighting a hot flash of anger, *if he thought I'd find this freak show even remotely entertaining.* She bit back a rude remark and instead asked, "Of what?"

Fester, who had been sitting in the corner, somehow suddenly flashed to Petra's side. She flinched from the strong, garlicky smell and the warmth of his body. Petra held her breath and took a step closer to the curtains that led outside.

He followed. "If you think your life is here and now, you are mistaken. Indeed, there is no time or space."

"My only mistake was putting twenty dollars in your jar." Petra's voice sounded screechy in her ears.

"Harbingers of ill will do not always mean you harm." Fester laid his fingers on Petra's arm and sent a jolt of electricity that lifted her off her feet.

Petra watched the crystal ball sail through the

air and the strings of hanging beads swayed, sounding like a rush of wind chimes. Potion jars spun in the air, tarot cards floated around her like large, one-dimensional snowflakes. The ball connected with a flying jar and shattered into thousands of pieces, crystal and potion glinting midair as the  poles supporting the draped damask groaned and teetered.

*Earthquake,* the rational part of Petra's mind told her, but Petra was listening to another voice, one that said, *run.* Amidst the fluttering curtains Petra flew, whirling her arms and feet, a mid-air mime pantomiming running.

When the earth settled, Petra found herself buried beneath a pile of fabric and pillows. She sat up, dazed. Other than the drapes of cloth and the swaying crystal beads, the tent looked about the same, give or take the tarot cards scattered about. She pushed them away so she wouldn't step on them.

Looking around, she didn't see the fortuneteller. She wondered where he was and if he was hurt. Dazed, she tried looking for him, but the incense stung the back of her throat and filled her head. Needing air, she pushed through the curtains, brushed off her dress and straightened her tiara. Taking a few faltering steps, she stopped.

The only other earthquake Petra remembered had been on Easter Sunday, less than a month earlier. She had been with her family at the dining room table and had watched the chandelier swing above the ham and creamed potatoes. That quake had rolled rather than shook and had lasted less than a minute but Zoe had wailed in terror. Zoe had to be frightened now.

*Where was Zoe?*

Too bad this town square didn't have stocks and pillory. They would have come in handy about five minutes ago. Then she would have known exactly where to find Zoe.

A three-legged, dog of indeterminate breed charged and took Petra off her feet. She landed hard on her butt in the dirt, legs splayed in front, dress around her thighs. She stared after the animal and watched the crowd filling the dusty street to see how they'd react to a dog breaking leash laws. No one seemed to notice.

Petra wanted to ask someone about the earthquake, but she didn't see anyone she knew. Where were the yellow jackets? Principal Soak-a-Bloke? Mrs. Brighton in her witch's hat? Petra stood, dusted off her dress and sat down on Zoe's abandoned stump.

Petra remembered the advice she'd been given

on a Girl's Scout hike, *when lost stay where you are.*
She didn't know if Zoe had ever received similar
advice, but it made sense that Zoe would
eventually return, if only for the funnel cake. Petra
closed her eyes, trying not to picture the trouble
she'd be in when Zoe blabbed. Maybe Robyn was
with Zoe. The thought made her feel a little better,
but when she opened her eyes, the fair looked as
strange as it had before.

Petra drew in the dirt with the toe of her slipper.
The blue shoes had a smattering of faux diamonds
across the top. She'd been annoyed about not being
able to wear heels to the prom until her dad
pointed out to her that last year's date, Micky
Lund, had yet to hit a growth spurt. Slippers were a
kinder choice. Petra hadn't cared that much about
the shoes or Micky, but she was glad now to be in
slippers.

Except none of that mattered anymore because
she was ready to go home. Not spotting Zoe's
familiar tangerine hair, Petra climbed onto the
stump for a better view. Standing with her hands
on her hips, she glanced back at the fortuneteller's
tent and then twisted around completely. Somehow
the tent had been replaced with a blacksmith's
shop. A giant fire blazed in a forge, and a thick
armed man wearing a leather apron and wielding a

hammer stood where only moments ago she'd visited Fester. Right? Petra climbed off the stump with weak knees.

The blacksmith swung his hammer onto a flaming red piece of metal and sparks flew. Again and again the hammer struck; the pounding rang in Petra's ears.

*Where is Zoe?* Petra's anger melted into confusion. She must have hit her head during the earthquake. That's why she thought she was flying mid-air. She must have had a concussion . Knowing that a head injury would soften her parents, Petra sat, waiting. Zoe and Robyn would turn up any minute…and maybe even Kyle.

But waiting didn't calm Petra. It reminded her of the very first time her mother hadn't met her after school. She'd stood at the corner near the crossing guard, surrounded by other second graders waiting for their moms, just as her mother had instructed. Eventually all the other kids disappeared into cars and she'd been left alone with the guard, who'd marched her to the office, where she had to sit on a hard plastic chair, while the gum chewing secretary  called her mom.

And then her dad.

During the second phone call, the secretary's voice had changed from cranky to hushed, and her gaze slid to Petra with a look of pity that Petra would later know too well. When her dad showed up, he seemed worried, harassed, and withdrawn. No one, not her mother or her father, had apologized for making Petra wait.

A donkey-pulled wagon rumbled by and brought Petra out of the memory. A trio of dirty-faced kids in brown cloth tunics gazed at her with wide eyes from their perch in the wagon. Their rags made Zoe's pillowcase look good.

Petra tried again to orient herself. She saw the jousting arena but not the funnel cake booth. She rubbed her head and decided that she must have left the tent from a different side. From this new angle the fortuneteller's tent looked different.

Perception can alter reality. In AP psychology they'd learned about mental maps and paradigm shifts. Thinking about Doctor Burns and the class bolstered Petra. She wasn't stupid, ditzy, or dizzy. Blonde jokes, in her case, didn't apply. Still, as she stood on the stump, she felt increasingly lost. Silly even.

She tried to recall Doctor Burn's words. *If you had an incorrect map of a city and were looking for a specific location, you would be both lost and frustrated. Experience determines perception.*

Right now she needed a map not of her psyche

but of the fair. She'd gotten lost. The three-legged dog, the blacksmith shop spouting flames and sparks (something she couldn't believe the fire marshal would allow), the three story-buildings and thatched roofed cottages, well, those were all things she hadn't noticed before when she'd been preoccupied with Kyle and his supposed prom invite.

She was on the wrong tree stump! Abandoning the stump, she wandered around looking for the fortuneteller's tent, but she couldn't find any bright colored fabrics or strings of crystal beads. Refusing to believe that she *would* have noticed a blacksmith shop spouting sparks, she squared her shoulders and set out to find the information booth where Mrs. Jordan handed out maps.

Ten minutes later when she couldn't find the booth or Mrs. Jordan, she turned toward what she hoped was the direction of the stables. She hoped to find Zoe with hot Horse Guy and thought about what she'd say to Zoe. The angry, *why did you leave the stump?* And, *why didn't you stay where I put you?* Quickly turned to, *I'm sorry I lost you.*

"Zoe!" Petra called out, her voice mingling with the calls of the vendors. "Robyn?" No one was paying any attention to her. "Zoe? Robyn? Anyone?"

\*\*\*

Emory tagged Chambers through the marketplace crowd. Farmers, artisans and peddlers shared the square, competing for business, breathing the same foul air. Hawkers called out, voices rising above the bellow of cows and the snorts of pigs, but no one called to Emory.

Two old men smoking long pipes and sitting in the shade of a vegetable cart looked up as Emory moved past them. A child teasing a cat with a bit of fish didn't see Emory, but the cat took note. Emory slipped into a dark alley, away from the market's chaos, and leaned against the wall. Dark, cool, the passage had a line of doors, but Chambers had chosen the furthest from the crowd, and, for perhaps the first time, Emory applauded Chambers' judgment.

Emory listened to the voices on the other side of the door: half past midnight, two nights hence, the rectory. Emory marveled at Chambers' audacity, at his ability to believe he worked in the name of God. Chambers didn't know Emory, or anyone, knew of his plans. Chambers' pride allowed him to believe that the Almighty would partner with such barbarians.

Emory felt no fear, although he knew if caught
Chambers would have him killed. Or try. Emory
smiled, pulled away from the door when he heard
the scratch of chairs on the stone floors. Footsteps,
shuffling, voices approaching, a rattle of the latch.
After a quick survey of the alley Emory realized the
entry, his means of escape, had been blocked by a
gaggle of geese. Not wanting to wade through
them and draw attention, Emory headed toward
the closest door. Finding it unlocked, he slipped
inside, praying the room would be uninhabited.

He saw a chair by the fire, tools spread across a
work bench and a floor strewn with wood
shavings. Emory leaned against the wall and
listened. He heard the geese, the rumble of
Chambers' voice on the other side of the wall,
villagers outside the window.

Then he heard another noise, much closer, and
more threatening.

A low growl.

Emory looked around and spotted an arthritic
mongrel slowly rising from his ragged mat. The
growl grew deeper as the dog lifted his lips
exposing jagged brown teeth.

Putting out a hand, Emory whispered, "Good
dog."

The dog's fur rose like a razorback along his

massive shoulders. His head lowered and his ears flattened. Drool gathered on his lips, and when he barked, the spittle flew.

Emory tried to listen for the men's voices, but the neighboring room now seemed hushed, while in Emory's room several noisy things happened at once. The dog lunged, sinking his teeth into Emory's breeches. A tall, apple-shaped woman wielding a large wooden spoon appeared from a back room.

"Out! Out," the woman cried, belting Emory with her spoon.

"I mean no harm," Emory said, covering his head with his arms and trying to shake the dog off his leg.

"Out! Out!" The wooden spoon beat on Emory's shoulders and back.

Tripping over the dog, which he'd managed to kick in the jaw, Emory made it to the window. The dog leaped for Emory's throat but missed as Emory clambered over the sill. Snapping at Emory's feet with brown and rotting teeth, the animal grew frantic. A tear in Emory's breeches caught on a wooden peg, but after a few moments of awkward hanging, Emory fell face first into a woodpile.

Above him, the woman shouted obscenities and the dog barked, but to Emory's relief, the room that

Chambers had occupied hadn't a window on the
woodpile side. Emory scooted off the wood,
scattering logs and planks, offered the woman a
lopsided grin and an apology. "A simple mistake,
good mistress. A wrong door, tis all." He ratcheted
up the charm in his smile and watched the
woman's expression soften. Her lips twitched as he
caught a log rolling down the street, picked it up
and waved it at her before returning it to the heap.
The gesture won him a toothless smile.

The dog, however, refused to be charmed. Paws
on the sill and head poking out, he continued to
bark, spraying slobber. He likely was too old and
rickety to clear the window, but Emory didn't stay
to find out. He ran through the alley, turned a
corner and stopped short when he saw a girl about
his age dressed in blue wandering through the
crowd. Blond hair piled on her head. Jewels
glistened in her hair and in her ears. She moved
like a feather on the wind, graceful yet aimless. A
tiny frown pulled at her lips and a worried scowl
creased her eyebrows. Turning, she faced him and
her eyes widened, as if in recognition. He took a
step toward her, pulled by an invisible cord. The
geese complained as he pushed through, honking
and pecking as they surrounded him.

"Give way, lad," the goose girl shouted.

But Emory wasn't listening to her. He strained to hear what the girl in blue was saying. Emory felt a flash of sudden, inexplicable pain, knowing she would never call for him.

*\*\*\**

A murmur ran through the crowd. Above their heads Petra caught sight of Kyle on a decked out horse. The Arabian gleamed in the late afternoon sun, mane and tail glistening like an onyx ring, and he wore a bright colored coat. Kyle had his eyes trained on a falcon flying toward the jousting arena.

"Kyle!" Petra called, relieved that the charade was near an end. Finally, he'd ask her to prom and together they could find Zoe. Mike had asked Blondie by hanging a sign on a freeway overpass. Mark had delivered a bouquet of helium balloons to Nicki. Ryan asked Heather while wearing a gorilla suit. But this had to be the most convoluted invitation ever. She swallowed her hysteria and felt a moment of relief.

A few people turned to look at Petra, but Kyle didn't. Anger flashed through her. She called again, but instead of turning Kyle spurred his horse down the dusty path. People moved for him like the Red

Sea had parted for Moses. In fact, some bowed, practically scraping the ground. Was this *really* an invitation to prom? Had egotism extraordinaire replaced hotitude? This skyrocketed Kyle's arrogance to a whole new stratosphere.

So over him and shaking in anger, Petra plucked a slimy vegetable off a nearby cart and lobbed it at Kyle. The discolored beet, slightly smaller and much more solid than a softball, would have landed true, squarely on the back of Kyle's head, except for another three-legged dog. The animal darted beneath the Arabian's hooves with a chicken in his mouth, and the horse danced away, carrying Kyle with him.

Wait. Where would a dog get a chicken? A live, white and black, squawking chicken? Had he stolen it from the petting zoo? She tried to imagine Frosty stealing a chicken. He didn't even chase rabbits. A child darted after the dog, shouting. She'd thought the three-legged dog from before had been dingo-looking and this was more shepherd mix. How many three-legged dogs running free could there be? One seemed over the top.

Even weirder, Kyle disliked riding. He called Petra's own thoroughbred a giant rodent and refused to even mount Laurel's fat, slow, Gwendolyn. Could that afternoon, three months ago, have been part of the ruse? Not likely.

*A bad dream then,* she reasoned. *I'm having a bad dream.* Doctor Burns said many cultures believe that dreams are a means for the soul to leave the body and experience other dimensions. Some psychologists believe that dreams represent the workings of the unconscious mind. So the dream couldn't exist outside her mind. None of this was real. She didn't think she was asleep, but if this was some peculiar life-like dream, what was her unconscious mind trying to tell her?

She didn't have a clue. She didn't know why she had suddenly been transported to Elizabethan England, but she did know Kyle. He needed to help her find Zoe so they could go home.

Petra picked up another beet and cocked her arm, but stopped short when a vice-like hand clamped her wrist. She struggled against the grip, fighting to send another missile at Kyle's big head. An arm snaked across her waist and pulled her against a solid chest. She squirmed and rammed her elbow into her captor's diaphragm. It hurt her funny bone, but he didn't even budge. She tried to stomp her feet, but soon realized she was at least two inches off the ground.

"Think twice, my lady," a voice whispered in her ear.

# Chapter Three

*Gold or silver coins - no paper currency. 240 pennies or 20 shillings equaled one pound. Each penny had a cross not only to symbolize Christianity but also to be used as a guideline for cutting the pennies into halves and quarters. The halfpenny was worth half a penny and the farthing was worth a quarter, or a fourth, of a penny.*

*What would be the cost of a rotting turnip?*
*—Petra's notes*

The breath against her neck sent shivers down her back. His hand on her wrist felt like fire. He stood behind her, holding her arm over her, so she couldn't see his face, but his voice had a Harry Potter accent.

An angry, muffin-faced woman bustled toward them gabbling, droplets of saliva flying from her loose, flapping lips.

Petra couldn't understand a thing.

"She wants to know how you'll be paying," the warm voice said. He didn't release her arm, but lowered it behind her back and plucked the beet from her fingers. Holding her against him, he whispered, "Offer her handsomely, and she'll not call the watch."

Petra looked at the sorry collection of spotted and bruised vegetables and then at the woman's fury. Muffin Face wore a mud colored shawl and an apron splattered with crusted blood. Most of Muffin's hair had been stuffed beneath a scarf, but bits of gray blond fuzz had escaped and framed her red, mottled skin.

"So sorry, of course," Petra said. The guy released her wrist. Petra fumbled through her bag, a tiny silk pouch held closed with a ribbon. She'd had it made to match the slippers and it held little more than a vial of perfume, Zoe's Girl Scout gadget, her phone and a few dollar bills. She handed the woman a five and the woman gawked.

Petra glimpsed at the guy who'd captured her wrist, instantly recognizing him from the stables. Solid, warm, and strong, he brought out in her the ridiculous desire to hide behind him from the insane woman. This bothered her for two reasons: She was still angry that he'd blocked her shot, and she wasn't the hiding sort.

Petra planted her feet, squared her shoulders and again held the bill out to the woman, embarrassed that her hand shook so badly that the bill flapped. Trying to sound reasonable even though everyone else had gone berserk, she said, "I'm sorry I don't have anything smaller." Petra looked pointedly at a small lumpy pouch tied to the woman's generous hips. "I'm sure you can make change."

When the woman didn't respond but stared with a slack-mouth, Petra sighed. "Very well. Keep it." There went Zoe's funnel cake, which served her right. Funnel cake denial, the high price of wandering off.

Muffin Face stared at Petra with beady, squinting eyes.

Horse Guy bent to retrieve the first beet she'd thrown, from the dusty road. It had rolled out of the way of the horses' hooves and wagon wheels and looked, to Petra, no worse than the other smelly vegetables in the woman's cart. Close up, it looked even uglier.

"No harm done, good mistress," the guy said to Muffin Face. He polished the beet, leaving a smear of dirt on his breeches, and handed it to the woman. Muffin Face sniffed, stretched her lips in a little smile and fluttered her lashes. Petra's lips twitched in a smile; the guy had swag. The woman gave Petra another scowl and turned her attention to a pair of women in dusty aprons.

Petra returned the bill to her purse and looked up to find herself nose to chest with Horse Guy. Taking a step back, she realized he was much younger than she'd thought, close, in fact, to her age. She peered at him, wondering what had made him seem older. His build? His swagger?

"I offered her a five," Petra said.

He looked at her, a smile tugging his lips. "Ah, but five what?"

His smile nearly disarmed her. Still, she tried to hold onto her anger. "A five dollar bill."

"You offered but one."

She again drew the bill from her purse. Horse Guy plucked it from her fingers and studied it, front and back, and then cocked his head. "A piece of parchment?"

She took it and waved the bill in his face. "It's money!"

He rocked back on his heels, considering her. "It has no value here."

Petra put her hands on her hips and blew a loose strand of hair from her eyes. "Five dollars is a lot for an anemic looking beet!"

"Perhaps, but I'm afraid it's an unfair price for a turnip."

"Turnip?"

"Yes, definitely a turnip. Do you not have such vegetables where you're from?"

She thought of the rows and rows of beautiful produce at Pavilions. She didn't think she'd ever seen a turnip, but she'd never looked, when passing the produce on the way to the Panda Express counter. She'd certainly never given any thought to discolored beets or turnips. Still, she was quite certain that one single, nasty looking whatever covered with dusty grime shouldn't cost five dollars. They had larger, prettier vegetables at the dollar store, not that she'd ever bought one.

He chuckled and took her wrist, sending a tingling current through Petra. He led her away from the glares of the gossiping women. Petra allowed him to lead her across the street to the stables, which somehow smelled better than the vegetable cart.

"Can you help me find my sister?" Her voice sounded small. "I really want to go home, and I can't leave without her."

"Who?" he asked.

"My stepsister. You saw us earlier."

"I saw her earlier?"

Petra nodded. "We saw you near the stables…" Her voice trailed away because those stables had looked nothing like where she was now. Sure, horses lined up in their stalls, flicking their tails and munching straw, but that was where the similarities ended. Here tack and whips hung on the wall, and dusty daylight peeked streamed between wooden slats. Straw covered the floor, and cobwebs filled the corners.

"And what does your sister look like?"

"You don't remember?" She thought of how his wink had sent a tingle up her spine. She wanted to remind him of the wink, but what if he hadn't been winking at her? He didn't even remember her. That stung more than it should. She held out her hand to show Zoe's height. "Kumquat-colored hair, tiny, freckled and bad tempered."

Petra tore her gaze away to look over the crowd. The square was full of fat, thin, hairy and bald people, not one of them Zoe. She thought of the one other person she had recognized. "How do you know Kyle?"

"What is a Kyle?" He rolled the name over his tongue, as if experimenting with its sound.

"He's not a what, but a who, and I saw you nodding to him in the street." Horse Guy was the only person who hadn't bowed. Her voice softened as she wondered over all the confusing things she'd recently seen. Kyle's riding a horse seemed even more unlikely than a three legged dog, because, quite simply, she'd never known Kyle to do one thing he didn't want to do. And three months ago he'd been adamantly opposed to riding a horse. "He was riding a horse."

Horse Guy blinked. "There are many horsemen in Dorrington."

"Wait," her voice squeaked, "Where did you say?"

"Dorrington. Did you think we were somewhere else?"

She opened her mouth to argue, but then closed it. "I need to find Kyle. Can you help me?" She shuffled her feet, sending dust into the air. "He is the only person I've seen riding a horse decked out like a rock star."

"Decked out like a rock star," he repeated the phrase slowly. "I do not know what that means, but perhaps you refer to the Earl's son. His horse wears the royal crest."

A royal crest? "His dad's name is John."

"Yes, John Falstaff."

"Like Shakespeare's dead-drunk Falstaff?" Her thoughts spun. In Larsen's AP English class she'd watched all the Shakespeare movies for extra credit. She wouldn't have thought that Kyle, who arranged his schedule around lacrosse practice, had ever heard of John Falstaff. If he had he'd pulled off the gag with an amazing attention to detail.

Petra frowned. Kyle wasn't good with details.

The guy's voice turned hard. "My lady, you are mistaken. *My Lord* Falstaff is no drunkard; he is a committed protector."

Kyle's dad owned a bunch of used car lots and ran commercials featuring girls in string bikinis. Lord and protector weren't names she'd have given him. "Fine. John Falstaff's son. I need to speak to him."

"That will be very difficult. Gaining an audience with the Earl—"

"An audience?" Petra thought of the girls in the TV ads, and her voice squeaked again. She cleared her throat. "I don't want an audience."

Horse Guy leaned against the stable wall and studied Petra. "You say you must speak with the Earl's son." His voice sounded calculating. "Why?"

Petra flushed. "He's my boyfriend."

Horse Guy looked at her blankly, and she tried to think of an old fashioned word, one he might understand. How would Juliette refer to Romeo? "My date."

He laughed. "Your date?"

"Yes." Okay, it hadn't been the best word choice, but since she couldn't think of a better one, she folded her arms and scowled at him. "Why is that funny?"

He chuckled, his brown eyes warm, his lips curled in a smile. "And who is your fig?"

"Fig?"

"Perhaps a pear or a peach…"

Petra, unused to being teased, clenched her fists and pushed past him. "This whole thing blows," she said over her shoulder.

He caught up to her in one stride and easily matched her pace. "Blows? What blows?"

Petra flung out her arms. "This! Everything about this blows!" She quickened her step yet he stayed at her side.

"By this, do you mean Dorrington? How can a village blow without wind? It is, perhaps, a bodily blow?"

*A bodily blow?* As she tried to figure out what exactly was a bodily blow, Petra fought a surge of panic. "This totally, completely sucks!" She sounded hysterical. She was losing it. Pressure mounted in her chest. Her head thrummed and her mouth went dry.

"It blows and then it sucks. Sucks what?" He seemed genuinely confused. Somehow this made things worse.

Petra wanted to scream. She wanted to throw more spotty and mushy vegetables. She wanted to go home. She was going to kill Zoe.

"Sucks blood? Sucks life?" Still, he matched her pace, but kept his voice low. People moved out of their way, staring after them.

"Yes! Yes! All of that."

He took her wrist and another current of warmth spread up her arm. He whirled her to face him, his expression earnest. "My lady, I beg you, for your health, do not make mention of witchcraft again."

*Witchcraft?* Who said anything about witchcraft? Shaking loose from his grip and turning her back, Petra lifted her skirt and ran down the street to the square.

Carts in a variety of sizes and shapes parked in the shade of the jousting arena. Farmers, bakers and cloth merchants all called out as she hurried past. Most wore rough cotton clothing in shades of dust. Their leather sandals matched the color of their feet.

Petra dashed through the crowd, overcome by animal odors and the press of too many bodies in too small a space. Looking at the ground, she closed her eyes and offered a silent prayer.

Opening her eyes, she thought she saw a pink flip-flop.

# Chapter Four

*A cock fight is a blood sport between two roosters (cocks), held in a ring called a cockpit. In Tudor times, the Palace of Westminster had a permanent cockpit, the Cockpit-in-Court. Cocks are almost as disgusting as the people that make them fight.*
*—Petra's notes*

"Zoe!" Petra pushed through the crowd and nearly tripped over a squealing pig. Grasping onto a vegetable cart, she watched the knee-high creature shoulder through a maze of wagon wheels, crates of produce, men in tights and women in skirts. The pig snorted as it went, as if stating its disapproval of the melee. Petra curled her fingers around the edge of the cart, letting the rough wood dig into her palms. She didn't recognize anyone. Not one single person wore normal clothes. The merchants, not even the kids looked like they belonged in Orange County. It wasn't one difference but a combination: Everyone seemed short, dirty and grim. Their mood matched their greasy hair, the chipped and broken fingernails. Everyone except Horse Guy. He didn't belong here, either.

She studied the people, searching for a few of the beauty standards of OC: a French manicure, the glistening of gloss hair products, the telltale perks of a boob job. But even the women in corsets looked saggy. Petra's gaze flashed around the square, searching, ignoring the hot Horse Guy.

A mop of bright curls flitted behind a crate of potatoes. "Zoe!" Petra followed, frustration and worry mounting.

The girl didn't turn but expertly navigated the crowd, expertly navigating through tight clad legs and dust lined skirts. The child held the pink flip-flop in her hand, which surprised Petra, but then when she thought about it, there were so many surprising things, too many to count. A pig on the loose? Toothless middle-aged women? Three-legged dogs? And maybe one three-legged dog was okay, but more than that was just wrong. Petra zigzagged between the carts, searching for Zoe's curls. Petra spotted the girl rounding a corner.

Thatched-roofed cottages with shuttered windows, white plaster buildings with timber frames, and wooden roofs—Petra hadn't noticed this area before. Could they be the drama department's backdrops? Most were two or three stories and quite often the second story leaned out over the first, looking like a beer belly protruding over a belt. All of it was pretty elaborate, even for Mrs. Brighton. Petra rounded the street corner and stopped short in the thick of a cheering crowd.

A sharp tug on her purse startled her, and she looked into the dirty face of a boy holding a sad looking knife. Both grabbed for her cut purse string, but Petra was quicker. She kicked at the kid and he sprinted away, disappearing into the press of bodies.

Clutching her purse, Petra was pushed from behind, jostled, tumbled to the ground. Pushing herself up onto her elbows, she faced an iron fence. A stream of red splattered the front of her dress.

Blood? Blood on her dress!

Around her, the people jeered, laughing, slapping each other on the backs and watching a pair of roosters battling on the other side of the iron fence. The birds, mottled brown, black, and white, dripped with gore and mud. The larger one had lost an eye, and blood and mucus stained the side of its face. The smaller, stringier bird lunged for his opponent's throat. When the larger rooster fell with a dying gurgle, the crowd roared.

Bile surged in Petra's throat. She gagged, clasped at her calves and laid her head against her knees. She spied her purse and she scooped it up. She uncurled, stood and pushed through the crowd until she reached a stand of trees at the edge of the square.

She tried to take several deep breaths, but she couldn't calm down. Where were the yellow jackets? No one liked the security guards, Hellsfire Helen or Wicked Will, but she'd wished they were here now. She wanted to hear them tooting their blow-horns and bellowing, "Slow down, Slick! Out of the flowerbeds! Back to Class! Quit killing roosters!"

Where were the flower beds? The parking lot filled with hot, shiny cars? She spotted a church steeple and walked toward it, remembering that after her hasty-prayer she'd thought she'd seen Zoe and her flip-flop.

Outside the church, a stone wall circled a small cemetery filled with headstones. Hitching her dress to her knees, Petra felt someone watching and turned to see a man built like a water-barrel but with noodle-thin limbs. He stared at her legs and licked his lips. Quickly, she dropped her skirts, patted them into place and turned her back on the man. She still felt his gaze.

Patchy grass and a smattering of dandelions and buttercups grew between the rough markers. Here were the flower beds—weeds sprouting up over graves. The chapel she attended with her family was made of red brick and had double glass doors and a shiny white steeple. This church was made of gray stone and had heavily carved wooden doors.

She looked over her shoulder. The man stood still, watching.

***

Emory had followed Chambers out of necessity and justice. Simply put, principle demanded he thwart Chambers' plan. He'd followed the girl why? Because it seemed she'd already tied him with an invisible string and he was as surely tethered as a donkey to a cart. No principles nor moral standards had anything to do with tagging her. He dodged a boy leading a sickly milk cow, and skirted past the vendors hawking their goods.

He would have walked past Anne without a glance and only stopped when she placed a hand on his arm. "Kind sir, consider my wares?"

Emory gave the girl's retreating back a long look before giving Anne his attention. He looked into his old friend's large, sad brown eyes. She had a cloud of brown hair that she wore swept away from her face, but in odd moments, when the hair escaped its pins, as it was wont to do, Anne reminded Emory of nothing so much as a spaniel.

"Are the colors not fine?" she asked.

Emory saw her puzzled expression that traveled from his face to the girl in blue who was quickly disappearing into the crowd. He sighed and smiled. "The finest," he agreed, his gaze barely touching the stand and its assembly of threads and dyes.

"I've also tapestries," she told him.

"They are well known, my lady. Your father's fame is well-established."

"Perhaps you would care to see his work," she urged.

By now the girl in blue had melded into the crowd. Fingering the threads, Emory said, "Not today, but in two evenings hence."

Anne's eyebrows rose. "A meeting, sir?"

"You may find me near the rectory."

He watched Anne's eyes light with fire. "But how—"

"'Tis just a meeting," he told her, modulating his tone so that a passerby would consider them strangers and not conspirators. "The plans are not set. There's still much to discuss."

She nodded, fussed over her threads, trying to hide her pleased and hopeful expression.

Worry stirred inside Emory. Anne's relentless

search for vengeance would surely prove dangerous. Emory had learned from hard experience that heaven meted out its own unique justice without need of human interference. The divine wheel of justice might appear slow, but it was steady and sure.

"We will meet," Anne said. Pink stained her cheeks.

Emory's gaze swept over the crowd. He'd lost the girl.

"Perhaps I can aid you further?" Anne's voice brought his attention back to where it belonged.

"No. I have no need." Emory shook his head, wishing it true.

\*\*\*

Petra walked through the cemetery, disregarding the dark, stained markers, and headed for a fresh grave. The headstone looked new; grass had yet to grow over the mound of dirt. Petra squatted beside the headstone. *Geoffery Carl, born 1589, died 1614.*

Forget the stalker. Forget the Royal Oaks Renaissance Faire. Somehow she had landed in the seventeenth century. Was this a dream? She didn't remember falling asleep. Had she hit her head in the fortuneteller's tent? At this very moment, was her body lying unconscious in Royal Oaks while her mind played tricks in Elizabethan England?

A tear rolled down her cheek. She brushed it away, knowing her hands, filthy from the fall, would leave a smear of dirt and mascara across her cheek. *It doesn't matter how I look in a dream,* she thought as the tears fell faster, bathing her face. She'd had such nightmares before, perhaps not quite realistic as this, but still she'd had those strange dreams where upon waking she'd been surprised to find herself in her own bed. Dreams where she'd forgotten to prepare for a history test, dreams where she'd lost her mother in a crowd, much like the crowd here. But she'd never dreamed of seventeenth-century England before. All those Shakespeare tragedies, Fritz, Richard, Hamlet, Lear, they were dead. No point in dreaming about them four hundred years later.

But what if it wasn't a dream? An alternate reality? A wormhole? A parallel universe? She needed to get a grip. Maybe at some point this would all make sense, but right now she would play along. She didn't need to worry about Zoe. What had the Fester the fortuneteller said? Some journeys must be taken alone. She didn't have to worry. Zoe wasn't shy–she knew how to ask for help. Just because Petra was lost in some sort of time warp didn't mean that Zoe hadn't found a way home. Or a funnel cake.

Petra squared her shoulders, sniffed, and looked inside her purse for a Kleenex. The light on her phone pulsed reassuringly. Of course, if she were really in seventeenth century England, there wouldn't be cell service, let alone towers or satellites, but she should at least *try* to call home. In private.

Hot Horse guy's witchcraft warning rang in her ear. Did they have public restrooms in the seventeenth century? Toilet paper? Aspirin? Anti-hallucinogenic drugs? Looking around, Petra saw nowhere to hide, but no one to pry either, so she sat on the spotty grass and pulled her knees to her chest. Keeping her head tucked over her lap, she opened her purse and fingered her phone. Three new texts. The familiar tiny red envelope cheered her, reminded her of who she was and where she belonged. She pressed a button and the phone chirped.

"Did you know him, my lady?" The voice over Petra's shoulder startled her.

Petra quickly closed her purse and glanced up, her heart and thoughts racing. A pretty brown haired girl close to Petra's age looked at her with curiosity. She reminded Petra of Robyn.

"Did you know my brother?" She sounded like Hermione. The girl's gaze swept down from Petra's tiara and lingered on the slippers. "Not a kinswoman…"

"Hmm." Petra tried to gather her scattered wits. She searched the tombstone for a clue and remembered something someone had said at her mother's funeral. "He was kind to me once." Everyone was kind at least once.

"Aye, he was kind to all." The girl's eyes grew misty, and, although she smiled, she still looked sad. "Particularly to those fair of face."

Petra raised a hand to her tousled hair and looked down at her dirty dress. "I'm sorry for your loss." She stuttered another stock sympathy phrase as she stood. "He was very young."

A shadow crossed over the young woman's face and Petra followed her gaze to an ox-like man at the edge of the cemetery. He watched, fingers touching the side of his thigh and a patch of leather that concealed something, possibly a knife.

"You are not familiar with his sad story?"

When Petra shook her head, the girl hesitated a fraction before clasping Petra's elbow and steering her away from the man with the leer.

"Perhaps 'tis best told over a cup of tea. Would

you care to join me?"

The invitation surprised Petra, and before she
could think of an answer, the girl continued, "My
name is Anne." She guided Petra down a path,
toward the noise of the village and away from the
ox-like man. Anne slowed slightly and visibly
relaxed when they emerged from the busy street
onto a quiet lane although she didn't relinquish
Petra's arm. She nodded at a cottage on the edge of
a wood. "My home, my lady."

A crude wooden fence surrounded the tiny
thatched-roof house and kept in three chickens and
a cow.

Petra followed Anne through the gate. All the
warnings self-defense classes and all the stranger-
danger instructions she'd received as a child
flashed through her mind. Never talk to strangers,
or go into their homes or into  cars, never accept
candy, or even tea. The words of a song her mother
had taught her sang in her head. *Go ahead and
scream and shout. Yell, holler and rat the bad guys out.*

But her mother wasn't here, hadn't been for
years. And her mother hadn't prepared her for a
delusion in the sixteen hundreds. Screaming, in this
case, didn't seem right. Her thoughts went back to
Zoe. Losing Zoe was the worst part of the
nightmare. Strange how losing her little sister had

never been a problem in her waking life, and yet here—whereever *here* was—losing her sister hurt the most. Petra lingered on Anne's doorstep, looking toward the busy marketplace, picturing Zoe wandering among the wagons and booths, looking for her, lost and frightened. Anne lived here, maybe she could help her find Zoe.

Anne latched the gate. "My home will be humble compared to what you are used to." The words held a question.

"Why do you say that?" Petra stared at the cow and noticed a goat. Not nearly as creepy as the water-barrel guy or the ox-like man, but she hoped they wouldn't get closer.

Anne stopped at the cottage door, her hand on the iron latch. Again, her gaze swept over Petra's dress and shoes.

"This is by far my nicest dress," Petra said, comprehending.

Anne raised her chin, the same look that Robyn had when Petra returned from a shopping trip with something Robyn envied. "You have many?"

"Dresses?" Petra thought of her closet at home bursting with clothes, skinny jeans, tank tops, t-shirts, camisoles, cardigans. She doubted that Anne had ever heard of Urban Outfitters or Anthropology. She replied truthfully, "No, not many dresses."

Anne pushed open the door. The cottage had few windows and was dark, cool and smelled of yeasty bread. A trestle table flanked by three stools stood in a corner, two tall wooden chairs sat near the fireplace, and a spinning wheel squatted beside a large loom. Petra had never seen a spinning wheel, except in the movie, Sleeping Beauty. Loose straw covered the wide planked wooden floor. The white-washed walls were nearly covered with large rugs that looked luxurious and out of place in the modest cottage.

In the dim light, Petra saw enough of the bright colors to see that each tapestry told a story. She wanted to study them, and yet, she hung in the doorway, uncertain, wary and still worried that Zoe was lost.

Anne bustled to a cupboard, pulled out a loaf of bread and a pot and placed them on the table. Then she picked up a long, sharp and gleaming knife. "Would you care for bread, my lady?" Anne raised the knife and Petra felt weak-kneed. The bread looked dark, thick and heavy. Petra's mouth watered.

*If this is a dream,* Petra wondered, *how can I be hungry?* Not a dream. There had to be some other explanation. When would food be offered again?

Petra slowly entered the room and let the door click behind her.

"Where you are from, are your meals as simple?"

More questions.

Petra thought of the Taco Bell's drive-through, McDonald's paper wrapped food. "In some ways, simpler." The preparation, at least.

Anne unhooked a kettle from a rod above a fire smoldering in the grate. "Do you keep a fire burning?"

Anne smiled. "How else would the tea and our bodies stay warm?"

"But it's nearly summer."

"Tis summer in your country?"

Trapped. If throwing a beet was witchy, then Petra couldn't tell Anne her bizarre mystery. "Almost summer, late spring." She guessed. "The same as here, of course."

Anne smiled as she poured the water into a cup and added a spoonful of dried herbs. Steam rose and scented the air with the thick aroma that reminded Petra of the fortuneteller's tent. "And from where does my lady hail?"

She thought back to her English lit class. Yorkshire, Herefordshire, Sherwood Forest, and London came to mind, but she rarely lied and the idea of remembering and keeping a story straight intimidated her, so Petra said, "Royal Oaks."

"Royal Oaks." Anne sounded out the words as she pushed a cup of steaming brew at Petra and motioned her to sit on a stool at the table. "Tis near the palace?"

"No…" her answer sounded weak, even in her own ears. She cleared her throat and promised herself she'd sound more confident in future lies. She would come up with a story, a good one. She was good at stories…although she had never had to pass them off as nonfiction before.

"'Tis far, then?" Anne looked pointedly at Petra's slippers. "How did you travel?" Anne's tone had turned confrontational.

Petra settled at the table and picked up the warm cup of tea. "By horse." She drove a Mustang, horsepower and all that, so it wasn't a complete lie. Petra swallowed a warm sip and watched Anne slather oozy butter over a slab of the brown bread. Anne dipped the knife into a brown jar. Flecks of something, perhaps pieces of honeycomb and bees, dotted the honey. Lauren would have loved this au-naturale meal, but Petra studied the bread, looking for tiny bee body parts.

"Do you live alone?" Petra asked, wondering if a girl of Anne's century could even own property.

"No, I live with my father. He's away purchasing dye."

Petra didn't want to sound like she was prying. "I live with my dad too. Well, it used to be just the two of us after my mom died." It never seemed to get easier to talk about. Feeling awkward, she took a bite of the bread and honey, despite the mystery specks. Nothing crunched. As she chewed, Petra glanced at the tapestries lining the walls. "Does your father make the tapestries?"

"The tapestries are commissioned by families of means." Anne poured herself tea and cradled the cup in her hands. "Do you like them?"

"They're amazing." Petra loved the vibrant colors and intricate designs. Most scenes depicted lovers, but a darker one featured an angel that seemed to transfigure from panel to panel. Wings lost, halo gone, pitchfork added. "Satan?" Petra guessed.

"An angel come from the presence of God who rebelled against the Only Begotten Son," Anne said, following Petra's gaze. "His name, Perdition."

Goosebumps rose on Petra's arms. Who would buy such a tapestry? She couldn't see it hanging in a church or heaven forbid someone's home. Imagine breakfast every day with Satan looking over your cornflakes, pointing his pitch fork at your latte. It was a gorgeous tapestry; the birds and flowers painted a deceptively pretty picture, but…Satan?

*This is a nightmare,* she reminded herself and her mind seemed to reply: *Well, if this is a nightmare, how can the tea sting the back of my throat?*

Had she ever eaten in a dream? Not seeing a napkin, she licked honey from her fingers and tried to remember her AP psychology class.

Dreams can be controlled. Trying to change the course of her nightmare, Petra closed her eyes on Anne and the tapestry and recalled a Robert Louis Stephenson poem her mother often read to Petra at bedtime.

> *From Breakfast on through all the day*
> *At home among my friends I stay,*
> *But every night I go abroad*
> *Afar into the land of Nod.*

"Bath, book and bed," her mother would say every evening. Sometimes Petra's dad would be there, often not. But bath, book and bed came as regularly as the sunset. The bath smelled of lavender, the books were piled in the shelves of her room. The day ended with her mother's kiss.

> *All by myself I have to go,*
> *With none to tell me what to do --*
> *All alone beside the streams*

*And up the mountain-sides of dreams.*

Her head felt heavy, her neck weak. Her toes and fingers tingled, and her cup wobbled as her strength eked away. Tea sloshed over the cup's rim and would have scalded her if it had been any hotter. Petra set the tea cup down and stared at her fingers curled around the handle as if they belonged to someone else. She opened her mouth to speak, but Anne had disappeared into the foggy haze that filled the room.

*The strangest things are there for me,*
*Both things to eat and things to see,*
*And many frightening sights abroad*
*Till morning in the land of Nod.*

# Chapter Five

*How to Make a Sleeping Draught*
*Valerian, a flowering plant, can be found throughout*
*Europe. Mix valerian, honey, apple cider vinegar and hot*
*milk. Valerian is also used as a perfume, so you can smell*
*good while you sleep.*
*—Petra's notes*

From the doorway, Emory stared into Anne's bedchamber, aware that this act alone breached a moral code, but he couldn't take his gaze off the girl on the hay stuffed mattress. She was everything he remembered—pink cheeks, red, full lips, clear skin and the most amazingly straight, white teeth. Her mouth hung open and a tiny trickle of drool stained the pillow beneath her hair. It was one of the loveliest things he'd ever seen in his long lifetime. "What have you done to her?" He cleared his throat because his voice sounded strangled.

Anne fidgeted and lowered her gaze to the floor. "I've done nothing. She is fine, merely sleeping."

"You should not have brought her here," Emory said. He wanted to ask how Anne had met her. It seemed remarkable that fate, by way of Anne, had delivered her to him again. "How long has she slept?"

"Since afternoon," Anne replied.

Rohan, standing behind Emory, softly swore, "Zounds."

Emory gave his old friend a cautionary look. Rohan shared Emory's disability when it came to women, although he did not have the effect on them that Emory seemed to. Rohan, in his dark and dusty robe, had a head as round and as bald as the moon, excepting the tufts of gray hair sprouting around his ears. Plus he had fingers and toes as thick as sausages. The women that cast come hither eyes at Emory spared Rohan hardly a glance.

"I pray she will sleep through the night. I believe she has traveled far." Anne's voice lilted upward, as if asking if anyone would believe her lie.

"Tis more than fatigue that has brought her to your bed, Miss Anne," Rohan said, his voice tinged with disapproval— and laughter.

Anne sighed. "'Tis but a sleeping draught. T'will not harm her."

"Such pride in your herbs, Anne." Rohan tisked his tongue. "'Tis a cardinal sin."

Another reason why women would not fawn over Rohan. No one loves a prude. Emory smiled before casting a questioning glance at Anne. "Why would you do such a thing?"

"Do not preach at me," Anne said, sounding more tired than annoyed. "I did not know ought to do. Left on her own, she would surely come to harm in the marketplace. A gentle woman wandering unattended, By faith, 'tis a wonder she made it here unscathed."

"'Til you drugged her?" Emory asked.

"When in doubt, take a nap," Rohan quipped. ""Tis a worthy motto."

Anne shrugged. "Perhaps she will see more clearly when she wakes."

"She is of quality," Emory said. "T'would be unwise to incur her family's wrath."

After a long pause, Anne said, "They need never know."

Soft candlelight bathed the cottage room. The moon and stars shone through the open window from which came the smell of the cow and chickens, yet Emory thought he smelled the girl's perfume, a scent foreign and intoxicating. He fought the urge to step closer.

The girl was still, but her mouth, which had been opened, was now pinched shut. Her nostrils flared.

*She is awake,* Emory thought, a tingle running

over his arms.

"Emory," Anne blew out his name with a sigh, as if she read his thoughts

Emory jumped, and tried to stop staring. "Of course her family will know. She will tell them," Emory said, loudly, trying to communicate to the girl what she must do.

"I'm not sure she will," Anne said. "She seems quite daft."

"These things doth the Lord hate, a proud look, a lying tongue." Rohan scolded Anne. He sounded good-natured, but his words were self-righteous.

"'Tis true. I lie not." Anne shook her head. "She seems to know nothing. Had all the intellectual capabilities of a turnip."

"Which she wouldn't recognize even if she held one in her hand." Emory chuckled. "This afternoon she mistook a turnip for a beet."

"You've met?"

"Briefly. She was throwing vegetables at Lord Garret."

Anne smiled. "Ah, so she has more intelligence than I supposed."

"Perhaps," Rohan said, "more sauce and mettle than intelligence."

"So, did his high and mightiness mind being targeted by vegetables?" Anne asked.

"He never knew. She can add poor athleticism to her list of attributes." He grinned, watching the girl stiffen beneath their onslaught of insults. He wondered what she would say when they met again? Because, although he knew they shouldn't, he also knew they would. He would make sure of it.

"They must be acquainted then," Anne continued. "It seems unlikely that even she would toss vegetables at strangers, especially royal strangers."

Emory watched the girl seethe in mock sleep.

"Perchance," Emory said. "She kept calling him Kyle."

"Kyle? What is a Kyle?" Rohan laughed long and deep and even Anne smiled. Emory watched the girl dig her fingernails into the palm of one hand as if to keep from slapping someone. He couldn't help staring.

"What is this?" The tone of Rohan's voice caught Emory's attention. He held a small, vibrant pink object with a little cap, made of a polished, thin, ore. Underneath the cap, a tiny red cylinder rose when Rohan twisted the tube. It smelled odd, a scent Emory didn't recognize.

Rohan raised it to his nose.

"Poison?" Emory asked, tone grave.

Rohan shook his head. He returned the cap to the cylinder, dropped it back into the purse and pulled out a small, leather book filled with glossy cards. One tag had an amazing likeness of the girl. He ran his finger over the image of her face in wonder.

Next they found a shiny object with characters that sprang to light when they touched it. Beeps in a variety of tones rang out. Rohan held the thing at arm length. "What evil is this?" he asked.

"A musical instrument, perhaps?" Anne guessed.

The thing screeched and Rohan dropped it. "Satan's tool," he gasped.

Outside the window a cow moaned.

"Anne, you said you found her crying over Geoffrey's grave?"

"She cried black tears." Anne gazed out the window. "I best be seeing Buttercup before she bursts."

Emory waited for Anne to leave and then demanded, "You know nothing of this?" Rohan grumbled in dissent. "She is but a lost child."

Emory put his hand on Rohan's arm and lowered his voice. "I need to know, is this your doing? Another trick, another ploy?"

"Come, Emory, be reasonable. Not every event

is a ruse of heaven or hell. The longer you live, the more you will learn that to be true."

Emory used an angry whisper. "You and I both know I do not live!"

"Hush, man." Rohan looked right and left, clearly not wanting to be overheard. "Anne said the girl knew Geoffrey."

"She lacks the look of a zealot." Emory motioned toward the thing on the floor. "And by all saints, what is that?"

"Let's see what it can do." Rohan picked it up and lumbered toward a chair. Sitting, he set the thing in front of him.

Emory watched while Rohan pressed buttons and used the tones to create a song. After a few minutes of mastery, Rohan began to sing along with his tune.

*"Come live with me and be my love,*
*And we will all the pleasures prove*
*That hill and valley, dale and field,*
*And all the craggy mountains yield."*

The lyrics made Emory uncomfortable, and he wondered if his friend had intentionally chosen the song. He sat beside Rohan and pulled the thing to him. He fiddled with the buttons until the device began to ring as if it possessed a hundred bells.

Rohan stopped singing and stared with an open

mouth. "Zounds."

*\*\**

Hours later, Petra woke. A cool breeze blew through the room carrying noise – crickets, a cow lowing, and a distant dog barking. She lay on her side, a scratchy wool blanket pulled to her shoulder and a feather pillow beneath her head.

Daft? Petra bit back a snort and fought the urge to spit out her SAT results. A flush of anger washed over her, but she held her tongue and body still.

How dare they look through her purse? How dare they drug her, study her, and discuss her as if she were an alien object, an insect on a pin, a brainless cockroach. She bet they didn't know cockroaches were one of earth's hardiest creatures, capable of surviving without food, water and even air for prolonged periods. And a dreamer or a time-traveler, even one caught in a nightmare, was much more clever and competent than a cockroach. A dreamer/time-traveler could accomplish anything, survive any physical hardship. Maybe.

Hoping she was alone, Petra opened her eyes and saw rough plastered walls, a three legged table beneath a window without glass, and the moon and stars.

*We both know I do not live. What does that even mean?* She didn't know, she didn't care, and she wasn't going to stick around to find out. After listening for sounds of movement in the house, she crawled from the bed. Her arms and legs felt heavy, detached, as if they belonged to someone else, and she needed extra humph to make them move. Standing in the center of the room, she plotted her escape. The door didn't have a knob, but a latch, a latch that would rattle if touched. She tried to think of where Anne and her father slept as the cottage appeared to have only two rooms.

*This Anne, even though she looks like Robyn, is not your friend,* she told herself as she listened at the door, trying to make sense out of the craziness. Would time continue in Royal Oaks while she was in Dorrington? Was her body here or there? Was she even really here?

And where was Zoe, what was happening at home? Had Zoe returned, reported her disappearance? Their parents would be furious about her abandoning Zoe at the fair, but at some point they would start to worry, right? Had that point arrived? They'd call Robyn, and her other friends.

They'd call the police.

She *had* to get home before she ended up on the

eleven clock news.

Hearing nothing from the other side of the door, she padded to the window. The shutters had been left open, but beyond the cottage gate the world looked dark and frightening. Tall pines swayed in the wind and threw dancing shadows across the road.

The wind screeched through the gaps of the wooden walls of a shed, as if to say "one good huff and away you go." A second structure on tall wooden legs stood beside the shed. Much too small and humble to be a barn, it had seed scattered outside the door. Chicken coop? She would have to walk past the roost, or coop, or whatever. Would chickens make noise? Did they sleep at night? Other than the KFC variety, Petra had never given chickens much thought.

*There's a fox in the hen house*, Grammy Jean would say when they were playing cards if someone tried to be tricky. Petra's grandmother, who spent all of her life in California, had once been on Hollywood's silver screen. If Grammy had lived to be seventy-something without ever seeing a chicken coop how was it that Petra, at 17, was now wondering about disturbing a herd—or was it a flock? of sleeping chickens?

She thought again of the Girl Scout advice.

*When lost, stay put until someone finds you.* Preferably someone without a sleeping potion. Okay, Girl Scout wisdom didn't always apply. Petra drew a deep breath. She wouldn't wait for the nightmare to end. She'd find her way home.

The wind teased at her hair and she remembered her tiara. Looking around, she spotted the faux diamonds sparkling on a bedside table. She scooped it up and pinned it on, thinking that if dollar bills hadn't any value, glass stones the size of pennies might come in handy.

Across the road lay the inky, black woods. She'd never been outside where there hadn't been a string of streetlights to dim the stars and moon. She thought of the crowded boardwalk that hugged Newport Beach, the lights over Royal's tennis courts, the fireworks bursting over the Angel Stadium. She'd never walked alone at night before.

Petra swung up onto the window ledge. Shivering, she dropped back into the room, grabbed the wool blanket off the bed, wrapped it over her shoulders and then slid out the window into the dark.

Without her purse.

Petra stifled a curse. Not that anything in her purse had any value in this Renaissance world, at least nothing worth the risk of climbing back into the room.  Petra brushed off her skirt and pulled the blanket over her head like a cloak. Trying to remember the way to town, she followed the dirt road down a steep hill that led to a fog bank.

The wind that had blown through the trees surrounding Anne's cottage had blown itself out. Mist swirled around the structures and trees lining the road.

Wrapping the wool blanket tighter across her shoulders, Petra tried to be brave, but random thoughts haunted her—highwaymen, wolves and other monsters, like  dragons. When she first heard hooves beating down the road she thought it might be her own heart, still she veered into the forest's shadows. The horses passed, but Petra remained in the woods, convinced she'd be safer among the animals than among men.

Unless there were wolves.

She didn't know if England had wolves, but the creatures were common enough in fairy tales. A blood-thirsty pack wouldn't have surprised her. Back home, coyotes, lean and rangy, roamed the canyons. They knocked over trash cans and scoured the neighborhoods for small dogs and errant cats. No one loved coyotes, but no one, other than pet owners, really feared them, either. A toot of a horn or a get-out-of-here shout typically scared them away. But wolves, at least the ones she'd seen in the zoo, were different. More solid. Menacing. From the edge of the woods she could still see the road, and if someone passed, she could easily fade into the thick woods, but if a wolf approached from the woods, she could run down the road. In her slippers.

A dense, cottony fog hung in the pines, blocking the moonlight. Petra tried singing softly, and night birds answered. Something skittered in a nearby thicket. A twig snapped. She wondered where she was and how far from home.

Suddenly a skin pricking sensation told Petra she wasn't alone. *What's not a wolf?* she thought, *a red fox, a raccoon, skunk, or a possum*? Harmless night creatures. Panic caught in Petra's throat. She leaned against a tree, feeling the scratchy bark through the thin fabric of her dress. The fog disguised the forest, turning each tree, shrub and stump into an ogre, troll or ghost. Someone, no something, hid in the dark, watching her. She was sure of it. Petra limped away from the tree, scolding herself for being tired, scared, and hysterical. Perhaps the sleeping draught hadn't worn off. Hunched beneath the blanket, she trudged along on wet noodle legs.

She thought she heard another twig break. She

swallowed and chose a stick off the ground and swung it as she walked in what she hoped was the direction of home. Her head thudded with every footfall, but she held it high, careful not to demonstrate weakness or fear. Another twig, closer this time, snapped. Clutching the blanket with one hand and the stick in the other, she broke into a run, praying for a straight path. Heavy breathing followed.

The ground became uneven and rocky, and Petra realized she was running in a dry river bed. She stumbled, mindful of her ankles, feeling every rock and pebble through her insubstantial, worthless slippers. Behind her, someone so close she imagined his breath on the back of her neck. Scrambling out of the riverbed and up the steep bank, she sprinted up an incline into a pasture and saw a roofline poking through the fog. As she raced toward it, her foot caught on something and she pitched forward.

The blanket flew and became lost in the dark. She felt exposed and naked without it. She scrambled blind, looking for her stick.

Hot breath that smelled of old meat blew down her neck. A wet muzzle brushed through her hair. Petra shuddered as waves of relief and terror washed through her. Not a highwayman, not a pack of wolves. She curled herself into a ball, tucking her head into her folded arms. The dog growled and pushed against her shoulder. The animal sounded a tiny bit like Frosty attacking a new chew toy.

Something zinged past her head. Another landed near her foot. The dog yelped.

Petra sat up to watch the biggest dog she'd ever seen lope into the forest. Thicker than a St. Bernard, taller than a Great Dane, a wolfhound? She'd never actually seen one before.

Hot Horse guy from the stables, the same guy she'd heard while pretending sleep, emerged through the fog.

His gaze flicked over her in concern. "Did you see him, then?"

Petra brushed her hair from her face and tugged her dress into place. "Of course I saw him. He had his nose in my hair." She studied the guy, remembering his words, *we both know I do not live*. He *looked* alive. Tall, strong, broad, most definitely alive.

His face twisted in pity. "I'm so sorry."

"Well, no harm done, thanks to you. Good aim." Still angry about his making fun of her and rummaging through her things while she slept, she added grudgingly, "I owe you."

Emory's laugh sounded bitter. He picked up her tiara, brushed it off and set it gently on top of her head. "You mustn't waste your time with repayment."

In the moonlight, he looked even more stunning. His hair thick and curly. His long lashes framed his deep brown eyes and his mouth turned down. Rock in hand, his build and stance reminded her of Michelangelo's David.

He must have felt her stare. "My lady?"

"How—why are you here?" Had he followed her?

"I would ask you the same."

"It must be after midnight."

He looked up at the moon clouded behind wispy fog. "Yes. Midnight. You have until midnight."

## Chapter Six

*The Gypsies had their own language and enjoyed a wandering, insular culture. They didn't mix or mingle with mainstream English society. Gypsies or Romas were said to have heightened psychic abilities, born with such gifts because of their close, respectful relationship with nature and the spirits of the elements. Supposedly, they could grant good fortune and hand out life destroying curses, but could they cause delusional dreams?*
*—Petra's notes*

Petra stood, brushed off her dress and wondered what he meant.

"Where are you heading at this late hour?" he asked.

"I'm going home." Her voice shook, and the unexpected emotion surprised her. *I can't remember the way. I'm lost,* she wanted to add. She held her voice steady. "My parents will be freaking out."

"Freaking?" He looked confused, but then his eyes turned sympathetic. "Yes, of course. Your father, your brothers, how would they take to your wandering in the dead of night?" He fell in step beside her. "With a strange man?"

How did her father feel about her wandering in the night? He'd never said, nor had he mentioned his thoughts on her roaming the woods with a guy who *didn't live*. What was he? Ghost? Vampire? Zombie? And why would he call himself a man when he was so young? She should be nervous, yet she was glad for his company, relieved to no longer be alone. "Tell me your name and then we won't be strangers."

He bowed slightly. "I'm called Emory Ravenswood."

She mimicked him with a curtsy. "And I am Petra Baron."

"Baron. You're a baroness."

She shook her head. "No. I don't think so. Not anymore, or at least, not the last I knew."

He squinted at her, clearly puzzled. "No brothers?"

She shook her head.

Emory took a step closer. "Just one mean tempered sister?"

Petra swallowed. "Stepsister."

"And she made the journey from Royal Oaks with you?"

"I thought so." Petra walked on as if she knew where she was headed and yelped when she stubbed her toe on a rock.

Emory reached out and took Petra's arm, sending tingles through her body. She decided that he felt real enough. So he wasn't a ghost, a poltergeist, or hallucination.

"But now you are undecided?" His brow crinkled and he let go of her. "When was the last time you saw her? You were searching the square this morning."

Petra bit her lip, wondering how much to share. She was glad she wasn't alone, but that didn't mean she wanted to confide in *the guy who does not live*. "I haven't seen her since the fortuneteller's tent."

"The tinkers!" Emory's face lit with understanding. "They are not to be trusted."

Did she hear him right? "Oh, and you are?"

He laughed. "You distrust me?"

"Trust," Petra channeled Laurel, "can't be given, it must be earned."

A smile tugged at his lips. "And what must I do to earn your trust?"

*You and I both know that I do not live.* She needed to know what that meant, but she didn't know how to ask. If it was tacky to ask after someone's digestion, religion, politics or  their bank account, it had to be at least equally rude to ask if they were dead. Especially someone who looked so red-blooded and hot. She shivered.

Emory slipped off his coat and put it across her shoulders. It felt warm and smelled of leather.

"Thank you, but a jacket doesn't buy trust." She slipped her arms into the sleeves of his coat anyway. "Won't you be cold?" Could a dead person feel temperature? He couldn't be dead. Was it possible that there was more than living or dead? Could there be various states in between? It sounded too creepy. She couldn't ask, so she thought of a different question. "You didn't tell me where you're going."

"For a walk." It sounded like a question.

She laughed. "To where?"

"Would you believe I'm following you?" Emory moved closer and folded down the coat's collar.

"Yes." Petra took a step back, out of his reach.

"So where are we going?"

She swallowed. "I'm not sure."

"In that case, perhaps you should follow me." Emory reached past her and pushed back a branch from a pine tree. He headed deeper into the forest.

She balked. "Where are *you* going?"

"I've been under the impression that you have not known your destination for some time now." She heard the laughter in his response.

Petra stamped her foot. She knew her

destination. What she didn't know was her current location in the time-space continuum. But she couldn't tell him that. "I'm not just going to randomly follow you."

"Following you was getting us nowhere except here." He gave a long and exaggerated sigh. "Very well, suit yourself." he let the branch snap back at her face.

Petra stepped away, and stared at the shadowy woods in front of her. Remembering the huge dog snorting through her hair, she shivered again. "Wait!" she called and hurried after Emory.

She caught up to him in a shaft of moonlight that pierced the forest's canopy. "Your coat," she began, breathless as she fumbled with the buttons.

"You keep it," he said, putting a hand over hers.

She sniffed. "So, where are you going?"

He headed into the dark and spoke over his shoulder. "To my home to consult a map. I want to find Royal Oats."

*Royal Oaks.* Petra thought about correcting him, but decided not to bother. She watched his back disappear into the woods. Putting one foot in front of the other she wondered if this was one of those no going back moments, one of those situations where one choice completely obliterates another. Like trying to return toothpaste to the tube, or taking back words. Some paths couldn't be doubled back, or as Grammy said, some bells couldn't be unrung.

She could still make out Emory's broad back.

Follow him or remain alone, in the dark, at the edge of the wood? She didn't know if following Emory would prove to be a course-changing decision, but she trailed after him anyway. He took a twisty path, and she did her best to keep up.

After what seemed like forever, they emerged from the woods and Petra took a deep breath when she saw that they stood at the edge of a cliff. She pushed her hair back from her face as an owl swoop over a noisy river. Trees, dark shifting shadows, protruded from the stone bank, and moonlight sparkled on the dew clinging to a stone building hugging the embankment.

*Is that his home?* she wondered, nerves worming in her belly.

She stopped at the cliff's edge when a gray, shaggy dog approached, wiggling a friendly welcome. Although not much smaller, he seemed totally different than the beast that had just snuffled through her hair. She allowed the dog to smell her hand before she scratched the fur between his ears. He sat and lifted a paw, a trick she'd taught to Frosty. They shook—hand to paw.

"How do you do?" she asked him.

He answered by wagging his tail, scattering fallen leaves on the path.

The windows of the house were dark, but a trail of smoke curled from the chimney. It would be possible for his family to be asleep; it was certainly late enough. But the house wore an empty look. "Do you live alone?" she asked.

"Just Cherub and I." Then, as if sensing her nerves, "You have nothing to fear here, my lady." He climbed onto the porch and paused, waiting for her. Two chairs stood to the side of the solid front door, and sawdust surrounded the chair that faced toward the river.

Petra took the step onto the porch. She wasn't allowed in a guy's house unless his parents were home. Until this moment, she'd thought that rule lame, easy to break and difficult to enforce. *But this is a dream, or something worse.* In her real life she'd never go into a deserted house with a stranger in the middle of the night, but this definitely was nothing like real life. Her heart quickened.

"Where's your family?" she asked.

"They passed on."

Dead? "All of them?" Of course, she knew people sometimes were orphaned and had to live with relatives or grandparents. In her world a foster care system existed, but she didn't know what became of orphans in 1610. She had a brief vision of starving pickpockets, Oliver Twist workhouses and scrawny kids picking through bare fields gleaning left behind potatoes. Emory didn't look like he was starving. And he definitely wasn't a kid. How old was he?

"I only know one person who's died." Her voice sounded small.

She wasn't sure what she believed about an afterlife. At her mother's funeral, the pastor had spoken at length of God and His kingdom, but Petra didn't know how she or her mother fit into that kingdom. But she did believe that when she died, she'd see her mother again.

"Just one?" Pain and puzzlement flashed across Emory's face. "No babes, sailors, a child?"

A chill ran up Petra's spine. "Not a baby or a child. That would be terrible." She paused. *Although, depending on who you've lost, it can be terrifying whatever their age*, she thought, remembering her mother lying still and silent in the hospital bed.

"How did your family die?" she asked, thinking of Dad, Frosty, Zoe, and even Laurel.

"Death comes early here. Perhaps where you're from—"

Instinctively, she reached for his hand and squeezed it. "I'm so sorry." She knew that in earlier generations life expectancy was shorter. A scratch could become fatally infected, childbirth was often deadly, and a cold could lead to pneumonia.

She held onto Emory's hand a little tighter, anxiety mounting. In the moonlight he looked like a Greek god.

Death had followed those guys too.

Emory pushed open the door, still holding Petra's hand. Coals in the grate glowed orange and red, casting large shadows. Stacks of leather bound books shared the shelves with cooking utensils. A trestle table, two benches and two chairs were all made of ornately carved wood. Maps in a variety of sizes of stained parchment nearly covered three of the walls. The fourth wall had two windows and the door through which they had entered. Another wall had a second door that presumably led to a bedroom.

He moved his hand to the small of her back. She felt its heat through the satiny dress, and her heart sped up. She'd never been so completely alone with anyone. At home, even alone, she was surrounded by neighbors within screaming distance and help was a telephone call away. Here, if she were to call out here, who, other than Cherub or perhaps a squirrel or two, would hear a cry for help?

"Are you tired, my lady? 'Tis the middle of the night." Emory closed the door behind the wiggling dog.

Cherub thumped his tail against the floorboards. It was so quiet. No ticking clocks. No humming refrigerator. No distant traffic or airplanes. She heard her own heart and hoped Emory couldn't hear it as well. "Not really. That sleeping potion messed me up."

Emory laughed and repeated slowly, "Messed me up."

"It's not funny."

"Anne meant you no harm."

*"Do you?"* Petra wondered, standing in the center of the room, unsure where to go or what to do, ready to run if necessary, And yet, she watched Emory and wondered if he felt the same tingling from their touch. "She could have killed me."

Emory smiled. "But she didn't."

Petra sniffed. "How do you know her?" The thought of Emory and Anne as a couple made her uncomfortable. She remembered them going through her things and frowned.

Emory motioned for her to sit at the table. "I have known Anne since she was a child."

He made it sound as if he was way older than

Anne, but that couldn't be true. "You were childhood friends."

She hadn't realized how tired she was until she sat. She took off the tiara and set it near her elbow. Wiggling her exhausted toes, she fought the desire to kick off her slippers. She needed to keep them on in case she needed to run away.

"Something akin to that." Emory reached for a scroll propped against the wall. "How did you know Geoffrey?"

"Geoffrey?"

"Anne's brother who recently died. You did not know? Anne thought you had met."

Petra shook her head.

"Geoffrey fought a battle for light and truth."

*Light and truth? What does that mean?* It sounded religious, and she'd learned in AP Euro about all the wars fought over religion. "Was he on a crusade?"

"Of sorts." Emory untied a string on a scroll and unrolled a massive map on the table. "I've never heard of Royal Oaks, but perhaps you can recognize it."

Petra put her elbows on the table, propped her head on her hand and studied the map while Emory weighed down the corners with smooth, round stones. Nothing looked familiar; many of the names lacked vowels. She doubted she'd be able to pronounce, let alone recognize, any of them. Her gaze strayed to maps on the walls.

"Those are all of lands much further away," Emory said. "I thought since you arrived by horse you must not have come from far." He took two other maps, and smoothed them flat.

Each of the three intricate maps had not only squiggly roads and winding rivers but also pictures of things like landmarks – a burnt stump, a cathedral, an inn. She studied them, impressed by the precision and detail. Emory stood behind her. She looked up at him. "Where did you get these? They're amazing."

Emory flushed. "I made them."

"You? How?" She felt his warmth. "Did you copy them by hand? It must have taken hours."

"By hand?"

"I mean, did you draw them yourself?"

He shifted as if uncomfortable. "I keep a journal and make sketches as I travel. In the evening hours I draw."

Morocco, Asia, the Holy Land. "You've been to all these places? On your own?" She'd thought him close to her age. Besides, how could someone in this century travel so far? "Was your dad a sailor? Did you apprentice on a ship?"

He smirked. "Something akin to that."

"Did you start sailing at age four?" she blurted, hoping she didn't sound rude. She imagined a trip across the ocean with the tide and winds the only engine, taking years. "How old are you?"

"I don't know my birth year," he admitted and because he sounded a little sad, she let it go. Perhaps the *I do not live* meant *I will not die* and he had lots of time to travel and draw maps. She caught sight of Jamestown, Virginia, sitting on the edge of a giant mass of borderless wilderness. He would never believe she came from the other side of nothing, just like she didn't believe that he'd traveled the world in some sort of perpetual youth.

He prodded. "Does anything remind you of your home?"

She shook her head and leaned against the table, frustrated and discouraged.

Cherub, who had been resting by the fire, bolted upright and ran to the door, barking.

"Who would come now?" Petra sat up, alarmed, and looked out the window. The moon had climbed high over the river's bank.

Knocking shook the door.

"Worry not." He placed his hands on her shoulders, and his warmth spread down her back and settled around her toes.

The rapping increased to pounding and the door shook.

Cherub barked louder and faster, fighting not to be drowned out.

Petra watched the door. "You should see what they want," she said, although hoping that he wouldn't.

Emory frowned. "I know what he wants." She tried to stand, but he held her.

"Sit, my lady. Study the maps." He pushed his fingers through his hair. "Perhaps you can find the way home while I dispose of my caller."

He stepped outside without her seeing who had knocked. She sagged against the chair, giving in to exhaustion and the heat of the fire. Like the chair from the Three Bears fairy tale, this chair wasn't comfortable: The back was too straight; the wood was too hard; the arm rests were anything but cushy. Still she found her head nodding.

Petra snapped to. She straightened her spine, pushed back her shoulders and rolled her neck. She wouldn't fall asleep. Again.

*Can you sleep in dreams?* Sleeping would make for a very boring dream. A dream within a dream? That would be new.

Petra looked around the room. Straw-strewn floor. Hand-carved furniture. Not one single modern convenience.

Sure, she'd always had a good imagination. Still, if this were all a hallucination or a dream, wouldn't something be off? Then again, nothing makes sense in dreams, it doesn't have to. The creature in the woods, the sleeping drug, the cockfight. Definitely nightmarish. But Emory? He was a part of a magical dream. *The best part.*

*In dreams, can you smell? Taste? Touch?* Petra didn't think so, yet here she smelled the parchment and ink from the maps. Tea had stung her throat. She flushed remembering Emory's touch and raised her hand to her cheek.

Petra stood and crossed the room. The dog followed her to the cupboard. "Shh," she told him.

She didn't mind if he watched, but she didn't want Emory to see her.

Cherub sat and cocked his head, staring at her with large, brown eyes. Petra pinched herself. It hurt and left a small red welt. She put a finger between her teeth and bit. *Ow.* Pain, she definitely felt pain.

She picked up the knife from the cupboard and held it above her finger. Gripping the handle, she paused. She hated blood – the sight, the smell – especially her own. She wiped the blade on her skirt, remembering the cockfight. She took the knife to the fireplace where coals glowed in the grate and she stuck the blade in a small flame until the point turned black.

If she slept, would the pain wake her? If she was dead, would she bleed? Taking a deep breath, she pressed the knife against her finger as the door opened and then slammed shut.

"My lady?"

The knife slipped. She caught it by the blade and nicked her thumb. Gasping, she stared at the blood oozing from her hand. Pounding sounded in her head, and she clenched her eyes and fists.

*Okay, I bleed.*

Emory reached her in two strides and grabbed her hand. "By all the saints!"

Cherub barked short, rapid woofs.

Petra tried to wrench away, but he took her elbow and drew her against his solid chest. He held her tight, trying to get at her thumb.

"It's no big deal," she said, her voice strangled, "just a prick."

Emory had her pinned to him with an arm around her waist; he held her wrist with the other. "No. Big. Deal?" he mimicked. "What can that mean? No big deal?"

"I know you think I'm an idiot." Her voice shook. She tucked her bleeding thumb into curled fingers and held her hand against her chest.

"As your bleeding hand would testify," he said into her hair.

She cradled her hand. "It's just my thumb and it made sense at the time. It was supposed to be a prick." Petra watched blood trickle through her fingers.

"Let me see," he said, his voice hard.

Petra shook her head, and he sighed. "Why do you distrust me?"

"Oh, I don't know. How about your friend poisoned me, you rifled through my things while I slept off her drugs, and then you brought me here to where we're isolated..." her voice rose and she felt dizzy.

"So you were trying to speed your death?"

"Of course not. Like I said, it was only to be a prick, but you slammed the door and the knife slipped."

"Why would you do such a thing?"

He already thought her crazy so she blurted, "I wanted to see if I'd bleed."

Emory turned her to face him, his hands on her shoulders. "Why would you think you wouldn't bleed?"

"If I were dead or sleeping, I wouldn't bleed." Her voice sounded small.

Emory clucked his tongue, sat her in a chair, and gently took her hand. "You are not dead, nor are you sleeping." He knelt before her, pressing the wound in her hand with the tail of his shirt. "Did you think I was a part of your dream?" He searched her face.

She nodded.

His lips twitched. "I am a nightmare?"

"Of course not." But she flushed.

"For the moment, you are very much awake and alive," he said with conviction. "Why would you think otherwise?"

"I can't think of any logical reason for my being here."

He reached out and cradled her head in his hand. "Perhaps you've had a bump on your head and have lost your way."

"Temporary amnesia?"

He looked confused.

"A case of forgetfulness." She liked the idea, even if she knew it wasn't true, it made much more sense than what had really happened.

With both of his hands clutching her wounded hand, he held her gaze. His eyes looked pained. "Tell me all you remember."

She took a deep breath and watched his face for signs of disbelief. "I was at a fair, a marketplace, and I went to see a fortuneteller. There was an earthquake, and when I left the tent, everything was different."

"Everything?" He stood, still holding her hand.

She thought back, cataloging all she'd seen: the cemetery, the blacksmith's forge, the tapestries. She shivered, remembering the cockfight.

"Unhappy memories?" he asked.

She shrugged, debating on how much to tell him. "I'm ruining your shirt."

He frowned at her effort to change the subject. "Was nothing the same?" he asked over his shoulder as he left the room.

"There was something, someone," she said when he returned moments later with a bucket and with a strip of white cloth.

He knelt beside her, took her hand in his, dipped a corner of the cloth in the water and began to clean the blood. "Who was that?" he asked gently.

"Kyle."

"Ah. Little Lord Falstaff," his voice hardened. "The Earl's son."

She wanted to see Kyle, but what would she say to him? *Hi, I'm a girl from the twenty-first century and I know someone from Orange County, California who looks just like you.* She grimaced. No, that didn't sound crazy.

"I think I know him."

Emory tore the cloth in two and dropped the bloody strip into the bucket. "I think that it is possible you do not know him at all."

Did she hear jealousy? "Then I shall get to know him."

He frowned while winding the dry cloth around her thumb. "If this is a ploy to engage the Earl's son, I promise, it won't be successful."

Petra straightened her spine. "I don't *ploy*."

"I must tell you, his father has plans for him that does not include a miss without memories." Emory pulled the cloth so tight it hurt.

Petra bit her lip to keep from crying out. "It doesn't matter. He's the one person I recognize."

"Only him?"

Petra stopped, mouth open, as she remembered Horse Guy's wink. But he hadn't remembered her at all. Besides, she'd known Kyle since kindergarten.

He'd brought her flowers when her mom died and had drawn a heart on her valentine in sixth grade. Emory had done little more than winked. "I have to speak with Kyle."

Emory stood. "Then you had better learn to call him my lord." He tucked in the edge of the bandage, making it a little too tight. "There's a gypsy camp a few miles outside of town. There's sure to be a chovihanis. Do you remember visiting a gypsy camp?"

She shook her head.

Emory's lips tightened. "If you did, it would make sense your sister is there still." He stood, picked up her tiara and held out a hand. "Shall we go look for her?"

## Chapter Seven

*The Chained Oak is a gargantuan tree whose branches are held together with yards of thick metal chain. Who did this and why? There are lots of local legends. Most likely the 16th Earl, responsible for planting thousands of trees on his estate, greatly prized the old oaks, whose massive boughs, so large and heavy, often broke because of their own weight. The Chained Oak's branches extended over a busy road. It's possible the Earl ordered the chains to save not only the tree but also anyone who happened along the road. The dark spot on the road beneath the tree is a shadow NOT century old soaked blood.*
*—Petra's notes*

The trail twisted through the forest and craggy outcroppings. Petra, worried about getting lost in the fog, stayed close to Emory. When they emerged from the woods, the mist dissipated and in the meadow stood an oak tree bound with chains. A wind whistled and the chains clinked together without rhythm.

Emory noticed her staring. "Are you not familiar with the legend of the chained oak?"

Petra shook her head, studying the massive tree.

The trunk looked as wide as a car, some branches considerably thicker than her waist. Corroded chains had carved grooves into the bark. Streaks ran down the tree like rust colored tears.

"Be very quiet as we pass," Emory said, taking her arm. "We would not want to be responsible for a falling branch."

"Are the chains to hold up the branches?"

Emory nodded. "Legend has it that many years ago on an autumn night while the Earl traveled this road he was approached by an old crone begging for food. When the Earl passed her by, the witch cursed him."

"That's harsh. It's not like the Earl would carry food." Petra looked around and imagined the old woman in the moonlight, standing in the center of the road, demanding a snack. "He was an earl, not a baker or a farmer."

"He might have given her a coin," Emory said. He sent her a sideways look. "The Earl is not the hero of the story. You mustn't sympathize with him."

"Is this Kyle's father?"

"No, a long-ago predecessor."

"Still, I'm not going to sympathize with a witch throwing out curses."

Emory coughed over what could have been a

laugh.

"I'm sorry I'm ruining your story, go on."

"The witch said that for every fallen branch of the Old Oak Tree, a member of the Earl's family will die."

"That's why we have to tiptoe past the tree, in case our thunderous footsteps send a branch to the ground?"

Emory, now a good distance from the chained oak, stopped and put a finger to her lips. "Like you, the Earl didn't take heed. In truth, he laughed and continued on his way, but moments later, a violent storm hit. Rain, thunder. A single bolt of lightning struck a branch of the oak. It burst into flames and fell to the ground." Emory's finger fell away from her lips, and he continued down the road.

Petra shook her head and muttered, "How tragic. A branch fell."

"When the Earl arrived home, he found his wife weeping over the loss of their only son. To prevent any further deaths the Earl ordered his servants to chain every branch of the tree."

"You can't believe in curses."

Emory looked grave. "A year later the Earl was out riding and as he passed the old oak a branch fell on him, knocked him from his horse, and killed him instantly."

"Here?" Petra asked.

Emory pointed to a spot on the dusty road. "Just there. Some say you can still see the blood."

Petra squinted. "I think that's a shadow."

He lifted an eyebrow.

Afraid that she'd been insensitive, Petra asked, "Did you know the Earl or his son?" She thought for a moment and then asked, "Or the old woman?"

"This was many, many years ago." He continued looking at her with dark, unreadable eyes.

"That's a horrible story," she said.

"You don't believe in legends."

"Or curses."

Emory considered. "Then why did you venture to the gypsy camp?"

Petra opened her mouth and then closed it.

"You said you last saw your sister at the fortuneteller's tent. I assume you went to have your fortune read. Yet if you don't believe in curses, it stands to reason you would not believe in fortune."

"Oh, I believe in fortune," Petra said, thinking of her home and everything she loved and missed. "I'm a fan of fortune." Good fortune, fortune cookies. Not misfortune.

His eyes swept over her gown. "Yes, I can see

that."

She put her hands on her hips, suspecting she'd been insulted. "What does that mean?"

He smiled softly. "Pray tell, my lady—"

"Please don't call me that." Her peevish tone surprised her. "I mean, why would you call me a lady?"

His gaze again swept over her clothes, resting on the tiara she clutched. "Are you not?" he asked, sounding skeptical.

Petra flushed and came to a decision. She couldn't tell him she walked into a 2014 fortuneteller's tent and exited into 1610, so she'd need a story, but one not too complicated. Something close to the truth. "I don't know what or who I am. I don't know where I'm from or how I got here."

A crease appeared between Emory's eyebrows. "I thought you said you were from Royal Oaks."

"Have you ever heard of Royal Oaks?" Panic tinged her voice. When he looked at her blankly, she continued, "Maybe it doesn't exist. Maybe *I* don't exist."

"And yet, here you are."

She nodded. "With you. Do you exist?"

"It is, perhaps a chance of fate, but am I to assume you don't believe in fate?"

When she shook her head, he said, "I thought as much. Then, please tell me why a gentlewoman such as yourself would venture into the gypsy camp alone."

"I wasn't alone."

"Ah, yes, you had taken a child."

She opened her mouth, but couldn't find a proper response. Nothing she said would make any sense to him.

"What did she tell you?" Emory pressed.

"Who?"

"The chovihanis."

"The what?"

"The fortuneteller. That is the Roma title."

"Well, the Chovi I met didn't tell me anything."

"A chovihanis tells not only the future, but also the past."

"I met a dude named Fester." She tried to think about Fester and his tarot cards. He had called her a fool...a fool on a journey. *If you think your life is here and now, you are mistaken. Indeed, there is no time or space.*

"A dude? Is that a bad thing?"

Petra smiled. "Sometimes."

"Because he may have arranged the kidnapping of your sister?"

Kidnapping. Petra hadn't considered that. She

slowed. "No one would steal my sister. I don't think."

"How did you become separated?"

Overcome by guilt, she couldn't make herself tell him she'd left her sister sitting on a stump outside the tent.

"Just because something seems improbable doesn't mean it is not true," Emory said, his voice kind. "Curse or no."

"I'm hoping Zoe is at home," Petra said.

"Then we must find your home."

Petra sighed. She read nearly everything that came in the house, so sure, she'd heard of wormholes and time machines. When she was young she'd read *A Wrinkle in Time*. She'd even seen the old *Back to the Future* movies from the eighties. "Don't mess up the time continuum" had been a common mantra. Until she found a way back home, she should interact with as few people as possible and look for a way to be struck by lightning. She needed to find a witch conveniently dead and wearing a pair of magical ruby slippers. Ruby slippers seemed much safer than a bolt of lightning.

She followed Emory's broad back through the woods, trusting him more than either one. The moon flickered through branches as a breeze tossed the leaves. Despite the dark she saw ferns and wild lilies along the path. Even the air smelled differently in 1610. She recognized pine, wood-smoke, and a pungent scent she associated with mushrooms.

They came to a turnstile and a wooden sign, much like one in *The Wizard of Oz* that told Jane to turn back, only this sign pointed in two directions, Dorrington and Leicester.

Wishing there was a sign that said Royal Oaks, Petra tramped after Emory past black and white timbered cottages with thatched roofs, millponds and barns. They arrived on a bluff that overlooked a meadow filled with brightly colored caravans. The whole world slept it seemed except for the gypsies.

Emory took her hand, drew her to a large stone and sat down, pulling her beside him. Again she had a sensation of comfort and familiarity as he held her hand.

"We should have done this earlier," Emory said as he pulled out a small knife. "The tinkers can be cunning."

"How cunning are you?" Petra asked, watching the blade glint in the moonlight.

He smiled gently. "We've had this discussion. Your crown, my lady."

She held the tiara, one of her last possessions.

"Why?"

"With the Romas, nothing is without price."

After a few minutes of watching him pry the jewels from the tiara, she blurted, "They're worthless. Fake."

Emory raised his eyebrows. "Since they look real to me, they'll look real enough to them." He cocked his head at the caravans. "So they are not worthless, Petra."

It was the first time anyone had said her name since she'd arrived in this strange place and time. She liked the way it reminded her of who she was. "I can't repay you."

He looked up from his work. "You're frowning. Have I upset you by taking the jewels from your crown? Everything has a value or a cost." He sounded serious.

She snorted.

"You disbelieve me?"

Petra thought of the Royal city dump, heaps of trash swarming with sea gulls and rodents.

Emory continued, "The Roma believe that all things are alive, that even the trees and rocks possess souls."

"Should I apologize to this stone for sitting on it?"

"Just because you can't see something doesn't

mean that it doesn't exist."

He sounded like Doctor Birch, her science teacher, talking about atoms, molecules, and germs.

Below them, brightly colored caravans clustered around smoldering camp fires. Raggedy, smiling children darted through the camp laughing. Above the bleating of goats, she heard a tune on a flute, reminding her of the Renaissance fair. She swallowed hard and stood.

"How will we find the fortuneteller?" she asked, although she knew the chivo-whatever wouldn't be Festus.

Emory rose also, folded his knife and returned it to his pocket. "She has already found us." He nodded at a group of men appeared through a thicket of trees. They arrived without sound, their faces impassive and shuttered.

The one in the middle seemed to be the leader, as he stood slightly ahead of the men on each side. He had an earring in his left ear and a ring on each finger. Gold chains draped around his neck and like Fester he wore red bloomers. His companions, one smaller and one larger, wore similar jewelry. Petra wondered how they had approached without jingling.

Emory greeted them in a strange language.

The leader returned the greeting without a

smile. Their gazes flickered over her dress and then rested on her face.

Emory took a defensive step in front of her, shielding her from the gypsies, and opened his palm to reveal one tiny, shining stone. The spokesman didn't flinch, but the small man on the right stepped in for a closer look.

The gypsies seemed to reach a silent agreement. The middle man replied in the strange, lilting tongue and then motioned for Emory and Petra to follow.

"Is gypsy like French?" Petra whispered to Emory as they followed the men.

"They call it the old language. It's unwritten." He placed a hand on her waist, drawing her against him.

"Did you ask about Zoe?"

"They denied seeing her, or you, for that matter."

"Well, of course they'd say that."

He chuckled. "Do you remember being here?"

"No."

"Please stay close. Romany value their women but have little regard for the Gaje fairer sex."

"Am I Gaje?" she asked.

His breath fanned her neck. "Yes."

"Are you Gaje too?"

He nodded. "But not nearly as fair."

As they entered the camp, Petra noticed the gypsies were small and dark, had curly hair and wore bright colored clothing. Petra looked away from their curious gazes as their escorts led them through the camp. A child clutching a rag doll ran forward to touch Petra's blue skirt. Petra smiled at the little girl, and the child grinned back, revealing crooked and brown teeth. A dog with a festering ear limped by, and an old man with one leg leered at her from a rug near a fire. Petra instinctively reached for Emory's hand.

He squeezed her hand. "Who is Mark Baron?"

She sent him a puzzled look and nearly tripped over a speckled goat. The goat bleated a complaint. "So sorry," she said to a young boy leading the creature by a knotty rope. "My father. Why?" She wondered how he knew her father's name, but then she remembered she carried an insurance card in her purse.

Emory stepped in front of her and leaned forward so his forehead nearly touched hers. "Not your husband?"

She shook her head, a nervous laugh bubbling in her throat as she looked into his dark eyes. "I'm not married."

A smile lit his face. He fingered a small gold

band that seemed to have appeared from nowhere. "Now you are," he said, slipping the ring onto her finger.

## Chapter Eight

*A wedding band is a symbol of:*
*Love*
*Commitment*
*Fidelity*
*Eternity*
*Honor*
*A wedding band is not a protection against kidnapping.*
—*Petra's notes*

"By my faith, my lady, this is the safest way," he said, taking her hands in one of his, hampering her futile efforts to remove his ring.

"I don't believe in your faith," Petra whispered as they moved through the camp.

One of their guides sent her a dark look over his shoulder and Petra stopped wrestling with Emory's hand and his ring. Emory chuckled softly. "Your beliefs are irrelevant against the truth."

"We are not married," she whispered in his ear. "That is the truth and we both know it." She suspecting that he referred to a larger, more universal truth, but with the gold ring weighing down her finger, she wasn't interested in metaphysics.

"Yes, thank the Almighty, we are not married. But for tonight, for your safety, we are."

Realization of her dependence on Emory started to sink in as their escorts paused in front of a caravan no bigger than her horses' trailer at home. Each of its four wooden side panels had a scene painted on it, the closest depicting lovers entwined in a dark forest, a doe and buck watching the pair from behind a pine while a flock of birds flew into a faded blue sky. On the next screen brightly speckled fish swimming in a bubbling sea.

"Each depicts an earthly element," Emory told her. "The Roma worship nature, the spirits of the sun, moon, air, earth, wind and fire."

When Earring Dude rapped on the caravan, a panel slid to the side and a gray-haired woman stuck out her head. The two conversed for a moment and then the panel slammed shut.

Emory whispered in her ear, "Is this your dude?"

Petra shook her head. She'd known she wouldn't find Fester—despite managing to find a Kyle look-a-like and Hot Horse Guy—yet disappointment still settled in the pit of her stomach.

The guides looked at Emory with a shrug and then all sat down on logs surrounding a fire. The small one drew a flask from his pocket, uncorked and took a swallow. After a moment, he passed his bottle to his companions.

Petra watched. They didn't seem to be going anywhere anytime soon. "What did they say? What just happened?"

Emory leaned close. "Our chovihanis is preparing for a healing. That takes precedence. We may as well sit." He settled on another log and one of the men offered him the flask. Emory held it out to Petra as she sat beside him.

She gave him her most disgusted look, one she'd perfected in middle school when she'd been assigned to sit by Lenny Jorgensen. Lenny was a paper chewer, tearing off bits of his assignments and masticating them into oozy tiny wads. He didn't do anything with his wads. He didn't throw them -- that Petra would have understood, even if she wouldn't have approved. No, Lenny collected his spit balls on top of his desk like a minuscule, useless munitions pile. Although Emory looked nothing like the concave- chested, slobbery Lenny, Petra felt a familiar frustration.

"We can't just sit here," she said so sharply their chaperones glared at her from beneath their thick eyebrows.

Emory frowned. "We're guests here, my lady.

This is their land, not yours."

Petra placed her hands on her hips. "But it's not their land, right?" She glanced around, wondering if any of the gypsies understood English. She spoke quickly and quietly. "Isn't that the point of being a gypsy? Vagabondness?"

"Vagabondness? Is there such a word in even Royal Oaks?" A smile curved his lips and she wondered if he was laughing at her. "Tell me, my lady Petra, if you were given the choice to shun the captivity of walls and ceilings and roam the earth, unburdened by possessions as the spirits direct, would you choose to stay at home?"

Petra swallowed a lump in her throat. She thought of her home, her dad. How since her mother's death, the walls and ceiling had stayed the same but the home itself had changed. Same house, same walls, same furniture, but the home had changed. Too large and too empty. Until Laurel and Zoe came. Since her dad's remarriage, the walls had shrunk and the volume had increased. Same house, different home.

Emory leaned forward and whispered in her ear. "A midnight ride across the earth? A sailing across the ocean at twilight?"

If she moved just an inch, her skin would touch his and she knew it would tingle, as it had before.

Whatever adventure she was on, she needed it to end so that she could continue with her life in Royal. Prom, AP classes, graduation, college, a career, marriage, two children, poodles, a house in the suburbs. No, not a house, a home.

Emory looked at her with intense steadiness. His gaze passed over her face, to her throat, to her waist, before rising back up to settle on her lips.

Petra felt woozy because she saw a life she never could have imagined, a life that defied time or space.

One of the men had lit a pipe, and its smoke curled with the revived campfire. Flames shot into the darkening sky. Embers popped midair. The stars, though faint, winked in the purpling haze. The night was fading. Where would she sleep? Did it matter?

Life in Royal had been perfectly arranged. There she knew exactly what she wanted, what was next on the agenda. As a freshman, she'd mapped out her high school schedule and had never deviated. Classes, clubs, service hours, she had everything she needed for graduation and UCLA. Here she knew next to nothing and had no idea what she needed other than a ticket back to her real life.

Emory picked up Petra's hand and held it in his lap. Nearby, a fiddler began to play, and someone beat a rhythm on a tambourine. Someone added drums. Through the wheels of the caravans she saw other fires burning. Women, barefoot and laughing danced. Their clothes, loose and flowing, billowed, their jewelry glinting.

Emory's thumb rubbed a circle against the pulse skittering in Petra's wrist. Behind her, she heard low chanting. She turned to watch an old woman, the chovihanis, was performing the healing. The jingling tambourines grew louder, drowning out the wail of the fiddle. The healer's voice matched the rising volume; the chants turned to moans and cries.

Emory looked over his shoulder. "She's calling out to the spirits in the Otherworld."

"The Otherworld? What other world?"

"You do not believe in the Otherworld?"

"Do you?"

"What you and I believe doesn't matter. It's the faith of the one being healed that's important." Emory listened. "The chovihanis is trying to stand in the shoes of the sick one."

Petra smiled.

"What?"

She shook her head. "It's just—well, they're all barefoot."

Emory sighed and continued his interpretation.

"It seems the lad is troubled by a malevolent spirit. The chovihanis is attempting to lead his problems into one of the three levels of the Otherworld where they belong."

"Do you think she can place me where I belong?"

Emory shook his head. "No."

"Why not?"

He reached out and touched her cheek. "Because you don't believe."

"Then why are we here?" Exasperation tinged Petra's voice.

Emory stroked her neck, pulling her closer. She knew she needed to lean away, to break the hypnotic contact. She couldn't trust Emory and yet, sitting beside him in the semi-darkness of the gypsy camp, inhaling the tangy smoke of mugwort and rosemary she felt powerless as he drew her against him.

Emory whispered in her ear. "If need be she can also travel to the three levels of the Otherworld for soul retrieval, which occurs when someone loses a part of their soul in a past or present life. Have you been lost?"

Emory's lips brushed across Petra's cheek, a hint of a kiss. She felt, rather than heard, him laugh softly as her lips looked for his. *This is it, then?* She wondered. *Is this why I'm here? To be with Emory?* Could she really give up her home, her family, her life plans to be with this person she'd just barely met?

No. Of course not.

But she didn't want to think that hard. She didn't want to think at all. Not about tomorrow or the next day. At this moment, she just wanted to *be*.

In this time, in this place, all she felt was Emory pressing against her, his lips looking for hers. And that was all she wanted.

Until the world exploded in fire, smoke, and the sound of guns.

# Chapter Nine

*Raids on Gypsy tribes were common sport in Elizabethan England because:*

*Gypsies were accused of spreading disease, particularly the plague.*

*Unprotected by the law, they were easy to blame for others' unexplained, dirty deeds.*

*Raiding Gypsy camps had about the same entertainment value as cockfighting.*
*—Petra's notes*

With a racing heart, Petra dropped to the prickly grass. Emory pushed her beneath a caravan and fell upon her. A small cry tore from her. He covered her completely, his knees digging into the ground on either side as he sheltered her with his body.

Another explosion pierced the air, and Petra bit back a scream. She tried to make sense of it, but all she felt was Emory pressing her to the ground, hard and heavy on her back, his ragged breath on her neck. She tried to push onto her elbows and his arms, rigid beside her, pinned her beneath him.

"Hush, Petra," he whispered. "For your health, be still."

Women, children and horses screamed. Goats bleated as horse hooves thundered past. Peering between his shoulder and the dirty ground, she saw scurrying feet, darting dogs and not much else.

"A gypsy hunt," Emory said in her ear. "This, I suppose, is your fortune."

"I don't want this fortune," Petra struggled for breath. Wriggling beneath him, she managed to turn over. Nose to nose with Emory, she debated on whether that had been wise. She tried to rise onto her elbows.

"Are you hurt?" Emory asked, without moving, his lips inches from hers.

Petra shook her head. She couldn't breathe beneath his weight.

"Good." He didn't flinch but remained firm and unmovable.

That's when she realized the pandemonium beyond the caravan had quieted.

Emory had lifted onto his elbows, his face still just inches from hers.

"What happened?" Petra gasped.

"Gunpowder, they must have thrown it into the fire."

Petra managed to get her other elbow beneath her. "But who? Why?"

"The gentry. Land owners hire thugs to drive

away the Roma. 'Tis common enough sport."

Petra, in an effort to distract her attention from Emory's body poised above hers, watched the feet and hooves scramble in the dust.

Then the caravan above them rolled away.

"Aye, what have we here?" A portly, bearded man smelling of beer wiped his mouth with the back of his sleeve. Lumbering, ox-like, he drew closer. As he leered at Petra, Emory peeled away from her in a fluid movement and stood in front of her, arms folded.

"We are not Roma," Emory began.

Petra sat up, instantly disliking the beefy man and his raunchy grin.

"But acting none better." The man laughed an unpleasant bark. "A bit of sport amongst the filthy Roms?"

Emory spread his arms, as if trying to hide Petra. "This is a gentle woman."

"A true lady wouldn't be here with the likes of you." The man looked Petra up and down and ran a hand through his beard. "She best be coming with me, boy."

As swift as a cat pouncing upon a mouse, Emory swung his fist into the older man's distended gut. The man whoofed out a puff of smelly breath and then lunged for Emory with a growl. Petra back-crawled away, pebbles and sticks hurting her hands.

"Now, my friend, be reasonable," Emory said, sounding casual and relaxed even as he blocked a heavy blow with his forearm. "You must know a treasure such as she would bring a fair price from her distraught father."

The man, stumbling, reeled toward Emory like a charging bull. "If she's such a treasure," he huffed, "then why is she rolling in the grass with the likes of you?"

"Good question," Emory said, taking a moment to swipe his hair from his eyes before sending his fist into the man's nose.

Petra scrambled to her feet.

Blood spurted down the man's face, and he howled in pain and anger. Emory placed his heel firmly in the man's groin and kicked him into the grass.

Petra, who had never seen a fight that hadn't been choreographed for TV or stage, stared. The spurting blood, the sound of flesh hitting flesh, the grunts and puffs of pain transfixed her. When the ox-like man fell to the ground, Emory grabbed her hand and she shook back to life.

"Let's take you home, my sweet," Emory said, pulling her away.

She followed mutely, and then screamed when another thug appeared from behind a caravan, raised his sword and plunged it into Emory's chest. Emory's knees buckled and Petra watched in horror as the sword sunk deeper and a silver tip protruded from his back.

A dark smelly and stiff shadow flew over her, plunging her into darkness. Petra clutched at the cloth covering her head. Someone tied something around her throat. The more she pulled, the more she choked. Petra kicked and flailed her legs when strong arms lifted her off the ground. She smelled yeasty breath and her stomach turned sick.

She tried to remember all that she'd learned in her self-defense class. Bash and dash – both difficult without the use of sight or arms. Breakaway techniques -- she struggled to think and then remembered to make her body limp. She slid from her captor's arms, but once her feet hit the ground, the man scooped her up and swung her around. Her head made contact with something solid. Inside the dark bag, Petra saw stars.

***

Moon and stars lit the valley. Emory didn't like being dragged by his heels, his head bouncing along the stone-studded path, but in his long existence he'd learned possum skills. So, eyes half open, body limp and an open wound in his chest, he held his peace while Petra's captors tossed his body down a river bank. He suppressed a grunt of pain when he smacked against a willow and silently thanked the tree for keeping him from the creek. Buried in the tall grass, he watched a man lift Petra onto a horse.

The ox-like man hauled himself up beside Petra, who was hooded and bound. It nauseated Emory to watch the man gather her against his barrel chest.

"Whatcha got, Marshall?" asked the youth who had stabbed Emory.

*Marshall.*

Marshall's beefy arms circled Petra's waist and rested against her breast. Emory thought he'd explode with pent-up anger.

"Bounty," Marshall grunted.

"Bounty or bootie?" The youth laughed.

Fire flamed behind Emory's eyes. He fought the urge to attack with nothing more than his hands. He tried gathering his thoughts.

He'd have to separate Marshall from the others without raising an alarm. Unless he could get the man off the horse first, the horse would need to fall without injuring Petra. If not for her, he could have startled the horse, causing him to rear and bolt and hopefully cast off Marshall. If she'd been awake, she could be of use, but from her slumped and compliant form he knew that she'd fainted. Normally he detested female vapors, but watching Petra's retreat, his heart twisted as the horses moved away. Marshall lumbered behind the others. Emory couldn't wait much longer; on foot he wouldn't be able to keep up with the overburdened horse.

Crouching, Emory hurried along the creek's grassy edge, jumping downed trees, dodging branches and tripping in and out of rabbit holes.

Ahead, Petra bounced against Marshall. Every jolt increased Emory's ratcheting fury. As they approached a bend in the road, Emory sprinted ahead to position himself behind a boulder. He picked up a couple of large rocks, tested them for loft and then aimed for Marshall's temple. When the other men and their horses disappeared around the bend, Emory let his rock fly.

"Good Gad," the man muttered as the rock whistled past his head. "Demmed bats." He turned in Emory's direction and Emory launched another rock. Marshall's oath died mid-mutter, as the stone smacked his forehead with a sickening thud. With Petra in his arms, Marshall wavered atop of the horse, leaning right and then left, like a leaf held to a branch by a thin stem.

The stallion, tall and beautiful, stood pawing the ground, waiting for the reins to tell him where to go. As Emory dashed forward, Marshall toppled to the right, taking Petra with him. Emory caught her while the big man hit the ground with an earth-shaking thud. Emory carried Petra away from Marshall's crumpled body. To Emory's surprise, the horse stepped over Marshall, and ambled after him.

Emory wondered how long it would be until Marshall's partners noticed his disappearance. Considering their apparent drunkenness, it might be hours. As the sound of horses and men gave way to crickets, creek and owls, Emory clucked to the stallion, picked up the reins and led him away from Marshall's moaning body. Safely hidden in a thicket of trees, Emory laid Petra across the horse's back and then hoisted himself up after her. Positioning in the saddle, he drew Petra against him and turned toward the village.

He debated on whether to remove Petra's hood and binds. His task would be easier if she remained inert. Her head bounced against his chest and he felt his breath matching her own in a gentle rhythm. Slowly, irrevocably, he felt himself melding into her.

*This has to stop,* he thought. *I am Emory Ravenswood, a man whose long life knows no end and no companion.* He couldn't keep her with him, tucking her into his home and bed, selfishly asking for her to share his half existence. What he wanted battled with what he knew was right. *She needs to return her to her family.* Not that he knew any better idea of how to find Royal Oaks than she did.

The horse plodded towards town, hoofs beating a soft cadence that seemed to say, *what now, what now, and what now?* If he couldn't have Petra, he could, at least, have the horse. He named him Centaur. Centaur could stay at Anne's, but surely both women would be angry if he deposited Petra back into Anne's bed.

The Earl then. Petra had said she knew his son, Little Lord Fartinstaff. He thought of Garret's blond pompadour lifting off his high forehead, his blue know-nothing-refuse-to-see-anything eyes.

Emory shifted, annoyed and uncomfortable. The son was young, he reminded himself. It was the do-nothing-but-collect-taxes father who deserved disdain. Emory could hardly blame the son for the father's misdeeds, or deeds of omission. Yet he did. The thought of leaving Petra in their care made him hate father and son. A new kind of revulsion, strong and bitter, rose from his stomach.

Petra sagged and bounced against him. Emory looked up at the moon as if expecting it to provide answers. It twinkled back at him. Petra's time was short: his time with her shorter still. It was a shame she had to die.

Petra would be gone by the time the Earl returned to Hampton Court. Young Falstaff was an impulsive idiot, but he was harmless and generally kind. He would ensure her final hours were spent in comfort. Perhaps Falstaff could locate her family and provide a fitting burial.

By the time the horse plodded over the last hill, giving Emory a clear view of the village, the chapel, and beyond that the imposing towers of Pennington Place, he knew what he had to do.

## Chapter Ten

*Bathing was rare but grooming frequent. Nails needed to be cleaned nightly, hair combed daily. Combs were made of ivory, horn or wood. They even had silver ear-spoons, small tools for cleaning out earwax. Ear-spoons can still be found in Asian markets, and there are professional ear cleaners in the streets of many Asian cities.*
—*Petra's notes*

The next time Petra opened her eyes she saw Kyle, leaning over her, his gaze warm and concerned. Her heart lifted. *I'm home, the nightmare has ended.* "Kyle," she breathed.

"My lady?"

Her elation crashed. Looking around, Petra saw a room of stone walls draped in tapestries and ornately carved bed posts draped in gossamer. A silver candelabrum with unlit candles sat on a bedside table.

Kyle wore a simple white tunic and tan breeches. A young woman behind him wore a blue gown and a white apron, and a man standing in a corner wore a dark, unreadable expression. How long had she slept? She tried to rise, but her head thundered. She slipped back down among the pillows.

Gypsies, music, healing, the Otherworld, rosemary and mug-wort, Emory, the sword. She was still trapped and, now, friendless. Tears of disappointment and loss came to her eyes. With her thumb, she felt Emory's ring.

*We both know I do not live.* That's what he'd said. Did that mean that he couldn't die? No. The shock on his face, the sudden stillness in his eyes, that horrible, ragged noise from his lips, and the blood gushing from his belly—his death had looked more real than anything she had seen in the movies, much more gruesome than her mother's slow fading.

Petra turned away from Kyle's gaze to look out the window at rolling acres of lawn, distant farmland, and a thick wood. "Where am I?"

"Pennington Place, my lady." Despite the Harry Potter accent, he even sounded like Kyle.

Petra clutched at the quilt and pulled it to her shoulders like a shield. "How did I come here?"

"My man Fritz found you by the front gate. You have suffered a head wound."

Petra clung to that. "A head wound. Yes."

The man with the frown and massive eyebrows left his corner and stepped closer. "If you would

tell us your family, we will send word of your
safety.

Safety? She'd seen her only friend in this time
warp run through with a sword. She'd been
kidnapped, bagged and beaten. No, she wasn't
safe. She rubbed the knot on her head, feeling its
size and wondering if it would turn purple. "I
remember little."

"You do not recall who brought you to our
gate?" Suspicion tinged the man's nasal voice. He
had a beak like a buzzard. Perhaps anyone doomed
to spend a lifetime with such a nose would be
cranky.

A line from the book of *Alice in Wonderland*
sprung to Petra's lips and she had to bite it back.
*One would never undertake a journey without a
porpoise.* Who had said that? The Caterpillar? The
Cheshire Cat? That was what she needed, Petra
decided, a mythical mentor.

Petra turned to Kyle, who, if not mythical, was
at least familiar. "Have we met?"

Kyle smiled and shook his head. "I do not
believe so. I would have remembered such good
fortune."

She smiled because he was so Kyle. Even if he
wasn't. "You look familiar, like someone I know
from somewhere else."

"What is your name, my lady?" the Buzzard Man in the corner asked. His question, though reasonable, sounded like an accusation.

"Petra Baron." She struggled to sit up and ended by bracing herself on her elbows.

The Kyle look-a-like stepped closer to the bed. "I am Garret Falstaff and this is Lord Chambers." He motioned to the man behind him, but didn't introduce the young woman, who was probably a maid. "You are safe here at Pennington Place."

\*\*\*

Petra watched a parade of maids fill a copper tub with a scalding, lavender-scented water. Mary, the tiny blond maid in charge of the brigade, scuttled between the bedroom and presumably the kitchen with brimming buckets.

"T'won't be but a minute now, miss," Mary huffed as she poured a final bucket into the copper tub. After dismissing the other girls, Mary pulled up a sleeve, exposed her forearm, and dipped her elbow in the steaming water. "Very good, miss." Mary placed her hands on her hips and gave Petra an encouraging smile.

When Petra didn't budge, Mary scowled and spoke slowly, encouragingly, as if Petra was a child. "Would you like me to undo your gown, miss?"

The dress had a row of tiny buttons parading down her back, but it also had a side zipper, making the buttons unnecessary. But Mary wouldn't know that.

"Um, no, I can manage." When Mary didn't budge, Petra slid a cautious glance at her and then unzipped the side of her dress.

"Coo?" the maid whispered, clearly fascinated. She stepped closer to inspect the zipper.

Mary circled Petra, and Petra rotated.

"You can go now," Petra said, trying to sound dismissive yet polite.

Mary's mouth dropped open, and she blinked hard. "But your bath --"

Petra cleared her throat. "I can handle it," she said, while stepping out of the dress.

When Mary remained motionless, Petra continued, "I like to bathe alone."

Mary's eyes widened to the point of bulging.

"It's how it's done in my country," Petra said. "We bathe privately." She spoke clearly, loudly, using the voice she used on her dog and her stepsister when she didn't want an argument.

Mary closed her mouth and blinked back tears.

Petra, unmoved and growing impatient, turned

her back on the girl and stepped out of her dress. "I really don't see the problem."

Mary's watery eyes had turned so huge she reminded Petra of a frog. "Gor, miss, is that your—"

Petra looked down at her bra and matching panties, both pink lace.

Mary choked, "But where are your-" she waved her hand toward Petra's midriff. Petra remembered once reading that the women of the earlier centuries wore pounds of undergarments. Her panties and bra although modest compared by Victoria's Secret standards, had to be shocking to poor Mary.

Mary shook her head, gathering Petra's dress from the floor. Then she stopped, frozen, as if in shock. "Your toes, miss. They're purple."

Petra didn't know how to explain Picasso Pinky's Salon.

"With flowers on them," Mary finished.

"Yes," Petra said.

"Did an artist *paint* —"

"Sort of."

Mary backed toward the door, Petra's dress a bundle in her arms.

"Where are you taking my dress?" Petra asked, panic in her voice.

Mary looked at the dress as if she'd forgotten its existence. "Why, to the washer woman, of course."

"But—"

To launder the dress without a drycleaners would take hours. The dress was dirty, but without it, what would she wear? She could hardly walk around in her underwear. Scandalizing Mary the maid was one thing but an entire village? She had a sudden image of Lady Godiva on a horse. When was Lady Godiva's time and what had become of her? Had they stoned her for her nudity? Made her wear a scarlet A attached to her ta-tas?

Mary gave her a tremulous smile. "My Lord has sent Jenny to retrieve some of the mistress' gowns for you."

"Won't the mistress mind?"

"She would have dreadfully," Mary said, her voice thick with emotion, "but she's passed away five long months ago and no longer has a say."

"And they kept her clothes?"

"Of course. What else would they have done?" Mary gave the tub of water a baleful glance. "Your water will be getting cold, miss."

"I'll get in after you've gone," she told Mary.

Mary looked doubtful. "I will come back?"

Petra folded her arms as a stiff breeze blew in through the window. "Not until I'm out."

"But your hair, miss?"

"I can do my hair," Petra said. It seemed odd to be standing near naked in front of an open window, but from their height she supposed only birds could see in. No airplanes, or helicopters, probably not even hot air balloons.

Mary's lip trembled.

"Fine," Petra said with a scowl. "You can do my hair."

Mary sniffed hard.

"Please go," Petra finally urged.

Mary didn't budge. "But what if you --"

Petra turned her back on her, listening for the door. She peeked and saw Mary give a despondent little shrug and then trundle out the door. At last the door snapped shut with a defiant click.

She was not only dirty, but also bruised and achy. Pulling her hair over the edge, she sank into the water up to her chin and closed her eyes. She tried to let go of everything, all her fears and concerns, but the scene in the gypsy camp kept replaying in her mind. She felt guilty soaking in the tub, being catered to by servants when people in the gypsy camp had been hunted down and maybe even killed.

Emory said the gentry led the hunts. Had Kyle, no, he'd called himself Garret, ordered the raid on the gypsies? What had happened to the children and babies? What about the sick boy who needed healing? How many besides Emory had died?

Emory. One tear rolled down her cheek and then another. Worried she'd break down, she tried to think of her biggest problem—how to get home?

But thinking of home didn't stop her tears.

She splashed her face with water. She was in England, home was in California. Even if she'd been in the right century, crossing an ocean and a continent, without cash, credit cards or passport would be difficult. But crossing four hundred years—impossible.

And yet not impossible, assuming she'd already done it once. Her mother used to say that if you did something once you could do it twice. Which wasn't really true. Some things you could only do once, as her mother's death had proved.

Which raised an interesting question. Had Petra died? Was this her afterlife? Her Otherworld? She wiggled her toes in the water, and the purple flowers made her feel a little better. She felt real, still herself. She didn't feel dead. Placing a hand over her heart, she felt its steady, reassuring thump.

She contemplated the tiny red prick on her finger. She bled and breathed; her heart beat. So, assuming she was still alive and had somehow fallen into a time warp—why this time? Why now?

If she had to time travel, why couldn't she have gone back to when her mother was alive, when she and her parents lived in the yellow house with the red roses, when going to the zoo and seeing the tiger roar was the most terrifying experience of her life? When building a sand castle at the beach and watching the tide demolish her work was her biggest disappointment?

And why was she here? Was that more relevant than how?

The kids in the Chronicles of Narnia were always finding ways in and out of Narnia—a wardrobe, the blast of a horn, a storm. Had she really gotten out of the twenty-first century through the wrong curtain of a fortuneteller's tent? Maybe she's missed the warning: *Beware, enter at your own risk; fortunetelling maybe hazardous to your life plans.*

"There are no coincidences," Laurel liked to say. Just like she said, "The Baron and McGee family was meant to be." As if in some great design, Petra's mother's death and Zoe's father's abandonment were lodged into their life maps, as inescapable and unavoidable as the setting sun.

Petra sat up and tried to shake off her funk

when the door creaked open.

"Just me, miss." Mary poked her head through the door. "I brought ye some gowns."  Mary flushed pink. "And if ye don't be minding, some under-things."

***

Standing in the center of the room, grasping a bedpost, Petra gasped as Mary gave a final tug on the corset. Then, before Petra had time to feel shocked, Mary deftly patted Petra's boobs into the chemise. Petra hadn't even the time to complain before Mary had moved on to the buttons. Petra closed her mouth, the grumble dying under the realization that she could hardly breathe, let alone complain. No wonder women on the covers of romance novels were always fainting into Fabio's arms. Either they couldn't breathe, or they were dying of embarrassment because their boobs were about to pop out. Petra blinked, one of the few movements she could manage, and said, "I won't be able to sit or lift a spoon."

Mary gave the laces on the brown velvet gown a tug and then stood back with a satisfied smile. "Gor, miss, you look lovely."

Mary held up a hand mirror for Petra to see.

What had been left of her makeup had disintegrated in the bath, but the steam had left her skin pink and moist. Her eyes sparkled blue, her lips red, and her hair had been swept into a thick twisty knot at her neck. She didn't recognize herself. She looked like one of the fainters from the romance novels.

Mary frowned, a tiny crease appearing between her eyebrows. She appeared to be on the verge of spouting a lecture. Petra recognized in Mary the tell-tale signals her stepmother always used just before a rant -- lowered eyebrows, clenched fists, tightened jaw. Petra wondered if scolding, primping and manhandling boobs was standard seventeenth century maid practice.

"Miss," Mary began, looking flustered, "to catch my lord's eye—"

Petra tried taking a deep breath. "Catch his eye?"

Mary sucked in her lower lip and began violently brushing Petra's gown. "You mustn't smack your lips or gnaw on bones. Remember to keep your fingers clean."

Etiquette lessons from the maid?

"Don't speak of politics," Mary continued.

As if she knew anything of the time. "Or, let me guess -- religion."

Mary stopped brushing, straightened and looked Petra in the eye. "They are the same." Mary placed her hands on her hips. "This is a beautiful dress, and I've made you just as lovely, miss." She sucked in a deep breath. "Don't be spoiling this."

"Spoiling what?"

Mary cocked her head. "Why are you here, then? If not to secure Lord Garret?"

"Secure Lord Garret?" Petra felt herself flush, heat and indignation rising. "Is he insecure?"

"Hush!" Mary hissed when a knock sounded at the door. "A footman, to escort you to the dining hall," Mary explained. "Keep your serviette in your lap."

Which might be easier if you knew what a serviette was.

If Mary thought Petra was there to "secure" Garret, who else might think the same thing? "Tell me again who will be at dinner."

"It's just you, Lord Garret, and Master Chambers."

Petra remembered Chambers with the frowning eyebrows. He radiated dislike and distrust. If he'd been a dog, the hairs on the back of his neck would have pointed upward. She wondered what role he played here. Mary had referred to him as *master*, so he wasn't a servant. "Where's Lord Garret's father?"

"In the city," Mary said and then added under her breath, "That's why we must hurry." She gave Petra's back a little push.

Petra discovered that, despite the corset, she could walk and breathe at the same time.

\*\*\*

Chambers and Garret stood when she entered the hall. Late afternoon sun slanted through two-story glass beveled windows and sparkled on the heavy pewter candlesticks on the table. Goblets, spoons and a knife that looked more appropriate for killing deer sat beside china plates.

A child in a blue tunic appeared at Petra's elbow, bearing a bowl of murky water. Petra flashed a look at Garret and Lord Chambers for direction, but Garret appeared to be looking at something outside a window. Lord Chambers frowned at her.

The child pressed the bowl closer to Petra, and she took a guess and dipped her hands into the water. That must have been the right thing to do, because the child then produced a small hand-cloth from his back pocket.

After the men washed their hands, they

remained standing and Petra, who had sat, bounced back up to her feet.

Lord Garrett nodded, and Chambers bowed his head. "The Lord is our rock, and our fortress, and our deliverer; in Him will we trust."

Garret had his head bowed and eyes closed, but Petra studied him from under her lashes. His resemblance to Kyle was spooky: height, sturdy build, blond hair, blue eyes, thin lips. Kyle had tan skin from his hours on the lacrosse field and she supposed Garret had his from hours outside doing… what? Hunting? Riding? Fishing? She didn't know what a young seventeenth century earl-to-be did. Kyle and Garret were *not* the same person; she couldn't forget that.

Petra tuned back into the grace.

"The Lord is our shield, and the horn of salvation, our high tower, and refuge, the Savior from violence."

Unless, of course, you happen to be a gypsy. Petra's heart twisted. Did Lord Garrett/Kyle had anything to do with the gypsy hunt? If he did, she wouldn't stay in his house.

Chambers droned on. By the time the food was finally served, she was hungry, but between a tight corset, Chambers' frown, and fending off Garret's questions, she found it increasingly difficult to chew and swallow.

"Perhaps you were on horseback and thrown from the saddle," Garret guessed. "That would explain the head injury."

"But where are her companions?" Chambers countered, speaking over her head as if she wasn't there. He narrowed his eyes. "The Romas. This is surely their doing."

Garret considered his forkful of pork and nodded.

Anger flashed through Petra. Did these men, the same who prayed for a really long time, order a hunt on the gypsies? How could Chambers go on and on and on about God's goodness and yet condone the raid? Treating people like pests? Hiring exterminators?

She took a bite of something steamy and brown and it tasted like sawdust. She remembered to use her napkin/serviette before speaking. "You can't blame the gypsies," Petra said, putting her napkin/serviette back into her lap.

"You said yourself you have no memory," Chambers said, looking at her from over the top of his goblet.

Petra rubbed her forehead where it had begun to throb. A tiny pulse beat in her temple. She wasn't used to lying. She had no idea what the

Renaissance people knew of amnesia, for all she knew those suffering memory loss were thrown into an asylum and spent the remainder of their lives trying to remember who might care enough to rescue them.

"A highwayman," she stammered, recalling a poem that she had memorized in eighth grade. "I think I remember a highwayman and moonlight." She tore into a roll and breathed in its yeasty smell. "A moor and an inn."

"But the moors are far to the north." Garret, fork poised mid-air, looked baffled.

It'd been silly to think that just because Kyle looked like Garret that they were somehow connected, that he would know how to help her home. *What I need is a fairy godmother, a wizard or a good witch. Too bad I don't believe in any of those things.* .

"It had to be the gypsies." Chambers frowned at his plate. "They kidnapped her from somewhere and brought her here."

"No," Petra said too loudly. She swallowed a lump of bread and it lodged in her throat.

Chambers studied her, eyes calculating.

"At least, I don't think so." Petra stirred the beans on her plate wishing they would turn into chicken nuggets. The limp beans weren't the green kind she knew; they were yellow and looked like worms. If she was going to have a magical moment why couldn't she be someplace that served Ben and Jerry's? If she had wished to be transported to another time and place, she wouldn't have picked this time or this place.

Unless she could have stayed with Emory. He had been the one good thing about her trip to Elizabethan England. By the time the pie arrived she was so angry and depressed she only picked at the berries and longed for ice-cream.

A footman came into the room and bowed before the table.

"Yes, Francis?" Garret said, tapping his lips with a square of linen.

"Sir, pray forgive the interruption, but the tapestry artisan has arrived. I took the liberty of having her sent to the first parlor."

"She?" Garret threw down his napkin, his eyes lit.

"Yes, Miss Carl, sir. It seems her father has been detained abroad."

"Excellent!" He turned to Chambers and Petra with outstretched hands. "Shall we?"

***

Pennington Place reminded Petra of Hogwarts. The first parlor had soaring ceilings and a fireplace with a mantel higher than her head. One wall had a flank of cut-glass windows, another had been lined with bookshelves, and another was blank.

Petra hung in the doorway, not knowing how to respond to Anne, who stood near the blank wall. A rolled tapestry lay near her feet like a colorful log.

Two footmen stood on either side of the tapestry. Anne, dressed in a modest gray gown, bowed her head at Garret, but when she saw Petra, her eyes widened in surprise. Petra held her gaze until Anne looked away.

What should she say to someone who'd drugged her? Petra wanted to forgive Anne simply because she had been friends with Emory. Did Anne know Emory had died? Petra watched Anne greet Garret and quote him the cost of her tapestry. Other than nervous energy, Anne seemed fine.

After moving chairs and tables to make room, the two footmen rolled the tapestry out over the carpet. Riotous colored flowers, coral and sapphire skies, silvery angels – the Satan tapestry. Petra gasped.

Garret leaned toward Anne. "Your work, it's extraordinary."

Anne accepted the compliment with stiff

shoulders, but stepped back. He followed at her heels like a sniffing beagle. "My father will purchase it, I've no doubt."

Chambers cleared his throat. "Maybe he'd like to see some of her others before he decides."

"Your father, is he not here?" Anne's face flushed as she shot Chambers a hostile glance.

Garret looked at his shoes. "No, he's away."

Anne's mouth dropped open with a sound as if the air had been knocked from her lungs.

"Tis of no matter. I'm confident my father will be pleased." Garret stood straighter. "I will purchase it."

"Are you sure?" Petra bit her tongue, assuming she shouldn't have spoken.

Chambers studying the tapestry became an unexpected ally. "I agree with Miss Petra."

Garret looked from Petra to Chambers as if they'd grown horns. "It's dazzling!" He shot Anne a warm glance. "It's poetry."

"Dante's Inferno, maybe," Petra muttered.

"What's that?" Garret asked.

Chambers paced the edge of the tapestry. "It's the story of the fall of Satan!"

The color seeped from Garret's face as confusion replaced his enthusiasm. "Ah, so it is," he said slowly. "So it is." Garret straightened and he looked at Anne. "When will your father return?"

Anne met his gaze with open hostility. "I do not know. He has gone abroad to purchase dye."

Petra remembered a second man in Anne's cottage. She'd assumed him to be her father. Maybe he wasn't. Or maybe he was and Anne was lying.

"Do you have other tapestries?" Garret asked.

Anne nodded.

"Then you must bring me another. Monday hence?"

"Perhaps it would be best to wait for the Earl's return," Chambers suggested.

"Nonsense. This room and this estate will soon be mine. I can purchase a tapestry," Garret said, his chest puffing out. "If I should so desire." The words sounded loaded and his eyes locked with Anne's.

Petra felt a current running between them like a live wire.

"Yes, my Lord." Anne ducked her head, but not before Petra saw a spark of defiance.

Garret rocked back on his heels. "Monday then, at the same time."

Anne's shoulders drooped as she watched the two footmen roll up her tapestry.

***

Petra had thought that she'd undress herself, but one look in the mirror at the army of buttons and the tiny tool that Mary used changed her mind. "Do you know how I got to Pennington Place?" Petra asked as Mary crouched behind her. She suspected Mary didn't believe her tale of memory loss.

Mary sighed, pushed back a lock of hair from her forehead and straightened. "According to Fitz t'was the thick of night, he answered the bell and found you dead to the world at the gatehouse door. A bag of jewels and a note had been tucked in your cape."

"A note?"

Mary raised the heavy brocade dress over Petra's head.

"It said to take good care of you until your father arrived," Mary said, lifting an eyebrow. "But aren't you the least bit wondering about your jewels?" She motioned for Petra to turn around.

"Oh, of course, the jewels," Petra said, taking a deep breath, her first since her corset encounter. "Did Garret just keep them?"

"He's keeping you, isn't he?" Mary shrugged.

Petra squirmed. The transaction made her feel more like Frosty at the kennel than Petra at the

Marriot. Of course, Frosty had to stay in a kennel surrounded by a choir of barking, whining dogs. She wasn't forced to stay in a cage, but she had to wear a corset, and that was sort of the same thing.

Mary flung a cottony nightgown over Petra's head. While Petra put her arms in the sleeves, she asked, "And Garret?"

"*My Lord* Garret --" Mary tugged the nightgown into place.

The nightgown, a soft shimmery and see-through affair, was a hundred times more comfortable than the dress. "Lord Garret wasn't suspicious?"

Mary smiled. "Suspicious and yet pleased, miss."

"Mary, you don't know me. Why are you pushing me on Garret?" She corrected herself. "My Lord Garret?"

"Pushing you on Garret?" Mary thought about that as she pulled pins from Petra's hair. "I spent years working my way up to being a lady's maid. Years, mind you. And in the five months since My Lady Falstaff's been gone I've been doing chores like the chamber and scullery maids." She paused the comb above Petra's head. "I don't like emptying chamber pots."

Petra got it. Spending time with other people's

pots would make her sick. "Can't you do something else?"

Mary looked like she wanted to use the hair comb as a weapon. "I'm a lady's maid," she said through gritted teeth. She set the comb down, deemed Petra ready and bustled her into bed.

Under the rustle of the covers, Petra heard Mary mumble, "Not all of us have the fortune to wander willy-nilly around the countryside with jewels in our pockets."

Even with the candle extinguished, Petra could easily see. Moonlight shone bright through the windows, and a fire smoldered in the fireplace. The feather bed had a down quilt, and Petra felt like she was floating in a white cloud, but she wasn't tired and didn't want to sleep. She didn't want to wander willy-nilly. She wanted to go home.

If she could Google...but before the Internet, there were libraries. A place like this would have a library, right? She crawled from the bed, shivering in the cold, and searched the room for something to wear.

*No clothes. No shoes. Night gown it is.*

The latch opened with a soft click, and the door swung silently open. The tapestry that ran down the hall felt soft beneath her feet. Candles flickered in sconces on the stone walls. It couldn't be too late because she heard the rattling and clinking of dishes from below.

Guessing that a library would be on the ground floor, Petra padded down the stairs, keeping an eye out for servants, or worse, Garret and Chambers. A stack of books sat on a table outside the third door to the left. A telling clue, her dad would say.

Biting her lower lip, Petra pushed open the door. Less a library, she decided and more like her dad's office, but some books and maybe some answers.

Petra stood at the threshold, hating that there were so many things she didn't know and didn't understand. She'd been in the seventeenth century for two days. Two days! Who has dreams that last two days?

A massive desk covered with ledgers and papers dominated the generous-sized room. Two chairs flanked a fireplace so large she could have stood among the embers and ashes without hitting her head on the flue.

At home, she knew exactly what to do, what to say, and if she made a mistake, which she almost never did, no one called her on it. Except for Zoe, who didn't count, because of her age and size. Zoe's freckles didn't help; they made her look comical, even when she was angry. Maybe especially when she was angry. Her skin flushed red, the freckles stood out and her hair seemed to stand on end. Furious Zoe looked like a cartoon character being electrocuted.

Petra leaned against the doorjamb, homesickness and loneliness overwhelming her. Casting a critical eye on the leather-bound books, she felt fairly confident that not one of them would provide directions on how to speed travel 400 years, but she stepped in for a closer look.

The books marched across the shelves and she recognized very few titles or authors. A great many had to do with agriculture. *The Modern Egg Farmer. How modern can a seventeenth century chicken be?* She passed poultry and poetry and spotted Copernicus. *Science.* A German bible. *Religion.* Could either help her?

While the shelves and book bindings were spotless, most of the book tops were covered with a thin layer of dust. Curious why *One Thousand and One Nights* was dust free, she pulled at it. The book slipped forward and the fireplace façade rotated nearly noiselessly. Where once there had been blackened bricks, now an opening.

Astounded, Petra watched the book slide in the shelf and the bricks whirred back into place. She tried it again with the same results -- bricks gone, dark passageway, earthy breeze, and moments later, all on its own, the bricks returned.

As did the voices.

# Chapter Eleven

*Some secret passageways lead to hidden rooms.
Hidden rooms are useful for kidnapping, smuggling
goods, and other illegal activities. Secret passageways
may also be private entrances or tunnels. They're
particularly common in episodes of "Scooby-Do."*
*—Petra's notes*

Out in the hall, Chambers spoke with
animation. "Of course your father must be
informed of the gypsy blight!"

Petra didn't want to explain why she'd
wandered from her room. With no time to consider
her options or consequences, Petra lifted her
nightgown and dashed through the fireplace.
Seconds later, the fireplace bricks closed behind
her.

Darkness engulfed her. She felt the walls on
either side. She stood stock still, afraid that perhaps
one wrong move would reopen the door and
expose her. She strained to hear, hoping they had
skipped the office, but Chambers' voice droned
closer and the tenor of his voice changed
dramatically after Garret interrupted with a
question.

"She cannot stay, my lord. Her people must be located and notified."

Garret said something unintelligible.

"Precisely why she's dangerous!" Chambers retorted.

Dangerous? Were they talking about her? Annoying, bossy, perhaps spoiled, but dangerous?

Petra didn't possess any weapons, or knowledge of how to use one if she happened to find one, but she knew things these men couldn't even dream. All the technological advancements, inventions and discoveries of the past four hundred years.

Of course, at this moment, she didn't have access to anything even slightly useful. *Beam me up, Scotty,* she thought, itching for a *Star Trek* gizmo that could rearrange her molecules and put her back where she belonged.

"She's but a chit," Garret laughed, his voice startlingly clear.

*Chit?* She didn't know what that meant, but she didn't like it. She also didn't like how close Garret sounded. What if they accessed the passageway and found her in the dark? In her nightgown?

As horrible as it would have been to be discovered in an office, being found in a secret passage would be much, much worse. There had to be a way out. Passageways always had a destination.

Cautiously, Petra toed the darkness ahead before taking a step. Nothing happened. Holding her breath, she took another step, and then another. Then she smacked into a wall.

She woofed in surprise, stepped back and rubbed her nose.

The voices rumbling in the office stopped. Petra froze until their murmurs resumed. Stretching out her arms, she felt along the walls, found a corner and slipped around it.

As her eyes adjusted to the gloom, she saw stone walls, hard-packed dirt floors and a timbered ceiling. She kept her fingertips against the wall to maintain her bearings. As she moved deeper, quiet and darkness seemed to swallow her. Then she heard a scraping noise.

Petra stopped, listening.

Silence.

Her nerves pricked, and her skin tingled as she continued to who-knew-where. Around a corner, she saw a flickering flash of light and smelled the acrid smoke of candles.

The footsteps fell in swift purposeful strides. Someone who knew where they were going, which put them at a distinct advantage. She had nowhere to hide.

Petra hadn't panicked when she'd been nose-to-beak with fighting roosters, or when she'd been drugged in Anne's cottage, or even when she saw Emory die, but now, in this gloomy corridor, adrenaline pumped through her. *Fight or flight?* Blood pounded in her ears as she picked up her nightgown with frantic hands and ran, stumbling in the dark.

The footsteps overtook her in moments. As she raced forward her foot caught on  something and she pitched forward.

She smelled a mix of cloves and leather as hands caught her and lifted her into the air. Imprisoned against a broad chest, Petra kicked as a thigh pressed between her legs. He held her so that her back arched against him, his arms curved under hers, his hand on the side of her neck, one pressing her head sideways.

He spoke quietly in her ear, his voice sending tremors down her spine. "My lady, do not move, or with one twist, I will snap your neck."

But Petra couldn't move. She could barely think. She couldn't hear her thoughts over her beating heart. His grip tightened. Stunned, she gasped, "I saw you die."

He dropped her to the dirt floor. "You?"

Petra craned her neck to look at Emory's face.

He grabbed her wrist, hauled her to her feet, held her against the wall with one hand and lightly ran his other hand over her arms and front as if searching for something. Knowing that she should be outraged, she still found herself grinning at him. They stood so closely that she saw the outline of his hard, chiseled chin and the glint in his dark eyes.

He stopped, as if struck by her expression, and his lips tugged upward. "What are you doing here?"

She suspected he wanted to sound angry and menacing. Disbelieving, she couldn't resist. She placed her hand on his belly where she'd seen the sword stab him. He didn't flinch.

"How?" she asked.

He held his finger to her lips, took her wrist and led her deeper into the passage. Then he turned her question back on her. "I saw you with Black Shuck." It sounded like an accusation.

"Who?"

He shook his head. "Black Shuck, the hound of hell."

She bit back a laugh. "The what?"

He shook his head again as if trying to clear it. "Pray thee, keep thy peace. What are you doing here? Who are you? Who sent you?"

"My answers haven't changed since yesterday. I don't know how I got here or why but… I've stopped wondering about myself and started thinking about you."

He took a step closer and leaned down so his nose nearly touched hers. "I don't know what sort of trick or trap you are, but I won't be fooled."

Her heart skipped as she stared into his eyes. "I'm not a trick. Or a trap."

He frowned and pushed away, but because he still held her wrist, she had no option but to follow. His eyes slid over her, and she suddenly felt grateful for the dark. "What are you wearing?" he asked through clenched teeth.

Petra glanced down at the thin cotton nightgown. By gathering it in a fistful in her middle she created folds that made it a little less sheer. "Mary called it a chemise."

His lips straightened and tightened. "'Tis nearly invisible."

She cut a quick glance at his face and then looked down at her pale, exposed ankles. She laughed. "Do you think this is an inappropriate nightie for creeping in hidden passageways?"

He didn't let go of her hand but towed her after him. "I do not mind for myself, of course --"

She tripped after him. "Of course…You do

realize, you haven't answered any of my questions."

"I'm not here to satisfy your curiosity."

"Which begs the question—*why* are you here? And that leads to *how* are you here?" Petra ground her heels into the dirt, a fair imitation of Frosty being led to the groomer. "I saw that man stab you." Her voice shook. "I saw the sword go through you!" She ran her hand over his back and felt his muscles quiver.

"Will you stop doing that?" He pressed forward.

"There has to be a wound." Dropping the folds of her chemise, she tugged at the back of his shirt and lifted it to expose the broad unblemished plane of his back. Reaching forward, she ran her hand up and under his shirt.

He stopped and faced her. The shirt, still in her hand, twisted around his waist.

"My lady, I do not know the customs of your Royal Oaks." He tugged the shirt out of her fingers and tucked it into his breeches but not before she saw his rippling, tan, perfect abs. "But I can assure you, in our country, young ladies do not remove a gentleman's clothing."

Embarrassment made her bolder. "Oh, are you a gentleman?" Her thoughts leaped to her stepmother's Regency romance novels hidden in a basket in the den. By Petra's calculations they were currently about two centuries prior to the Regency period, but a gentleman was a gentleman, right?

"If I weren't a gentleman, I wouldn't be worried about your sheer shift."

"Good point," she said. As he stood before her, glowering, she took the opportunity to touch his belly again.

He roared and grabbed her other hand, so that he now held both hands.

She laughed.

He gave her hands a shake, rattling her to the teeth. "This is not a lark!"

She sobered slightly. "I'm just so relieved you are alive."

The frown between his eyebrows eased. "As I am you." He released her and turned away. She trailed after him.

"You must stop touching me," he said over his shoulder.

She sniffed, offended. "As if I wanted to."

He lifted his chin. "Apparently, you do."

She trotted by his side. "I just wanted to see where the sword went in."

He sent her a swift glance. "You thought you saw something. You were mistaken."

Moving through the gloom with grace and speed, he seemed remarkably healthy and fit. He also seemed to know where he was going. "There was a lot of noise, a lot of confusion. You were kidnapped."

"Kidnapped?" She gathered her nightgown in her fists so she could keep up. She wished he'd slow down so she could see his face. She knew he was lying.

"Did you think you flew to the manor?"

She opened her mouth. She didn't remember traveling or arriving at the manor. "Someone put something over my head. If you weren't lying on the ground dying as I'd thought, did you see who it was?"

"If you remember, I had problems of my own."

She grabbed his arm, and he looked down at her face and then at her exposed legs. "Me too. Black Muck and all those hell hounds."

He brushed her off, turned his back and walked away. "It's Shuck," he said over his shoulder.

His indifference stung. Staring after his retreating back, she dropped her nightgown and said, "Well, shuck you."

He paused, as if he understood her near-obscenity and the anger and frustration that'd brought it on. "Go to bed, my lady. You've no business here."

"I don't know where to go," she said in a small voice.

"Left, then right, follow the passageway until you reach the orangery."

*Orangery? What the shuck is an orangery?* She remained rooted as he turned a corner. A minute later she heard the low murmur of voices coming from further down the passage. A light glowed in the distance.

She really couldn't go back the way she came. Return to the library and face Garret and Chambers? She didn't want to return to her room with more questions than when she'd started out. Not knowing what else to do, she went after Emory, but at a distance, hoping he would lead her out of the passageway.

The path sloped downward, and the deeper they went the more putrid the air. The rank smell made her think of bats. The light grew brighter and Petra recognized the deep voice that had belonged to the second man at Anne's. She turned a corner and bit back a gasp. She ducked, afraid that Emory had seen or heard her, but after a moment, she peeked to watch Emory, a large man in a friar's frock and a heavily bleeding gypsy.

The gypsy lay on a cot, wrapped in what

appeared to be gory rags. The passageway opened up to a slightly wider hall lined with a cell made of cut stone with iron doors. The cell where the gypsy lay had a thick chain draped through the bars. A padlock dangled from the links and a key protruded from its hole.

Emory bent over the gypsy, pressing down the wounded man's shoulders while the friar cut away the rags that had presumably once been the gypsy's clothes. The gypsy moaned and writhed. The friar muttered something.

The friar took a clean cloth from the bag lying beside the cot and folded it. With Emory's help, he rolled the gypsy onto his side and wrapped the cloth around the man's middle.

The wound in his belly seemed to match the one in his back, like the sword wound she'd seen on Emory. The gypsy groaned and let out a string of curses Petra didn't recognize but completely understood. Sweat rolled down his pain-contorted face.

The bandage secure, Emory and the friar gently returned the gypsy to his back and Emory mopped the man's face. No longer pinned, the gypsy contorted on the cot. The friar stood still, eyes closed and head bowed. After a moment he raised his eyes to the ceiling as if asking a question. Then the friar and Emory exchanged places, but instead of holding the gypsy's shoulders, the friar put his hands on the gypsy's head and uttered what sounded like a prayer. He took a tiny vile from his pocket, unplugged its cork and poured a drop of slow moving liquid onto the gypsy's head. Immediately the man quieted.

The friar and Emory looked at each other and then the friar looked up and directly into Petra's eyes. Startled, she ducked back around the corner, embarrassed to have been caught spying on such a private moment of…What had she seen? A faith healing? What had been in that bottle?

Petra leaned against the wall, listening. An iron door swung shut with a creak and clank. Footsteps padded away. Clearly, the friar had seen her; Emory probably suspected she hadn't left, but neither approached. The candle light blew out, leaving Petra in the dark.

She heard the gypsy's labored breathing. Must and mildew mingled with the smell of his blood, leaving a metallic taste in her mouth. Confident that the friar and Emory had gone, she went to the wounded man.

Eyes closed, lips slack with sleep, his face gleamed with sweat. He looked oddly at peace, despite the bandage wrapped tightly around his torso. She thought she recognized the rings on his fingers and knew she'd seen him earlier in the camp. She had a dozen questions for him, but she didn't want to wake him and she wasn't even sure if he spoke English. Besides, he looked like he needed rest more than she needed answers.

Petra headed in what she hoped was the direction of her room.

\*\*\*

Emory followed Rohan through the door that led to the chapel's basement. Dungeons and chapels seemed unlikely bedfellows, but they shared a roof and a plot of land. Thumbscrews beneath the alter, chains beneath the choir loft, a scold's bridle beneath the confessional, and a meeting of zealots in the rectory.

Rohan's wide body filled the narrow stairwell and Emory tagged after him. Hearing a noise behind him, he looked over his shoulder and saw rats scurrying in shadowy corners. He smiled, wondering if Petra suffered from squeamishness, if she would turn back, return to her warm bed in the manor. Falstaff's manor.

He knew what he had to do; Petra or no. The time approached. They emerged through a side door that opened to a cloister. Damp night air filled Emory's lungs and he inhaled deeply, feeling a renewed sense of purpose.

Rohan, as if reading his thoughts, took note of the moon's position in the sky and said, "They will be here within the hour. I can do this on my own."

Emory cast a swift glance at his friend and saw a rare steely determination. Normally Rohan had the disposition of a sunny day, but at the moment he looked stern.

"I'm going with you," Emory told him.

Rohan cocked his head, motioning for Emory to follow him around the corner. The dark windows of the rectory looked upon them, promising their secrets. Although the rectory looked asleep, Emory knew that Father Priestly must be awake, preparing for the night's tryst. Chambers and perhaps others would soon join him. From the shelter of a lilac bush beneath the front window, Emory and Rohan would listen to the men's plans.

"I'm afraid you are needed elsewhere," Rohan said, his voice a whisper.

Emory shook his head, uncomprehending, until Rohan pointed at the side chapel door creaking open. Breath caught in Emory's throat.

Petra stood in the moonlight, framed by the inky black of the doorway. The moonlight pierced her chemise, revealing every one of her curves. Her hair fell about her shoulders and shone like the color of stars. She moved through the cloister and stopped at the well, staring into it as if lost in thought.

What was she doing here? How had she escaped the curse of Black Shuck? How had she managed to twist her way into his life? Because he'd thought she would die, he'd allowed himself kindness. Knowing she would be but a brief interlude, he'd let down his guard.

Emory flinched beneath his friend's scrutiny. "Who is she?"

"Who is she to you?" Rohan asked.

Emroy flushed. "Is she your doing?"

Rohan shook his head, the smile returning to his eyes. "She is your problem, not mine."

Emory folded his arms across his chest. "No, she is not."

"We can't allow her to stay. We risk exposure."

Exposure. Unable to tear his eyes away from the shimmery chemise, exposure seemed the appropriate word. Emory let out a small groan and hung his head. *Damn heaven. Damn hell.*

## Chapter Twelve

*Everyone in Elizabethan England was expected to receive basic religious training. By law, every minister held services on alternate Sundays and on holy days. All children over the age of six had to attend. Parents who didn't send their children might be prosecuted in church courts. Court or church with corrupt priests in charge? Tough call.*
*—Petra's notes*

Had Rohan been speaking? If so, very little had registered. He'd been completely absorbed by Petra's appearance. Nothing could be accomplished if he allowed her to stay. Sighing, he cast Rohan a pained glance and left the rectory's shadow.

She didn't hear his approach. She seemed to be whispering while staring into the well's depth. Perhaps she was making a wish. Her shoulders were slumped, her head bowed, her arms and hands dangled at her side. Even from behind she looked profoundly unhappy.

Emory crept from the shadows and into the moonlight. Four stone paths dissected the cloister and met at the well. Emory stayed on the grass, his gaze never leaving her.

The moon bathed her in a glow. He was close enough to know she smelled of lavender. Looking up, she caught sight of the manor's turrets and her face cleared. Picking up her chemise by the handfuls, she started toward the manor. He trailed after her, past the rectory, past the chapel to a path through the woods to the place where the manor's iron fence had a few missing bars. He wondered how she knew of the short cut.

Across the grounds, the small flicker of a lantern approached. Emory wondered if Petra also saw it and knew the potential danger. He had to warn her. He wouldn't let her stumble into a disastrous meeting.

Emory ducked beneath the low branches of a pine tree, his heart racing. Through the boughs he watched the lantern flash toward where, until moments ago, Petra had walked.

Where had she gone? He held his breath as he searched. Pines, alders, wild brambles, no Petra. Never had he felt so vulnerable. The lantern passed, but Emory stayed in the shelter of the pine.

No voices, no questions. She must have passed Chambers without notice. How had he lost her? He cursed as he headed across the broad lawn toward the manor. Stone-built, the manor had turrets, annexes, towers, and wings.

It embarrassed Emory that despite the size and scope of the place, he knew exactly which window belonged to Petra. He had watched from the woods as a gatekeeper had carried Petra to the manor, as a young footman received her into his arms, as young Falstaff had directed the staff and a parade of candlelight had made its way to a window in the northwest corner. Hours later, as he stood in the shelter of the woods in the early morning light, he had seen Petra standing at the same window.

He knew where she belonged.

Upon reaching the manor, he began the long, slow scale of the wall. One foot up and then another, each hand and foothold searched for and then found in the stone. Midway, he stopped to catch his breath. From his perch he saw the rolling river that led to the village, the sharp point of the chapel's steeple. He hoped Petra had beaten him to her room. He told himself that he only needed to be sure that she had returned safely. He did not intend to hang from a sill waiting for her.

He wondered how Rohan fared and whether they would be able to stop Chambers. If Chambers discovered Rohan's interference, Chambers would have him killed. How many deaths had Rohan endured? Anger and another emotion he couldn't identify flared through him. He reached Petra's windowsill seconds later.

The room was empty. He debated only a moment and then swung over the ledge.

The fire in the grate burned orange. If Petra returned he'd have nowhere to hide and no excuse for being in her bedchamber. If she called out, if he were discovered, conventions would force an immediate marriage. Still, he stood in the center of the room, because he couldn't leave, even though he knew he couldn't stay.

Someone had taken the quilt off her bed and a trail of dirty, Petra sized foot prints led out the door.

He smiled because even though he did not know Petra well, he knew her well enough to know that she would give her quilt to the wounded Roma.

***

Petra woke the next morning when Mary arrived carrying a tray of food. Sitting up on her elbows, Petra pushed the hair out of her eyes.

"Good morning, miss," Mary nearly sang.

Petra grumbled a sleepy reply. "Is breakfast in bed typical?" The day before she'd found it awkward to balance her tray. She hated the thought of spilling something sticky on her sheets.

"Oh, no, miss. Breakfast trays are only for when the master is away." Mary lowered her voice to a whisper. "Lord Garret likes his lie-a-bed." Mary winked as if Petra would find this interesting.

"And the Earl, does he like to lie-whatever too?"

Mary settled the tray beside Petra's knees and looked calculating. "A little lie-about does no harm."

Petra looked at her breakfast and wondered if it could cause any harm. Of course, she really hadn't expected pop-tarts, but she did miss them. Maybe the gypsy would appreciate the hard boiled eggs, slabs of ham, and a scoop of what looked like it might be beans of an unknown variety.

"Does the Earl know I'm here?" Petra asked, sitting up slowly, careful not to jostle the tray.

"How would he know that, miss?"

Petra shrugged and thought about texting, e-mails and instant messaging, not to mention phones, cell phones, telegrams, and the pony express. "If he knew, do you think he'd mind?"

Mary mumbled something like, "Not if he got to keep your jewels," before she went out the door.

Petra picked at a piece of bread and realized that Mary probably wouldn't discuss the Earl, *her master*, for fear of endangering her job. Through the window Petra saw a tinge of pink. Birds began to call, the morning was waking, but she hoped the occupants of the manor were still asleep. Three outings in her nightie seemed like three too many, but she couldn't wait much longer. Mary would be back for the tray soon.

Slipping out the door with the food tray, Petra tried to think of an excuse for wandering the halls half-clothed but gave up. *No one asked much of a half-clothed half-wit.* It was a liberating thought. She walked fast, watching the eggs tumble around the tray.

The sudden clamor of church bells almost made her drop the breakfast. Wedding bells? That reminded her that Mary *did* have expectations…impossible expectations. Petra passed a window and looked out over the rolling estate to the normally busy square beyond the manor's gates. The square looked vacant. No farmers, no vendors.

*It's Sunday*, she realized. *They observe the Sabbath.* The thought cheered her and she practically skipped. Would she be invited to attend services? Would Emory and The friar be there? She had plenty of questions for them both.

Thankfully, she didn't pass anyone on the way to the office. Inside, she kicked the door closed with her foot and leaned against the wall, catching her breath. Moments later she was in the now familiar passageway where she couldn't help thinking of Emory.

She flushed remembering how it felt to be in his arms. Just before the attack on the gypsy camp, she had been sure he was going to kiss her. And she had planned on kissing him back. She hadn't wanted anything more or less than that.

And then everything went wrong. She'd thought, she was *sure*, he'd been killed. The sickness and horror of that moment washed over her.

And then she'd found him in the passageway.

And he wasn't happy to see her.

That hurt. That he hadn't been as touched and moved by seeing her as she'd been hurt. A lot. He'd been shocked to see her, but definitely not happy. The thought of never seeing him again, again, twisted in her belly. It was becoming a familiar feeling.

She turned a corner and told herself to forget Emory. She needed to talk to the man in the monk garb. He'd administered some sort of prayer or blessing on the wounded gypsy and he had found peace as quickly as if the friar had pressed a button. Petra knew that there wasn't a button or potion that could send her home, but maybe…

But she didn't really know that, did she? She'd arrived in Dorrington, England, in the year 1614 without a lot of pain or fanfare, so why shouldn't she be able to return as easily? The friar had some sort of gift. She simply had to persuade him to work his magic on her.

When she turned the corner and came face to face with the empty cells, she asked herself if he had made the gypsy disappear. Where had he gone? Where was her quilt? And now what was she to do with the food? She didn't want to feed the rats.

This was what she really hated about 1614. There were too many questions.

And rats.

\*\*\*

Dressed in a soft gray dress with a pearl trim bodice, Petra followed Garret and Chambers into the tiny stone church. The congregation of villagers gathered in the chapel, even the flock of sheep trapped in the stained glass window, seemed to stare as she tried to sit in the back pew.

Chambers gave her a heavy frown and Garret sighed deeply when she settled her skirts around her. A family with six children stared at her–six round little mouths hanging open at the sight of a stranger in their spot.

"Oh, do you sit here?" she whispered. She apologized and hurried after Garret, feeling Chambers' frown between her shoulder blades.

As the town's leading citizen it seemed Garret had to sit on the front pew, directly beneath the stern gaze of the priest. Apparently, as the Falstaffs' guest, Petra was expected to also.

The hymns blaring through the organ pipes were giving her a headache and the service hadn't even started.

Garret sat like a statue, clasping a hymnal. Petra tried to peer around him to search for Emory or the friar. Instead she saw Anne slip into the back of the chapel and arrange her blue skirts as her flushed face struggled for calm.

Petra tightened her jaw, straightened her shoulders and fixed her eyes on the priest. She didn't care and wasn't curious about Anne's relationship with Emory.

After the opening prayer, Petra kept her gaze on the pulpit, but her attention wandered. She found it hard to focus, and when she managed to tune in she found the sermon silly. Who, other than a priest with porcupine sideburns, could seriously blame a drought on scandalous behavior?

The priest began droning the Beatitudes, but his message barely scratched Petra's thoughts. *I don't want to inherit the earth,* she thought; *I just want to go home.* It didn't seem an unreasonable request when the Lord was promising much greater blessings. The poor, the hungry, the mourners, the meek, the pure in heart, the peacemakers- where did she fit? What about Emory? Where was he and why had he been so mean?

During the closing hymn, Garret's strong bass voice belted out a song Petra didn't know. She mouthed along in monotone and cast him a glance. What if she told him her experiences, how would he react? Would he think her insane? Have her locked away? Would he protect her? Could she hide behind him? Possibly, but that wouldn't be fair. She hadn't a romantic interest in Garret, although she wondered why not. He looked exactly like Kyle. Tall, handsome and kind, yes, but he has the sense of humor of a toad, a small voice in the back of her head told her. Exactly like Kyle. She wondered what she ever saw in him.

Garret caught her watching him, and the corners of his lips lifted, but Petra didn't know if it was a smile or the just the necessary movement to sing *chart and compass come from thee.*

After the benediction, Petra looked beyond Garret's broad back to watch the friar slipping through the broad double doors. When had he come in? No sign of Emory. Maybe since he couldn't be harmed, he also couldn't walk on hallowed ground, a vampire or demon sort of thing. Not that the congregation appeared so holy. She recognized a few of the parishioners--including Muffin Face, Anne, and some of the men from the cock fighting rink.

Petra didn't believe in vampires or demons, but until a few days ago she hadn't believed in time travel. Maybe she needed to be open minded about all sorts of things including fortunetellers, and even tarot cards. The thought weighed on her. Everything she'd known, or believed to be true, wasn't. When everything seemed possible, then nothing was impossible.

"Absorbing sermon, wouldn't you agree, Miss Baron?" Garret stood between her and the retreating friar as solid and immovable as Mount Sinai.

Petra nodded and tried to snake by, but he followed so close she worried he'd step on her dress.

Outside on the steps of the chapel, the late morning sun streamed through the shade of a maple tree and cast a dappled sunlight on Anne's face as she chatted with the friar and the priest.

Petra stopped beside the priest and laid her hand on Garret's arm. "Good morning." She gave Anne a brief unfriendly nod that she hoped conveyed a small bit of her dislike and then turned to the priest. "Father Knightly, I so enjoyed your sermon."

The priest had an unfortunate resemblance to Abraham Lincoln, the same build and craggy facial features, but with more hair. His eyebrows, dark, thick and long, poked from his forehead like a thorn bush and the front of his hairline had a cowlick that made his hair stand on end.

"Good morning, Miss Carl," Garret sputtered out a greeting to Anne.

Anne lowered her eyes and bobbed a curtsey, looking humble, and yet somehow not.

Petra watched, curious. Did Anne hate Garret, when he so obviously felt differently? Petra's attention flicked from Garret's flushed cheeks and eager eyes to Anne's shuttered face and ramrod-straight back, but then she saw the friar moving down the path toward the church's gates and lost interest in Garret and Anne.

She'd seen historical movies of women running in skirts and decided that they must have been computer animated. Trying to move quickly while wearing a hundred pounds of clothing wasn't going to happen for her. She moved past Muffin Face, navigated through a herd of children, and nearly tripped over an aged woman draped in a shawl.

Spinning around, she didn't see the friar but she caught sight of a plaque nailed on the wooden gate.

*"In loving memory of those who fell to Black Shuck, May 1557.*

*All down the church in midst of fire, the hellish monster flew,*

*and, passing onward to the quire, he many people slew. "*

Beneath the plaque, scorch marks scarred the gate.

"Tis the devil's own fingerprints, that," the woman said, noting Petra's interest.

## Chapter Thirteen

*Legends as old as the Vikings claim a doom dog
known as Black Shuck roams England. It's said that
seeing him means certain death within twenty-four
hours. He haunts graveyards, side roads, lakes and dark
forests. In other tales, he's a protector of lone women.
He's also big, ugly and has breath that smells of rotting
meat.*
*—Petra's notes*

Petra turned to the woman who came barely to
her elbow. Wrapped in the shawl, she must have
been warm in the early morning sun, but she
looked cold and wizened. Her black eyes stared
into Petra's face.

"Black Shuck…is he the devil then?" Petra
licked her lips, feeling foolish yet scared.

The woman bent her head. "Not the devil, a
hound of hell."

This woman was clearly a relic from the Dark
Ages, steeped in what Grammy would have called
hoo-hah. Petra tried not to think of her practical
Grammy rolling her eyes when she asked, "Black
Shuck came here? Others have seen him?"

The woman cackled, exposing a mouth without

teeth. "No one lives more than a day after catching sight of Black Shuck."

Petra fought back the shiver that crawled down her spine as she remembered her conversation with Emory. *"I'm just so relieved you are alive,"* she'd said. *"As I am you,"* he'd replied. She'd wondered what he'd meant. He couldn't believe in hell hounds, could he? He had whispered about the legend of the chained oak. Shivering, "No one? Were you here then?"

The woman sniffed and wiped her nose on the back of her filthy sleeve. "I was but a bairn on that terrible day."

"Black Shuck came here and everyone who saw him died?" Sarcasm laced Petra's voice as she studied the old woman. She looked as old as a mummy, but according to the plaque, Black Shuck had visited the church only 40 some years ago.

Death comes early, Emory had said, and looking at the woman she supposed that old age came almost as quickly. Petra put her hand to her cheek, wondering if she'd be old in ten or twenty years. She felt a flutter of panic and a renewed sense of urgency to find her way home.

"This black dog, or the devil in such a likeness," the woman said. "God, only He knows how the devil works."

Petra wanted to get away from the witchy old woman; she reminded Petra of the one in the story who cursed the unlucky Earl. She didn't want to hear about a killer canine on a rampage or the devil disguised as a doom dog, and she certainly didn't want to be cursed. But maybe she already was. Was that why she was here? She moved away from the chapel doors, but no longer caring that she might be thought rude.

The woman trailed after her. "Running all along down the body of the church with great swiftness and incredible haste."

Petra hastened toward the gate, but the woman managed to stay at her elbow, speaking and spraying spit.

"He came among the people in a visible form and shape. He passed between two persons as they were kneeling in prayer and wrung the necks off them both at one instant. Clean backward."

Petra managed to reach the cemetery's gate, a stone and wrought iron contraption, but she hadn't been able to shake the old woman.

"Where they kneeled they died," the woman said, leering up at Petra, revealing nostrils ringed with hair.

"That's a terrible story." Petra frowned at the woman. "That's the second worst story I've heard since I've come here."

"Tis not a story --"

"Yes it is!" Even in her own ears her voice sounded screechy. "None of it's true. It's all..." She fought to find the word, "hullabaloo, hoo-hah!" Frustrated that she'd been reduced to her grandmother's terminology, she nearly shouted. "Superstition!"

The woman gaped, her mouth a terrible, smelly hole.

"There are no such things as curses, or hags, or devil dogs!" Petra put a hand on her forehead as if to stop all her wild thoughts. "Please excuse me."

As she stumbled into the cemetery, she realized she'd returned to the spot where she'd first met Anne. Lifting her skirts, Petra walked briskly among the tombstones, as if she knew where she was headed, as if she had a destination to pin point on a map.

She heard a low chuckle. "Hoo-hah? Hullabaloo?"

With her hands on her hips, she turned, ready to defend her vocabulary.

The friar stood among the tombstones, amusement on his face. "Come, my dear, no need to resort to obscenities."

"Hoo-hah and hullabaloo are hardly

obscenities." Petra's face flushed with anger.

"But it is derogatory."

"I can be much more derogatorial."

The friar laughed till he had to wipe his eyes.

Despite her aggravation, Petra found herself warming to him. She sat on a tombstone and watched him laugh at her.

"I can do insulting, would you like to hear more?"

Scathing retorts, insulting barbs, the subtle diss—she had a repertory. Not that reducing others to tears was something to brag about, but in the jungle of high school halls, it was a useful tool. One that she intended to use on Emory if she got the chance.

"Will they all be as amusing?" the friar asked. "Perhaps we should first be introduced. I find it very useful to know whom I am insulting." He cleared his throat. "Perhaps that's a lesson you might do well to learn. I am Friar Rohan."

She cocked her head at him, debating on whether or not to remind him that they'd spent some time together last night. "Friar Rohan, I'm Petra, but you already know that. I think Emory told you about me."

"My dear," Rohan said. "I pray that you do not consider yourself the central topic of everyone's conversation."

Petra bit back a sharp remark, one that could perhaps hurt as badly as his, but she knew she needed Friar Rohan, miracle man. She needed a miracle badly. "*Has* Emory mentioned me?" she asked more meekly.

He nodded, and his eyes twinkled as if he were having a wonderful time.

"I thought so." Petra felt annoyance tingling up her back. "Did he also tell you about mangy Black Shuck, and how I've apparently bucked tradition?"

"Mangy?" Rohan's eyebrows twitched. "Black Shuck is a magnificent beast. I'm sure it'd ruffle his fur to be described as mangy."

"So you've seen him, too? Does Emory know?"

"Not everyone is susceptible to hell's wiles."

Petra snorted. "Or superstition."

"Do not mock what you don't understand," he gently cautioned, not unkindly.

"I'm not mocking. I'm sad and scared."

"Ah yes, so I can see." He squinted at her. "Well, happy up."

Petra inhaled sharply. "What did you say?"

Rohan blinked as he lowered his girth onto a headstone. The marker disappeared beneath the spread of his frock. "Happy up? It's not, perhaps, as derogatorial --"

"Who are you?" Petra asked, studying his face. He looked like a clean-shaven Santa Claus. She'd expect him to say "ho, ho, ho, merry Christmas," or even "happy Christmas," but not "happy up." That was her father's expression. "Happy up," her father would say right before he called her Peevish Petra. She didn't know anyone else who used the saying and she doubted it was a common expression in 1610. Nothing about this man seemed common or ordinary.

He returned her gaze with kind, blue eyes. "I am your friend."

Petra shook her head. "We've just met. Besides, I get the feeling you're not very picky who is, or who isn't, your friend."

Rohan smiled at her. "Not true. For example, Black Shuck is not my friend."

"Is there such a thing?"

Rohan lifted his eyebrows at her. "Any friend of Emory's—"

"Emory is not my friend."

"He most certainly is," Rohan put his hands on his knees and leaned forward. "He just doesn't know it yet."

"And how would you know?"

"Heaven helps me."

*Heaven helps me or, heaven help me? An odd thing*

*to say*, Petra thought.

"Or, perhaps more fitting to say, I help heaven." He winked. "We're on the same team."

"Whose team do you think I'm on?"

"Your own of course. 'Tis true for most of us, I'm afraid."

"But not you?"

Rohan raised his eyebrows. "He who's not with me is against me."

"You're the easiest person to understand I've met since I've gotten here, and yet, it's like you're talking in riddles. I'm not against you and I'm not on a team."

He chuckled. "Are we not sitting together? And if you are not here, where are you?"

When she didn't answer, he pressed, "Where would you like to be?"

"Home," she said.

"And how will you get there?"

She frowned at him. "What has Emory told you about me?"

He laughed and it seemed to come from deep within his belly. She couldn't help smiling.

"With his words, you mean?"

"Of course with his words! How else would he tell you anything?"

Rohan gave her a teasing smile. "Words are

perhaps the least effectual form of communication, which our dear Father Knightly so aptly demonstrated in this morning's sermon." He gave a great sigh and looked at the church.

Father Knightly stood on the steps. The two men scowled at each other. Rohan looked sad for a moment and contemplated his hairy toes sticking out of his leather sandals. Then he looked up at her. "For example, the good father and I just enjoyed a little exchange. Did you notice?"

"Would 'enjoy' be the right word?"

"Much more fitting, I believe, than derogatorial." Rohan gave her a small smile. "Forgive my demonstration. I just wanted to prove that there are more means of communication than words. So, do you want to know what Emory said of you with his words? Or otherwise?"

Words could be insulting, but the otherwise? She'd really like to know the otherwise.

"I thought so." Rohan laughed again, looking a fraction wicked. "Last night he said you were...shall we say, derogatorial."

"He was mean, not me." *I just wanted to see where he'd been hurt. I still want to see that.*

"He said you said to him, 'shuck you.' He didn't know what it meant, but he didn't like it."

"He wasn't meant to." She hated that she

sounded contrite. Should she apologize? It did sound pretty offensive, even if it didn't mean a thing. "Did Emory tell you I want to go home?"

"You've lost your way?"

"Yes!" Petra's heart leapt. "Can you help me?"

"Maybe, but you may not like it."

"I really want to go home. I'm *desperate* to go home."

Rohan considered her and then asked, "Then why don't you?"

"I don't know how!" She would if she could. Of course, she would. Even if it meant never seeing Emory again. He meant nothing to her. She needed to tell him that he was rude and mean, she'd be doing the world a favor by teaching him to be polite.

"Last night I saw you heal the gypsy. He was writhing in pain, and then you did something, said something, and he...calmed down. Now he's gone. He was so bloody and hurt. He couldn't have just walked out. You did something."

Rohan shook his head. "I can't bring you peace, Petra."

She flung out her hands. "But you worked some sort of magic."

"It's not magic, my dear." He sighed. "You're asking the wrong questions."

"What do you mean?"

Rohan scratched the top of his head. "Perhaps instead of asking how, you should ask why."

"Why do I want to go home?" Petra's voice squeaked.

"No, my dear." He studied her with patience. "Why are you here?"

Petra placed her hands on her hips. "I don't know that either."

"But have you asked?"

"And who would I ask? You?" She took a step closer and lowered her face even to his. "Do you know why I'm here?" she asked slowly and steadily, as if she was talking to someone who had difficulty understanding English.

"You're here for the same reason I'm here. Indeed, wherever any of us may be." He grinned at her, which made her even angrier. "To help."

"To help? Help who? Help with what?"

"Ask, and it shall be given you; seek, and ye shall find; knock, and it shall be opened."

She balled her hands into fists and thought of knocking Rohan on the head. "Show me where to knock, because I'd really like to know."

"Ask and receive not because ye ask amiss."

Petra applauded herself for not knocking the man to the ground.

"Some questions just don't have easy answers."

A snapping twig interrupted their conversation. Petra looked up as a shadow fell across the bench.

"Ah, Miss Baron." Garret took a deep breath and brushed the hair from his eyes. "I've found you." He looked uncomfortable. "Good day, sir, I'd come to accompany Miss Petra to the manor."

Petra didn't consider her conversation with Rohan over; she still had plenty of questions for him, questions she didn't want to ask in front of Garret.

"Shall we go?" Garret asked, his tone the same he'd use if he were asking if she'd like to witness a hanging.

Petra looked over her shoulder and saw Anne talking to Emory. Her heart pinged. He wore dark breeches, a white open shirt, a low-slung belt and despite his simple attire he looked like royalty. She couldn't hear their conversation, but she managed to hear the words 'rendezvous' and 'this afternoon.' From the expression on Garret's face, she knew that he had also heard their plans.

Garret followed her gaze and his scowl deepened. "Come," he urged her toward the waiting carriage. As he took her arm and tucked it into the crook of his elbow, he patted her hand as if to console her. "Good day, sir," he said to Rohan, leading Petra away.

\*\*\*

Garret looked worse than she felt. He sat in the carriage and stared out the window with lowered eyebrows. He had one leg crossed over the other and the top leg swung like a pendulum. Petra sat across from him, carefully avoiding his boot.

Carriages looked romantic with their velvet interiors and gold gilded paneling, but they smelled of horse poop and bumped and jostled over every rock and pothole. Petra and Garret bounced toward the manor in uneasy, teeth-rattling silence.

Until they stopped.

Garret reached forward and pounded on the dash. "I say, Fritz, how now?"

When Fritz didn't respond, Garret pushed back the curtain that separated the cabin from the driver's perch. No Fritz. Garret muttered a curse that she'd never heard before, but because it must have been bad, he gave her a sideways look and muttered an apology.

Seconds later Fritz appeared at the carriage door holding a large metal contraption in his hand. Garret asked what Petra was wondering. "What is that?"

A pink tinge stained Fritz's neck. "I beg your pardon sir, this is an axle." He cleared his throat. "A broken axle, to be more exact."

"Well, by faith, fix it."

The pink tinge moved to Fritz's cheeks. "I haven't the proper tools with me, sir." He looked balefully at the contraption.

Garret pushed out of the carriage, and Petra watched through the window. "Then how will we get home?" Garret demanded.

"It's not far," Petra said, considering her satin shoes and wondering how they'd hold up in a cow pasture before she said, "We could walk."

"Walk?" Garret's expression said he wouldn't have been more surprised if she had suggested they turned themselves into birds and fly across the field.

She saw the towers of Pennington Place on the other side of the hill. It wouldn't take long. She'd walked much farther last night. "It's right there."

"Walk through the field? With the cows?" Petra smiled because he looked so much like Kyle when he'd been told he had to drive his Uncle Billy's Oldsmobile to school because his Volvo needed an oil change.

She pulled her lips down, attempting to look

serious. "Well, they won't hurt us, will they?"

"They're filthy."

"But slow, right?" She didn't know anything about cows, but the ones on the cheese commercials always seemed good-natured.

The pink dominated Fritz's face. Sweat ran down his forehead and he pulled at his collar. *He's hiding something,* Petra thought. *But why?*

# Chapter Fourteen

*A bull is different from cows:*

*A bull is much more muscular, has larger hooves, a very strong neck, and a big, bony head.*

*A bull is taller and weighs a lot more.*

*A bull becomes fertile at about seven months of age.*

*A bull is nothing like the California happy cows in the TV commercials.*

*—Petra's notes*


Fritz answered by pulling down a basket from the driver's perch. The warm smell of fresh baked bread escaped from beneath the check cloth covering the basket and wafted her way.

*Mary, you sly match-making dog,* Petra thought.

"Sir, if you and my lady wish to retire in the shade of the tree," Fritz said, his words stiff, as if rehearsed. "I will fix the axle and return herewith." He pulled a quilt from his perch and tucked it over his arm.

*Herewith?* The blanket suggested a stay overnight. Petra glanced at the cloudless sky, grateful for the sun and warm breeze. "My lord, we can walk," she insisted.

"No!" Fritz said at the same time Garret

bellowed, "We will not!"

Petra rolled her eyes, annoyed, but then her annoyance turned to distrust. "Wait. If I stay here, with you, doesn't that…I mean, couldn't that…" she searched her memory. In Laurel's Regency romance novels, there were complicated rules of etiquette and if any were breached a marriage always seemed to be the punishment. Alcoves, terraces, and bed chambers were off limits, of course, but what about a tree in the middle of nowhere? Garret, as the son of an Earl, would be expected to uphold certain standards, but what were those standards? "If we stay too long together, alone, wouldn't that be bad for my reputation?"

Fritz blinked rapidly, his lips forming words he didn't say. Petra watched him through lowered eyelids. What was it with these people? Fritz, Mary, why were they so anxious for her to hook up with Garret?

"I will walk." Petra announced, scrambling out of the carriage. Her skirts caught on the door jamb, pulling her dress up around her thighs. She yanked them free.

Garret stared at her legs with an open mouth. "Alone?"

"Yes, alone." Petra swept a disgusted gaze over

him as she righted her skirts and headed for the split-rail fence.

"My lady, I beg of you," Fritz began. "I'll return shortly, you have my oath, but if you're in the field, I won't be able to find you."

"We could have been halfway home by now," Petra said over her shoulder. She pulled up her skirts to climb over the fence. Behind her, she heard gasps.

A hand on her arm stopped her mid climb. "My lady," Garret said. "Please, I know another way. We will be home within an hour."

The panicked expression on Fritz's face had eased, the pink had left his cheeks and returned to his neck.

"We'll have to go through the woods," Garret said in a tone that sounded like, *we'll have to go through hell.*

They walked silently up the hill beneath sun dappled trees. Garret matched his long stride to Petra's shorter one and she was glad for his quiet, if hostile company. Although she'd ridden to church in the carriage, supposedly on this same road, nothing looked familiar. They could have been transported to Italy for all she knew. "You do know where we are, right?"

"We aren't far from the village," Garret told her.

From a distance, the church bells began to toll long and low and Petra wondered why. It felt bizarre to be walking through the countryside with a strange man in a foreign place while church bells rang an ominous rhythm.

They rounded a corner and came face to face with a monster. Not literally a monster, maybe, but definitely monster-like compared to any creature Petra had ever seen up close and for real. Her mind said bull, but her gut said wooly mammoth. His horns glistened in the midday sun. Leaves of grass poked out of his mouth and twitched as he chewed. Standing three feet away in the middle of the road he seemed larger than any of his family members, distant brown menaces in a field.

Garret took a step backward and put a protective arm in front of Petra. "Let's hope he has already eaten his supper," he said softly.

The creature snorted, as if to say that he preferred humans to grass.

***

Emory squinted through the dust motes that filled the tiny wooden structure's air and counted the powder kegs. Sunlight peeked through broken, gaping slats. Spiders spun in the corners and hay, like a golden mountain, covered nine kegs. The gun powder was easily enough ammunition to blow a wing off Hampton court, destroy the translations, the translators and a few members of the king's court as well.

"My life for tinder and flame," Anne said.

Emory glanced at her. Her fever-bright eyes told him that she was only partly jesting. "Come," he said, putting a hand on her shoulder to draw her away. "We are halfway home. It is almost done."

Anne refused to budge. "But it tempts me so. We should set it now. Imagine the flames."

Emory, who had his own fearful memories of fire and flame, took her hand and pulled her down a cart path. "If we act too soon, they will have time to recover. The distribution is key. Until then, we cannot risk disclosure, nor can we endanger you."

"I have no fear of them," Anne said, shuffling and kicking up small dust devils.

"You should," Emory told her. "I fear for you."

"Because I am a gentle woman? Because you believe I should keep my concerns to home and hearth? But who is to say that the word of God isn't a womanly concern?"

"Chambers and his lot are dangerous, Anne. As you well know, this is not a game."

"Why have you no fear for yourself? Or for

Rohan?" Anne asked. "Rohan is not in his youth; he should be safely tucked into a monastery tending herbs and perfecting Latin."

Hearing voices, Emory stopped and placed his hand on Anne's back.

Anne also heard the raised voices and whispered, "Tis the Sabbath. Have they no care?"

Emory slid his gaze toward her, smiling at her hypocrisy and indignation. "Hush, perhaps it is our zealots," he murmured. Then he recognized the voices. Slowing, he crested a small hill and saw Petra, Falstaff carrying what appeared to be a picnic basket, and a bull standing in the middle of the road.

Petra waved a large stick in front of the bull's nose, but the animal didn't seem even mildly threatened. Further down the road was the carriage, lilting to one side with a wheel lying alongside of it.

Watching Falstaff and Petra battling the bull, Emory fought a wave of unreasonable irritation. "It would appear your would-be suitor is seeking another's favor."

"He is not my suitor," Anne said through gritted teeth. She dropped her hand and turned away.

"Not for lack of effort," Emory said. His heart

thumped, suddenly off rhythm, when Falstaff pulled Petra against his back.

"I'm glad he's turned his attentions elsewhere," Anne said, lifting her chin and sounding small and young.

Then Emory realized that he was responsible for the roaming bull. "Did you close the gate?" he whispered to Anne.

She leaned toward him. "A manly chore, much too difficult for a gentlewoman such as myself."

Emory's lips twitched. "We must help them."

Anne shielded her eyes from the sun. "They are as helpless as children." She said it casually, fondly even, but Emory heard a steely note in her voice.

Emory knew he had to take Anne home. He had only brought her because she had refused to tell him the information, Rohan's information, unless he'd let her join him. He should have left her in the churchyard and found Rohan himself, but Rohan had been speaking with Petra and he would rather compromise Anne than face Petra.

A bad decision and here he faced another decision. Turn away from Petra, Falstaff and the bull? Before he drew Anne away and bypassed the trio, he heard distant horse hooves. *It might be anyone,* he thought, but the chill down his spine warned him it was Chambers or his men.

It seemed Petra was not to be avoided.

# Chapter Fifteen

*King James authorized the Church of England's translation of the Bible in 1604. He appointed 47 clergymen who completed their task in 1611. Many factions of the church disapproved of the availability of the Bible to the common man.*
*—Petra's notes*

"He sounds unfriendly," Garret said.

The bull snorted, pawed the ground and made guttural noises in the back of his throat, but another noise caught Petra's attention. She looked around Garret's back to watch Emory and Anne at the fence.

"And what is friendlier than a Sunday afternoon picnic?" Emory said, stepping onto the road, before helping Anne over the sty. "May we join you?"

"Emory, can you not see they are already dealing with one uninvited guest?" Anne smiled but her eyes were calculating. She shook out her skirts; the hem was dirty and smudged.

In a world where it seemed very few of the opposite sex were on a first name basis, why did Anne get to call him Emory? Why did they get to wander through pastures together when she and Garret had to watch their toes for fear of being punished by marriage?

She looked to see if Garret shared her thoughts, but his attention was firmly focused on the bull. Petra's gaze flew from Emory to Anne and back to the bull, who, snorting and pawing, refused to be ignored.

Emory undid his belt buckle and fashioned a lasso. Petra's heartbeat accelerated as Emory looped his belt over the monster's horns. The bull fought, but Emory, avoiding horns, teeth and hooves pulled the creature behind the fence. Anne locked the gate and Emory vaulted to safety.

The entire episode had taken less than a minute. With his nose to the ground and grass sticking from his mouth, the bull seemed happy enough.

Petra wondered how long she and Garret had faced off with the bull. Maybe it'd only been minutes, but it had seemed like forever. How long would they have stayed there, trying to out-stare the bull if Emory hadn't shown up? She felt a smidgeon of reluctant gratitude.

"Well done, sir," Garret said. He glanced at the basket and quilt, as if he'd forgotten their existence. Gathering his resolve, he turned to Anne and said, "Let us retire to the shade of the oak and share some wine." It was a statement, but Garret made it sounded like a question.

Anne clapped her hands and said, "Splendid idea." All smiles and giddiness, Anne rang false.

"Splendid," Petra muttered. She stood apart, watching Garret spread the blanket over the spotty grass and buttercups. Anne settled on the quilt and drew her skirts over her tiny shoes. Garret drew bread, cloth wrapped cheese, apples and a pair of tin goblets from the basket and set them in front of Anne with a shy smile and a flourish.

"It appears a luncheon made for two," Anne said, cocking her head and smiling at him.

"Tis plenty for all," Garret said, a flush staining his cheeks, "especially for you."

Petra scowled, watching Garret fawn over Anne. Why had Emory and Anne both turned on their charm? What were they doing on this deserted road? Didn't Garret even wonder? What did he see in her? Why was he so into her? And was that hay on the hem of Anne's skirt? Beyond the hill stood some sort of a barn, had Emory and Anne been in the barn? Where were the etiquette police when they were needed?

Not that she wanted to force Anne and Emory into marriage.

"Are you not joining us, Miss Petra?" Anne

said, sweetly.

Emory, who'd been looking over her shoulder turned to smile at Petra's left ear. He didn't meet her gaze. She turned to see what he'd been watching. In the far distance, two men on horseback approached the barn. If they came closer, they would have to square off with the bull. She faced Emory and wondered if his sudden save the bull act had anything to do with the men on horses. Were Emory and Anne hiding from them?

A flicker in the back of Petra's mind told her that something more than hunger had brought Emory and Anne to their bull rescue.

"Please, Miss Petra," Garret said, motioning toward the quilt. "As gentlemen, we must remain standing until you sit."

"Or, should we defy convention, we risk of getting cricks in our necks conversing," Emory picked up the wine bottle and studied its markings.

"You must sit down, dear," Anne cooed. "The heat and the excitement of encountering the bull must have frightened you and you wouldn't want to cause yourself further harm."

Petra opened her mouth and then shut it quickly. She wanted to cause serious harm. The two men smiled at her. At that moment, she hated them all, but not knowing what else to do or where to go, she sat.

Garret sliced the apples with a knife that looked capable of taking down the bull. He laid cloth napkins before Petra and Anne and then placed thin apple slices on the cloth.

"Miss Petra, you employ the most interesting turns of phrases," Anne said, picking up an apple slice. "They are charmingly original to my ear."

"Yes," Emory agreed, accepting a slice of cheese from Garret. "Just last night I heard her say shuck you and I've been baffled ever since."

"Oh, I think you know what that means," Petra said, frowning at the apple slices. One had a brown spot, like a worm hole.

Garret looked at their faces. "I was not aware that the two of you had met before."

"Briefly," Petra said.

Emory flinched beneath Garret's gaze.

"Then perchance you can settle the mystery of Lady Baron's sudden arrival," Garret said.

"I am afraid not," Emory said. "Lady Baron is as much a mystery to me as to you."

"But if as you say, you met last night -- " Garret pressed.

"Tell us about your village," Anne said, smiling, but definitely interrupting. "Maybe something you say will ring true."

*Ring true?* As if she was lying? Of course she was lying. She couldn't very well tell the truth, no one would believe her. This was one of those instances where honesty was the worst policy.

"Yes, tell us more of your village, my lady," Emory said.

Petra took a deep breath. "Well, in Royal Oaks, if a *gentlemen* is nice one day, he'd also be nice the next."

Garret looked at Emory and Anne. "Nicety surely knows no geography," he said.

"You're kindness doesn't," Petra said, smiling into his eyes.

Garrett poured the wine into a goblet and set it in front of Petra.

She shook her head. "I don't drink, especially if there's a possibility of a sleeping potion."

Anne had the grace to blush.

"Suspicion, a malady, I'm afraid," Emory murmured, taking the goblet in front of her. "May I?"

Petra looked over his shoulder and watched horsemen at the shed. She was sure Emory was playing some sort of game and she didn't know the rules, was perhaps, even incapable of learning how to play. She didn't understand any of them. She felt like Alice at the Mad Hatter's tea party.

She stood, determined to not stay another minute. She didn't need funky mushrooms or drugged cakes to help her get away.

The men, surprised, slowly, reluctantly, climbed to their feet.

She nodded stiffly. "Goodbye." She knew she was ruining their party, but she didn't care. Anything seemed better than this. Emory made her feel like he was a cat and she was mouse.

Anne and Garret made her feel in the way.

***

Emory felt sick as he watched Petra leave. He'd caused her pain. Guilt settled across his shoulders. He tried to shake it off, tried to engage in Anne's and Falstaff's conversation, but he kept watching Petra, small and sad, walk away.

Anne laughed, and he supposed it shouldn't surprise him, but it did. He stared at his friend. The anger, where had it gone? What had Falstaff said to make her forget her vengeance for her brother's death?

Falstaff leaned forward. To Emory's amazement, Anne also leaned in. They were practically nose to nose. She looked…mesmerized. Laughter in her eyes, pink staining her cheeks,

Emory couldn't watch. It was too intimate.

"Excuse me," Emory said, quickly standing and brushing off his breeches. He cleared his throat and started again. "I'll walk Miss Baron to the manor."

Falstaff and Anne had their eyes locked on each other.

"Would you like us to accompany you?" Falstaff asked without breaking eye contact with Anne. He spoke like at school, saying something he knew that he should, but didn't mean.

Emory wondered what Falstaff would do if he said yes. Emory considered accepting Falstaff's offer, just to see what would happen. But Garret and Anne, caught in their trance, captivated by one another, were unpleasant company. "Thank you, no. I'll be off."

Anne didn't look up when he left.

Emory sped to catch up to Petra. He'd never known a lady who walked so fast. With her skirts clutched in her hands, she was near as brisk as many a man. Although, she looked nothing like a man. With her chin up she looked like an avenging angel.

Once he caught up with her, he wished he'd taken more time, because now, a few strides away, he didn't know what to say.

"If I've given cause for grief, I apologize,"

Emory addressed Petra's back.

She started to turn toward him, but then caught herself and poked her chin an inch higher, revealing her soft white throat. He waited for her to speak, but she didn't.

"I did not mean to be unkind," Emory said softly.

Petra stared straight ahead and after a few beats of thickening silence said, "You were kind the night before. You gave me a ring."

"To keep you safe."

Her chin lowered a fraction, but she continued to take long, fast strides. "Safe wouldn't be the word I would use to describe that night."

"And yet, here we are, a few days past, quite safe."

She pressed her lips together. "No thanks to you."

He gave a small laugh. "And how, my lady, do you think you landed at the gatehouse?"

She looked at him then. He saw anger, perhaps wounded pride, in her eyes.

"I don't know how you did that since I saw a man run a sword through you, but if you rescued me, why did you take me there?" She tramped ahead. When he didn't respond, she pressed, "Why couldn't I be safe with you?"

He racked his brain for something to say. *Turn around, walk away, do not ever look upon her again,* a voice in his head urged. He didn't know if he was prolonging both of their pain by matching her stride for stride, but he didn't listen to the voice. He couldn't leave. "You are safe at the manor."

She turned, fists clenched at her side. "With the men who ordered a gypsy hunt?"

"They would never harm you."

"And you would?"

"To your reputation I should cause irreparable damage --"

"And Anne's reputation? What about that? She gets to roll around in the hay with you, but I have to be packed off to the manor for safe-keeping?"

Emory's voice turned hard. "I assure you, Anne and I were not rolling in hay."

Petra sniffed. "You were with her, alone. Hay must have been involved because I saw it on her skirt."

Emory didn't answer.

"Besides, how can I have a reputation when no one here knows me?" Petra asked.

"They will come to know you," Emory said softly. "They will grow to love you."

She flounced away. "I don't want to know them!" she flung over her shoulder. "I don't want them to know me, let alone love me."

He caught up to her in two steps.

"And who is the ominous They?" she asked. "Who are you worried about offending?"

"Everyone lives by the rules dictated by society --"

"You say that, but I don't think it's true." Petra stopped in front of him and pointed her finger at his chest. "Not for you, at least. You might think it's true for me and all mere mortals like me, yet somehow you're above all that." Reaching out, she jabbed him in the belly where the sword wound should have been.

He didn't flinch. Too late, he realized he should have.

"You saw Black Shuck," she made it sound like he'd committed high treason. "Why didn't you die?" Taking a step closer she lowered her voice. "Why are *you* immune to the devil dog?"

He shook his head and said softly, "Do not mock what you don't understand."

She stood directly in front of him, her face lifted. A frisson tingled through him. *One step back, take the step, one and then two, do it.* The voice, normally so effective, didn't sway him. He couldn't leave.

Maybe that's why it was so surprising when she did. She was able to do what he dare not. He watched her go.

***

Petra prided herself on grand exits. She knew she did them well. Nothing said "you're zilch to me" as a little butt-swagger. No looking back. Looking back made the grand strut a lie. So when she looked back, she told herself she was looking for Garret and Anne with a cautious over the shoulder glimpse. When she saw Emory's attention fixated, not on her butt as it should be, but on a dusty wagon filled with straw, she flushed with anger.

Slowing, she considered her options. Backtrack to find Anne and Garret or go to the manor? She could look for Rohan and try to persuade him to help her go home, again. Not that she would know where to find him.

The manor's towers poked up over a distant hill. She supposed if she stayed on the same road she'd get there eventually. Garret wouldn't be there, but Chambers might be. Despite the warm sun, she shivered. She knew it was wrong to dislike someone because of their eyebrows, but she did. If she went to the manor, she'd be forced to hide in her room to avoid Chambers.

The dusty road passed farmhouses and barns. Her shoes weren't the walking type and after a few minutes, she stopped and leaned against a fence to remove them. Balancing on one foot, she slipped off her shoe and rubbed her tender heel. She looked up in time to see a hay wagon disappearing into a barn.

A crouching shadow crossed the field. Straightening, Petra watched. The shadow moved to the barn's gaping entrance. Petra stepped closer, just in time to see Emory slip inside.

Crouching, creeping, skulking— stalker words. Why would Emory stalk a hay wagon? It had to have something to do with the horsemen she'd seen him watching earlier. Her cheeks flamed. Covert action. She'd read the term in some book and she'd never had a reason to use it before, but it seemed to fit. Emory had used her for covert action. He and Anne had acted all friendly, but really they were hiding from the horsemen.

Petra climbed the fence and after a careful look for the bull, trailed Emory to the barn. Horses and cows milled around the pasture. The bull, a distant lump of brown, dozed in the shade of an oak.

A sheep trotted forward to inspect Petra's gown. Then, as if reading Petra's mood, bleated away. Petra peeked inside the barn. Dark and smelly, the barn appeared mostly empty, except for a hay wagon.

She caught sight of a pair of pitchforks stabbing and lifting hay off the wagon. She could only see the tops of the hats belonging to the two men. No sign of Emory, she thought, searching the barn's dark corners for movement. A ladder ran to a loft filled with hay. She watched the shifting straw. Not even a breeze moved through the barn.

"Chambers, he be wanting this loaded onto a boat," the man in the straw hat said. "Must be some boat."

*Chambers? Boat?*

"Laws, man," said the man in black hat. "I told you no names be mentioned!"

A pitch fork pointed at a cow watching them through an open window. "Who you think Betsy goin' be telling? The King?"

A hand swooped off the straw hat and swatted the black hat with it. Black Hat speared the straw hat with his pitchfork and lifted it high into the air.

"Curse you, Darby!" The pitchfork and hat fell to the barn floor, sending up a spray of dust motes.

Petra squelched a sneeze and then another. Turning, she smacked into a broad chest.

An arm went around her waist, pulling her against him, a hand clasped over her mouth. She knew it was him. The arm around her waist was too tight and the hand on her mouth too fixed. She marshaled all her self-defense know-how and elbowed him in the abs. She grinned at his surprised woof. After a quick glance at the hats, who continued their pitch fork work without breaking rhythm or conversation she brought her elbow up to deliver a blow to his nose.

Emory caught her elbow and used it to drag her to the far side of the barn. She let herself go limp and when he was unguarded, she threw her arm back, breaking his hold. Breathing heavily, she faced him.

Emory rubbed his nose. "What are you doing here?" He spoke quietly yet forcibly. With his eyebrows lowered he looked so haughty she wanted to rub his nose in a cow pie. There were plenty to choose from. She thought quickly and remembered the one name she'd overheard from the hats. "Spying on Chambers," she whispered, watching his reaction. He took a step back, obviously surprised. She took a step toward him. "What are you doing here?"

He glared.

"If I scream those men with pitchforks will make short work of you. Maybe you're not afraid of pitchforks, but I bet you're afraid of Chambers."

She cocked her head. "Why?"

He shook his head and ran his hand through his hair. "Why what?"

"Why aren't you afraid of pitchforks? Why are you interested in the hay wagon? What is Chambers loading onto a boat?"

He didn't reply and so she continued. "I could help you, you know. I'm staying at the manor. I could spend much more time with Chambers…not that he's pleasant company, but I could keep my eye on him."

"Keep your eye on him," he repeated slowly, a smile tugging at his lips. "That sounds uncomfortable." He reached for her, but she twisted away.

"You know what I mean."

"Yes. I find it frightening that I do." He folded his arms across his chest.

She mimicked his stance. "Tell me what's going on or I scream."

He tugged her to a stand of trees where they could talk above whispers. "You are *going* back to the manor."

She took a deep breath. "One."

He fought back a smile. "One what?"

She lifted an eyebrow. "Tell me by the count of three, or I scream."

"Don't be a fool." He looked toward the barn, uncertain.

"Two." She took a step closer to him. "I'm not a fool. I'm an AP scholar and top student in my honors English course." Tears sprang to her eyes when she considered the muddle she was in and far removed she felt from her real life.

"I do not know what any of that means, but I think you mean me to be impressed." Emory rubbed his nose again.

Petra blinked back another tear. This surprised her. She never cried, but everything was a huge mishmash. She felt like she'd lost not only her way home, but also her identity. Taking another deep breath, she steadied herself and opened her mouth to scream. Screaming was better than crying.

Emory rushed forward, took her in his arms, and silenced her.

# Chapter Sixteen

*Scientists once believed that people found kissing pleasurable because kissing lips generate an electrical current. This may not be true, but kissing can be shocking.*
*—Petra's notes*

His mouth tasted warm and slightly of wine. A warning somewhere deep within her sounded, but she pushed it away.

"Why would you help me?" he asked softly and she felt his breath and the movement of his lips against her throat. His hands spanned her waist. Before she could answer, his lips found hers again and he bent her backward, leaning over her.

For a few dizzy seconds she couldn't think of anything other than the kiss. "Everyone needs a little help," Petra said, struggling to find her voice. His lips returned to her throat, trailed down the side of her neck and stopped below her ear.

"I do not want or need your help," Emory said, running his hands up and down her back.

"Not exactly true," Petra said, pulling away so she could see his face. "Kissing, for example, is very difficult to do alone. Tell me what you want with

Chambers and I'll kiss you again."

He laughed. "You want to kiss me. Again."

She backed away and tucked a strand of her hair behind her ear. "I think I learned in biology class that you want to kiss me more."

He took a step toward her, and she bit her lip.

"Biology class? What other secrets did you learn in this biology class?"

She thought about everything science had learned since the 1600s and smiled. At the moment, she didn't want to talk about micro-matter.

"Tell me your secrets, and I'll tell you mine," she said, trying to sound calm, despite the rioting inside. Self preservation told her to run. Her emotions told her to lean into him. Her sensible self said she didn't know Emory and what she did know didn't make any sense. But he could hurt her. A lot. *I'm not safe with Emory,* she told herself and managed to take two steps back.

"I'm sure you'd find my secrets impossible to believe," he said in a ragged voice, running his hand through his hair.

"I'm pretty sure you won't believe my secrets, either. *I* wouldn't believe me, but you can trust me to spy on Chambers."

He reached her in one step and placed his hands on either side of her face. Staring into her eyes, he said, "I don't want you around Chambers --"

"You're the one who put me there," she reminded him.

He opened his mouth to speak, but she cut him off. "Tell me what to look for." She leaned toward him and kissed him on the lips. Remembering what Rohan had said, she whispered, "I can help. Tomorrow Anne is coming to the manor with another tapestry. I can watch Chambers and pass information to Anne, but first, I need to know what I'm looking for. And why."

"I am not as interested in Chambers as I am in you." Emory let her go and turned. "I shouldn't be interested in you. This is wrong."

She touched his arm, gently. "I agree." She steeled herself and tried to sound more rational than her clamoring emotions. She knew girls who hooked up with a different guy every weekend; they seemed to be able to casual kiss. That she'd never been interested in making out for make-out sake didn't mean it couldn't be done. Girls in the locker-room called it NCMO, noncommittal make-out. "A kiss *can* just be a kiss."

"It wasn't just a kiss for me." He intertwined their fingers and rubbed his thumb on the inside of her wrist.

Her blood thrummed beneath his touch. "It has

to be," she said, squeezing his hand as he pulled her to him. "I don't belong here."

"But you're here now." He leaned forward and rested his forehead against hers. "How long will you stay?"

She smiled. "Until I can find my way home. And until then, as long as I'm at the manor, I'll help you with your Chambers problem."

"Why?"

"You tell me."

He sighed. "You mustn't endanger yourself. Or take unnecessary risks."

She frowned. *Why is he such an adult?* she wondered. *Why does he act older than my dad?*

Then he placed his hand on the back of her neck and kissed her deeply. Suddenly even putting him in the same sentence as her dad seemed creepy. He murmured, "Promise me or the discussion is over."

She wanted him to kiss her again, but held his lips just a few inches away from hers. Finally, she said, "I promise I'll be very, very careful."

"Good." He stepped away, and she felt cold without him near her. "Chambers is dangerous. Worse, he's impassioned."

"About what?"

"He wants to destroy the translations of the King James Bible."

"The King James Bible?"

"You know of it?"

"Sure, the whole world knows of it." Petra immediately realized her mistake.

He looked baffled. "How can that be? It has yet to be distributed."

Petra thought quickly and avoided the question. Remembering the long and boring prayer Chambers had given over every meal at the manor, she thought, *What a hypocrite. Why pray if you don't believe?*

Turning from Emory's gaze, she stared up into the leaves of the alders and watched the shadows filtering through the branches.  She didn't know what she thought about God, but the universe seemed too perfectly balanced to exist without a creator. "Is Chambers an atheist? Is that why he's trying to stop the translations?"

Emory held up his hand. "No more questions. Why would you say the whole world knows of the King James Bible, when I assure you, the whole world does not. A vast majority of the world knows nothing of any Bible."

"That was a question." Petra folded her arms across her chest.

He opened his mouth and then quickly shut it. Obviously, he'd told her more than he thought safe.

She was struggling too. She'd just met Emory and sometime soon, she had to return to Royal Oaks and never see him again.

Emory took a step closer. "What I meant was no more questions from you."

"That's a double standard, isn't it? You're allowed questions, but I'm not?" Petra backed away, and twigs snapped beneath her feet. He didn't get to make up rules.

"That was, I believe, two questions." Emory stood in a shaft of sunlight, looking annoyed.

Petra sighed and wished they'd go back to kissing, but that didn't seem right or responsible. "How's this, I'll answer every question you ask for every question you answer."

He looked at her through narrowed eyes.

"You don't have to play my game," she told him, "but then I don't have to play yours."

He rolled his eyes, but nodded.

"Why weren't you hurt when I saw the sword go through you?"

"Who said you got to go first?" He shook his head. "Where are you really from?"

"You already know that, Royal Oaks." She stamped her foot. "I answered you, now you have to answer me."

Looking up at the heavens, Emory said, "I am

immortal."

He had to be lying, yet goose-bumps rose on her arms.

"I believe it is your turn," he said, his voice hard.

She sniffed and her voice wavered. "You don't get to just say you're immortal, because that doesn't happen without... something."

"Hmm." He rubbed his chin. "Would you believe in pixie dust? Dragon's blood? Or, perchance a magical potion?"

"If you have to think up options, you're lying."

"I gave you my answer. Do I get another question?"

"No!"

He took her hand and pulled her to him so that she rested against his chest. She thought about pulling away, but not much. She let his warmth swallow her.

"I refuse to play this fool's game any longer," he said.

"That's because you're lying and losing," she said, smiling.

He wrapped his arms around her and lowered his lips to hers. "I definitely think I am winning. I am the victor."

"Me, too," she said, and for a few minutes, she

felt lost to everything else.

"Come," he said, pulling her with him. "I must return you to the manor."

"And to my spy duties," Petra said, smoothing down her dress.

Emory groaned. "Is there any chance you might remain in your room?"

"You didn't tell me why Chambers wants to destroy the Bible," she said, as they walked toward the distant spires.

"I suppose that means no."

She cut him a glance. "What do you think?"

"I think that you would be safe in your room."

She laughed. "Sure. Whatever. Don't tell me, but I could help."

Emory held her hand as they walked through the grove. After a moment of obvious internal debate he said, "Chambers and unfortunately many others believe that only priests, those who have studied and been ordained by the church, should be allowed access to the Bible. They believe all laymen need a mediator with God." He must have read her puzzled expression because he added, "In other words, priests."

"It's a power thing," Petra guessed.

Emory smiled. "Yes. A power thing."

"Well, they won't be successful."

He studied her. "How can you be sure?"

Thinking about all the hotels all over the world with a Bible on every bedside table, she smiled. "I just am."

Suddenly, Anne's being there made perfect sense. "You'd said Anne's brother had been killed for truth and light."

Emory nodded. "He was killed protecting the translators."

# Chapter Seventeen

*Servants are not just employees. They are members of the household who live with the family. A good maid is attentive, discreet and a little bit psychic. She was there when you needed her but never in the way. She should be gentle with hairpins and corset laces.*
*—Petra's notes*

"You must ask him about falconry, miss," Mary said as she ran the comb through Petra's hair.

At the dressing table, Petra caught the maid's glance in the mirror. "Falconry? I know nothing about falconry."

Mary poised the comb above Petra's head. "It matters not." She might as well have added the word "duh."

"How can I talk of something I know nothing about? I'll look like an idiot."

Mary raised her eyebrows as if to say *so what?*

Mary dragged the comb through Petra's hair with brutal force. Her face screwed with intensity. "He's *into* falconry. If a bird can capture his interest, then I am sure my lady might do the same."

"Okay, I get you dislike being a chambermaid, but at least you have a job," Petra said.

Mary blurted, "What if he marries someone who already has a maid? I would be emptying pots for a lifetime." Mary shuddered.

"Since I don't have a maid, that you know of, you think Lord Garret should choose me? That seems a weak basis for a marriage."

Mary placed the comb on the table, giving Petra a moment of relief before she began to vigorously twist Petra's hair into long coils. "Unless haste is taken, Lord Garret will not choose his wife."

"No?"

"No." Mary blew out a sigh and thrust pins into Petra's hair with such force that her scalp tingled. "The master will decide."

*The master*, she knew it was a turn of phrase common to the day, but it gave her a sinking feeling. What if Anne and Garret belonged together?

"And the master has chosen the Bevan estate," Mary continued. "Mistress Bevan has her own maid."

"Most would, wouldn't they, but not me." Petra studied Mary's unhappy face, there was more the maid wasn't saying. "Is Miss Bevan so bad?"

Mary sniffed. "I have friends at the Bevan estate

and have heard stories of their mistress."

Although it was difficult to feel very sympathetic to someone poking her scalp with hairpins, she watched Mary with more compassion. "I'm sorry, Mary, there is no way I'm going to marry Lord Garret."

Mary closed her eyes and pursed her lips as if in pain and suddenly Petra remembered what Rohan had said, *"You are here for the same reason I am here. To help."* Mary's position could mean her survival. "I can't make Lord Garret fall in love with me, and I certainly won't marry him." She saved this last sentence for when Mary had finished with her hair.

Standing in front of the mirror, liking the way the deep blue gown matched her eyes, Petra thought about how she *could* help Mary. "You know, I think Lord Garret likes Anne."

Mary looked baffled.

"The tapestry girl."

Behind her, Mary shook her head, addressing the mirror. "Impossible."

"Why not?"

"Because earls sons do not marry artisans."

"I think he might be in love with her." Petra pulled at the lace of her cuffed sleeve. "I'm not sure about her, though."

Mary scoffed. "They'll not be looking for a love

match."

"We should all be looking for a love match," Petra argued.

Mary inhaled deeply. "What makes you think he favors her?"

"It's in his body language," Petra said.

"His what?"

Petra thought back to her AP psychology class. She folded her arms and leaned away. "See, this means I'm closed."

"Closed, like a shop?"

"Sort of," Petra said. "It means I'm not interested in what you have to say. But if I lean forward, connect my eyes with yours, like this," she demonstrated, "it means I'm engaged."

"Engaged?" Mary squeaked.

"Not that kind of engaged. It means I'm open to what you have to say."

"Gor, miss, this is a lot to remember."

"Most people don't remember. They just act instinctively, and others pick up on it. For example, if someone wants to kiss someone, they look at their lips."

"Kiss?" Mary muttered, looking doubtful.

"And another sign that they're interested is they cock their head, like this," Petra tilted her head at a forty-five degree angle. Mary imitated her, and they both laughed.

"Anne is coming this afternoon with a tapestry, right? Let's watch their body language."

After Mary left, Petra sat down at the dressing table and studied herself in the mirror. She looked different here. It was more than simply the lack of makeup, the dolled up hair and fancy dress. She felt different.

Putting her chin in her hands, Petra realized she'd been thinking so hard it was making her head hurt. Nothing at home had caused this much --- perplexion. Was that a word? If it wasn't, then it needed to be. She creased her forehead, dragging her thoughts back to her problem.

If she helped with the distribution of the King James Bible, that would be huge. She couldn't think of anything having more of an impact than the Bible, yet bibles dotted the globe and were found in grocery stores, mansions and huts. It wasn't as if she were here to right a wrong. But what if she didn't help? Then maybe they wouldn't. But of course, they would. Right? After all, it was the Bible.

There had to be another reason for her being here. Had she come to the seventeenth century to play matchmaker for Anne and Garret? That didn't make sense. Nothing made sense. Her being in the

1600s seemed like an elaborate and cruel joke. It might make a smidgeon of sense, perhaps, if Garret and Anne were her long forgotten ancestors, but Petra knew her father's people came from Denmark and her mother's family was German.

And Emory? Her heart twisted when she thought of Emory. She wouldn't think about him. He was like a guy at summer camp. A month of fun and then back to reality. Without him. A month? No. A week, tops. It'd already been three days.

Three days. What was her family thinking? That she'd run away? Were there posters with her picture up on telephone poles? Was her profile circling the web? Were police and dogs roaming the canyons searching for her?

What if Rohan was wrong and her being here was random? She couldn't help anyone, could she? In this place she wasn't even capable of taking off her own dress. What if the fortuneteller had sent her here just to be mean? Could a fortuneteller have that kind of power?

A rattle of stones on the drive announced visitors. Petra moved from the mirror to the window. Anne and her tapestries had arrived.

\*\*\*

Garret studied the tapestry with his head at a
forty-five degree angle. Petra sent Mary a glance to
see if she'd noted the telling "I'm interested" head
tilt. Mary's shrug said it was a hopeless match.

Garret appeared to be considering the tapestry's
colors and scenery, but to Petra everything in his
face said that all he saw was Anne. No footmen,
Petra, Mary, or Chamber—for Garret there was
only Anne. Chambers cleared his throat, clearly
hauling Garret back to the heavily populated first
parlor.

Anne stood at his shoulder, oblivious, and
waiting.

"The birds." Garret waved a hand at the
tapestry. "And the flowers."

Garret was tongue-tied. Petra wanted to help
him, but he had his gaze fixed on Anne's lips. Petra
decided there was little she could do about that.

"Possibly you would like to see it on the wall?"
Anne suggested. "In a different light?"

"Have you others?" Garret blurted.

"Is this not to your favor, my lord?" Anne
looked hurt.

"Tis not that. Not that at all. I just thought that if
you have others, perchance I might consider those
as well. Before I make a decision." Garret cleared
his throat. "Before I commit to a purchase."

"Yes, I suppose." Anne cocked her head at Garret.

Petra wanted to raise her hands and cheer. She'd known that Garret had a thing for Anne. Now, given the head cock, she guessed that Anne felt the same. Petra had to at least try and fuel the fire. "Perhaps Miss Gilroy has more at her home," Petra said.

Anne flashed her a startled look. "T'would be highly irregular for Lord Garret—"

"I will come to your home," Garret said, a happy flush staining his cheeks.

"But my father is away," Anne stammered.

"Mine too," Garret said, as if thrilled by this shared commonality.

"My Lord, it would be highly unseemly," Chambers said, stepping forward.

"We shall go now. Prepare the carriage." Garret turned to Fitz, his back to Chambers. "Will you do me the honor of escorting me to your studio?" he said, offering Anne his arm.

*Studio?* Anne had little more than a two room cottage, but she didn't look embarrassed or unhappy about Garret dropping in. In fact, she glowed.

"My Lord, your father would not approve," Chambers began. As he moved to block Anne and

Garret's departure, he stepped onto the tapestry.

Garret cleared his throat and looked pointedly at Chambers' boots. Chambers looked down at the lovers he had stepped upon, but didn't budge.

"My father would wish me to make an informed acquisition." Garret turned to Petra. "My Lady Baron, would you please accompany us?"

"Oh, yeah," Petra said.

Chambers cleared his throat.

"Of course, Chambers, you may also come." Garret rose to his toes. "And because I am hungry we will stop at the bakery for tarts." He looked at Anne and Petra as if daring them to contradict. "Which flavor do you prefer, Miss Clar?"

Anne looked pleased. "Currant jelly?"

Garret laughed as if she'd said the cleverest and wittiest thing. "Is that an answer or a question?" He snapped his fingers at Fitz. "Tell Chester to prepare the carriage."

Because Garret and Anne spent the ride to the bakery discussing tart flavors, Garret bought one of each flavor. At the cottage, Garret took Anne's hand to help her down from the carriage and then touched her face with a finger to wipe away a small smear of jelly.

Chambers wore a sour expression, and Petra guessed it had nothing to do with his rhubarb tart.

***

"I must see her again," Garret said, leaning into the velvet cushions.

"You've already bought her entire tapestry collection and commissioned another," Petra said, tapping her chin and thinking.

The carriage passed fields, a collection of barns, geese, and mill wheels; it looked like a perfect backdrop for fairy tales. Garret and Anne were like Prince Charming and Cinderella and everyone knew how that turned out. Although Petra knew not every romance had a happily ever after, she wanted to nudge Anne and Garret together.

Chambers glowered at her, as if he read her thoughts. "My lord, your father will never approve."

"Stuff and nonsense," Garret began. "I can afford tapestries."

Chambers sat up. "It is *nonsense* to engage the girl's affections."

Garret flushed red and studied the landscape flashing past. "I have said nothing of her affections."

"It is a great unkindness to trifle with her," Chambers said.

Garret looked at first at Petra and then at Chambers. "Do you think I have engaged her affections?"

"My Lord, have pity on the girl, I pray," Chambers said. "Do not lead her to where you cannot follow."

Garret returned his attention to the passing countryside, his face sad.

"It would never do," Chambers persisted. "You know your father."

"Yes, but—"

Hooves beat after the coach and a man's voice called, "Hail!" The carriage lurched to a stop. The horseman drew even with the coach, pulled the reins and brought his horse to a prancing halt. A horse tethered behind him pulled up short.

The horseman took off his black hat and Petra recognized one of the pitchfork-wielding men from the barn. "My lord, well met," he said, catching his breath.

"Well met, my good man," Garret said.

"I've come from Hampton Court," the man said, "with news from the Earl."

"My father?" Garret leaned out the window. "Is he well?"

The man tipped his head. "He is well. He sends his regard and requests your immediate attendance, my lord."

"Now?" Garret asked. "That seems highly irregular."

The man cleared his throat. "I beg your pardon, not you, my lord. 'Tis Master Chambers he wishes to see."

"Ah, very well then." Garret leaned back into the carriage, looking pleased.

Chambers did not look pleased. Petra watched Chambers and the horseman exchange loaded looks. The horseman rubbed a hand over his horse's neck, trying to calm the animal. "Post haste, sir. I have taken the liberty of bringing you a mount."

Garret smiled, but Chambers did not.

"Please ask my father to send word of when he plans to return," Garret said to Chambers.

Chambers climbed out of the carriage and leveled a glance at Garret from under his heavy eyebrows. "I will do that, my lord."

"Good day then, Chambers." Garret's voice had a singsong quality. "God speed."

"Good day," Chambers said, sounding as if he expected nothing good to come of it.

The carriage seemed empty without him, but empty in a nice, friendly way, as if a bad-tempered dog had been removed. They continued down the road in an easy silence and after a moment Petra asked, "How about a ball? A masquerade ball!"

Garret stared at her, considering. "But what if... *no one* will come?"

"I think everyone you want to come will come." Petra knew by "no one" he meant Anne. She tapped her chin.

"What makes you say so?"

Petra shrugged, liking her idea. "I just know but it will have to be soon. Chambers probably won't stay long. He didn't even take a bag."

"Chambers I can manage," Garret said. Left unspoken was, *but not my father*. Which to Petra, sounded very brave and a little stupid, but she didn't challenge him.

\*\*\*

Within the hour Petra, Mary and Fitz arrived at Anne's cottage. Fitz set down the trunk on the porch with a woof, and rolled his shoulders. Mary laughed. "I will be making it up to you, Mr. Fitzroy," she said.

Petra smiled. She didn't want to know how Mary planned on repaying Fitz. She rapped on Anne's door, and Anne answered with a puzzled look.

"Good day, Anne," Petra said, smiling and pushing her way into the room. "I'm here for two things."

Anne, who had her hair tied in a knot on her head and a smudge of ash on her nose, looked flustered and unhappy to have Petra in her home.

"First, I've brought you this." Petra handed Anne an envelope. "It's to a ball."

Anne looked at the invitation with a pained expression.

"And this," Petra motioned to the trunk, "is full of ball gowns."

Anne opened her mouth to protest.

Petra put up a hand. "Oh, you'll go. And you'll wear one of the gowns. You might even have a wonderful time."

Anne shook her head, but Petra stepped forward and opened the trunk. Inside were three of the Countess' dresses: a red brocade, a blue silk, and a creamy lace. "I'm sure they'll fit," Petra said, smiling. She knelt by the trunk and held up the red one. The edge of a note peeked out from the bodice.

Anne stepped forward, curious.

Petra stood. After an over-the-shoulder glance at Mary and Fitz who waited like statues at the door, she turned and whispered, "I have a message for Emory. You'll both be interested."

She didn't know if Mary or Fitz had an allegiance with Chambers, but she was sure Anne would read the note and pass on the information. Glancing down at her ink spotted hands, she hoped her struggle with the quill would pay off and that Emory would follow Chambers to Hampton Court immediately.

Anne's expression turned from wary to curious.

"You have to come to the ball tomorrow night," Petra said, no longer whispering. "Promise me."

Anne looked at the invitation and then at the slip of paper poking out of the red bodice, a small crease between her eyebrows.

"I think the red will look stunning," Petra said.

# Chapter Eighteen

*Masquerade balls were elaborate dances held by and for members of the upper classes. The parties became notorious throughout mainland Europe in the 17th and 18th centuries. They had a reputation for "improper" behavior such as unescorted women, lover trysts, and other secret activities. They deserved their bad reputation.*
*—Petra's notes*

"Dorrington has not changed in one hundred years," Rohan sighed over his glass of ale. "Babies are born, grow old and die, but the families remain."

"Carrying on where their fathers left off," Emory agreed, watching the crowd milling around the packed ballroom. Despite the masks, he picked out the Biddens with their carrot red hair and the Trents' characteristic baboon length arms.

"Bakers still bake, cobblers still cobble, farmers till and plow." Rohan set down his glass of ale and frowned at the musicians stumbling, already worse for drink. "Why are we still here?"

"Tired of me, old friend?" Emory asked.

Rohan grunted and then nodded toward the

door where Petra stood, holding the arm of Falstaff. She looked stunning in the blue gown, as nearly all the Dorringtons took note.

The villagers expected a match. Surely, the future earl would marry the wealthy, mysterious beauty; it was all anyone spoke of.

Typically Emory didn't listen to gossip, but tonight he heard it swirling around him. He set down his drink with enough force to shake the table.

Dorrington remained a small village a stone's throw from London. All those who frequented social events inevitably rubbed shoulders. Which is why Emory kept his shoulders to the sideline. In a world where children grew to parents, he couldn't risk recognition. He safeguarded his solitude. The sleepy village had grown in the past decade. Shops, farms, and a host of other businesses sprouted like weeds along the smelly river port, over the hills, and out into the countryside. A few even came close to his territory. He grimaced, at the thought of neighbors. He'd have to disappear again. Soon.

"What is Petra Baron doing here?" Emory asked. What had caused her to leave wherever she'd come from and rouse him from seclusion? How had she managed to get him to a ball? In a mask?

"An even better question, why are you at a masquerade ball?" Rohan echoed his thoughts.

Emory sighed. It had once bothered him how Rohan had an uncanny ability to read his mind, but he'd long grown used to Rohan and his ways. "You know I need to speak to her."

"A task I happily would have undertaken in your stead," Rohan muttered, bemused.

As usual, Rohan was right. Emory should have asked Rohan to make the request. Anne, given her new…giddiness, Emory couldn't depend upon, but he completely trusted Rohan. "I should leave." Emory stared into his ale, his voice heavy.

"No, you should stay," Rohan said, settling back against his chair and propping his fat feet in front of him. He wore a mask and his frock, which did little to disguise his pot-belly.

Emory also wore a mask, but he had changed from his everyday brown breeches to black velvet breeches and a ruffled white shirt. He felt ridiculous and not just because of the peacock feathers in his hat. His attendance had been wildly imprudent. He and Chambers had been practically nose to nose at Hampton Court, and his appearance at the ball would be all the more suspicious.

The musicians picked up their fiddles. The men, obviously self-trained, burst into a rousing rendition of *Barbra Jean*. Perhaps they were the best Falstaff could do on short notice. Their noise mingled with Emory's jumbled thoughts. He would go mad if he stayed. He pushed away from the table to seek out Petra.

"Will you dance?" Rohan asked, laughing.

Emory sent him a withering look and bumped into a woman with furiously batting eyelashes. He brushed past with a quick apology and scanned the room for Petra, but instead his gaze landed on Anne.

Anne typically had a calm, practical, almost level-headed approach to her plots of revenge, but when he had last seen her, she'd seemed almost flighty. Why?

He flushed, because he knew. Young Falstaff. Or rather, Young Falstaff's feelings for her. Her feelings for him. The emotions had changed her from the sad, angry fighter he'd known, into a lovesick girl. This worried him. He didn't wish her further pain.

Speaking of pain, he ran his finger along his collar, pulling at the ruffles. He hated constantly changing fashion in general and ruffled collars in particular.

Mrs. Livingston and her daughter, Jane, had spotted him. If they recognized him, so would

Chambers. He'd managed to skirt the attention of most of the villagers, but somehow he'd fallen into Mrs. Livingston's path and she refused to let him be. Tonight she wore a ruby red dress with faux jewels studded across her enormous bosom. Jane, who lacked her mother's impressive prow, looked hot and uncomfortable in a yellow dress that gave her a jaundiced appearance. The feathers on her mask matched the color of her skin, giving her a washed out raccoon look. He tried not to watch as they twittered behind Mrs. Livingston's fan.

His being here, hobnobbing with gentry, this was Petra's doing. He should be angry with her, but he felt desperate to see her. Alone.

***

Petra tried to keep track of Anne and Garret, but they kept weaving in and out of the dancing couples. From the whispers she'd heard, no one recognized Anne in the late countess' ball gown and everyone wanted to know about the mysterious stranger dancing with the future earl.

Petra clung to the back wall, trying to eavesdrop and yet be invisible, but a growing collection of men bounced around her. Who were these guys and why were they hounding her? Had Garret sent flunkies? Irritation flashed through her. He'd promised that she wouldn't be a *wallflower*, his word, and an interesting one, that obviously meant some sort of party pity person. What had he told his... what were they, these guys? Friends? Dorchester with the concave chest, Littleton with the hair sprouting from his ears, the duke of something with a wart on the side of his nose. Who were these people to Garret and what did he expect her to do with them? Dance, she supposed, but she had other ideas. She sighed, looking over the crowd for Emory.

"Excuse me, Miss." A guy with a ruddy-cheeked fresh-scrubbed look touched Petra's elbow. He had red hair brushed off his forehead and freckles dotting his skin. "Would you do me the honor?" He held out his hand.

"Honor? Oh, you mean dance." She wouldn't look him in the face. "No, I'm sorry," she said, addressing his boots. "But no. I've a headache." True. Technically, her head didn't hurt, but these guys were a headache. Besides, she didn't dare dance in this odd parade of bows, curtsies and the occasional foot stomp. She wondered what these people would think of the Royal High school prom.

"Perhaps I might fetch you lemonade?" he asked.

Petra smiled. "That would be awesome."

"Awesome?" Behind the mask, his eyes looked confused.

"Hum...lovely?"

After the guy left, Petra felt a touch on her arm and she knew who it was even before he spoke in her ear.

"That's the fourth partner you have turned down," Emory said.

Petra attempted a laugh to cover her rising temperature. How did he do this to her? Why did his touch skyrocket her blood pressure? When did he get this power over her? She kept her voice light. "You're keeping score? I thought you've been too busy lurking in dark corners to keep track of my dance card."

She looked down at the card in her hand with its lines and signatures. She didn't know exactly how it worked and she'd been too embarrassed or afraid to ask. She wished Mary had come with her, so that she'd have at least one friend in the crowded room. She looked at Emory in his black velvet breeches and feathered mask. Was he her friend, or something more?

They both watched the ruddy boy weave through the crowd bearing the lemonade like a lantern. "And now you will have to chat with him to repay his kindness, and he looks about as conversational as a turnip. Or a beet."

Petra, refusing to be teased, pointed across the room at Anne and Garret. She'd convinced Garret to wear a red scarf and vest thingy and she'd told Anne to wear the red dress. "They match."

"Is that your doing?" Emory's mouth turned down.

"You know it's Garret's doing."

"And where did Anne find a gown at such a late hour?"

Petra sniffed. "I think they look sweet."

"It will never do."

"Why not? I mean, I know they're young."

"Everyone here expects him to marry you, the wealthy, mysterious stranger." Emory leaned forward and murmured in her ear.

The whisper of his breath on her throat sent her blood swooshing which she tried to ignore. She opened her mouth to protest.

He stepped back. "You did not know?"

She shook her head. "I'm as dull as a turnip or a beet, remember?"

"Your beauty is the subject of all of Dorrington's gossips."

"Then I'm glad I can provide some entertainment." She swallowed and tried to turn the conversation to something less personal. "How about you? Did you find any of my information useful?"

He glanced over his shoulder at the approaching Mrs. Livingston.

Petra followed his gaze and laughed. "Is she why you're hiding out with me?"

"There is little I prefer to hiding with you." He took her arm. "Perhaps we should have this conversation on the terrace."

"The terrace?" A nervous laugh, bordering on a giggle, escaped. She abhorred giggling, but she couldn't stop. "Isn't that where lovers go for scandalous activities?"

Emory ran his fingers through his hair. "I promise no scandalous behavior."

Petra frowned. "Well, that's disappointing. If you won't promise scandalous behavior then I think I want to stay here and watch you face off with Mrs. Tremendous Tatas."

Emory scowled and groaned. "Pray tell, what are tremendous tatas?"

"Do you really need to ask?" She laughed when he blushed.

"Outside, lest we're overheard."

"So you admit it," Petra said. "You are hiding."

"As are you!" Emory said.

Petra tried to recall the social rules of Laurel's Regency romances. "I remember young women became somehow tainted if go on terraces or into alcoves with men."

"I thought you hadn't a memory."

She balked.

"A walk in the garden then?" he persisted. "We have walked in gardens before."

"I will not marry you, really marry you, no matter who finds us where." She knew she shouldn't go. She knew her resolve, when it came to Emory, was weak. He was like chocolate, a sticky mess, impossible to resist.

"Good." Laughing, Emory took her elbow and led her through the back of the room. Above the center of the dance floor hung a chandelier strung with innumerable candles and pieces of cut crystal, but Emory stayed where the chairs lined the walls, mindful to stay in the corners where flickering sconces did little to break the darkness.

The double doors stood open, and a cool breeze blew down the deserted hall. Petra took a deep breath. It felt good to be free of the perfume and body odors that filled the ballroom. The music, blaring and jingling, was now muted to background noise, and she found the tension in her shoulders easing. A cool moist breeze blew in from the river and played with her curls. The night air felt good.

"Wait here," Emory said. Seconds later he returned with a heavy cloak that he threw around her shoulders. It smelled of leather and cloves.

Emory stopped beneath an arbor, swearing beneath his breath. "Chambers saw me when I retrieved my cloak. I hope the mask had been ample disguise."

Rose buds dotted the thorny vines climbing the trellis. In a few weeks the buds would blossom, but for the moment, they were pinched closed, each a promise. Heady-scented honeysuckle spread over the soggy ground. Petra swallowed as a dark figure in a swirling cape emerged from the manor's wide double doors and paused on the steps. He looked over the garden and Petra saw his porcupine eyebrows and the long shadow he cast over the stone walk. She took a deep breath and clutched Emory's arm.

"Follow me," she whispered, pulling at Emory's sleeve. She raised the hood of the cloak and hurried around the manor, unaware if Emory had followed. Careful to keep her footing on the uneven bricks, she stopped at the kitchen garden's picket fence. With a quick glance over her shoulder, she saw Emory right behind.

Emory pulled her to him as she lifted her skirts and attempted to step into the garden. "There's a fence for a reason," Emory said.

"Yes, to keep out rabbits." Petra shook off his arm.

Emory tightened his hold, forcing her to straddle the knee-high fence which snagged her skirts and exposed her ankles. He watched Chambers and then turned back to Petra.

Petra climbed to the far side of the fence and Emory followed. Keeping her face averted from the approaching Chambers, she whispered, "Tell me what happened in Hampton Court. You went, didn't you?"

"You there!" Chambers called from across the grounds. "A word!"

With her head turned she whispered, "You should see what he wants. He might get suspicious if you don't."

"He already is suspicious. We met at Hampton Court."

Petra's jaw and stomach dropped. "What will you do?"

"As I have previously planned. The true question is, what will you do?"

"Me? Why?" Petra asked, nerves jangling. "Is our being together in the dark garden, how did you say it, damaging to my reputation?"

Emory released her elbow and pulled the hood of the cloak to cover more of her face. Tucking her hair into the hood, he asked, "You would rather I leave you alone in the dark?"

Petra waved her arm in the general direction of the crowd emerging from the manor's double doors. The moon beneath the clouds had risen to its zenith. The hour was late, and departing guests trooped down the broad steps and lingered on the walk. Carriages stood waiting in the moonlight, horses shook their harnesses and stamped their hooves, impatient to leave. "I'm hardly alone."

Suddenly from inside the manor came a clamor of bells and the beating of a drum. Chambers, who had stood on the edge of the departing crowd, disappeared in the crush.

"What's going on?" Petra asked, watching the villagers rush into the manor.

"There must be an announcement." Emory took her arm and guided her toward the stables. "Come."

Petra shook off his hold and started toward the ballroom, but he captured her hand. "I thought you wanted to hear about Hampton Court," he said.

She pushed her hair out of her eyes. "I do, but aren't you curious?"

"Perchance, but I would not risk another meeting with Chambers."

When cheers and applause erupted from the manor, Petra felt like she'd missed the final touchdown of a close football game.

"We will never have a better opportunity to speak," Emory said.

She raised her eyebrows. "Really? Why not just break into my room again and we can talk there." She smiled when he started. "Who else would return my quilt?"

He flushed, and turned.

"Did you eat the food as well?"

Emory studied the moon, but after a few moments, he replied, "Tam ate the food."

"Tam the gypsy?" She moved to stand in front of him.

He folded his arms. "They prefer to be called Roma."

The music and the noise of the crowd rose to a deafening level. Petra cocked her head at the manor and asked, almost yelling, "Don't you want to know --"

Emory shook his head, frowning. "I believe I already know."

"You do? What is it?"

"Young Falstaff's announced his engagement."

Petra stared at the manor wishing she could see inside. She had an image of a crumpled Anne lost in a dark corner, pompous Garret standing on the platform with the plain and rich Miss Bevan. "Poor Anne."

Emory looked grim. "Indeed. She'll have a hard time of it."

Anger flashed through Petra. Why would Garret spend the evening dancing with Anne when he knew he would marry Miss Bevan? Why would he lead her on, buy her tarts, commission her tapestries when his marriage to the Bevan estate was a signed and sealed deal? "I guess his dad will be happy."

Emory looked surprised. "No. He'll be furious, which is exactly why Young Falstaff acted during his father's absence."

"Do you mean he's marrying Anne?" Petra's voice nearly squeaked. "How can he, they just barely --"

"When an earl, or in his case, an almost earl, decides what he wants, he generally gets it."

Petra closed her open mouth. It sounded so like herself. "But she's so sensible; I'm surprised she said yes."

Emory barked a small laugh. "Do you suppose he *asked* for her hand?"

"Wait. What? He didn't ask? He just assumed she'd say yes?"

"If he'd asked her, as you said, perchance she'd refuse." Emory took her hand and led her to the side of the manor where it was quieter. Away from the crowd's clamor she heard crickets, a hoot owl, and animal noises coming from the stables.

"Young Falstaff had to act quickly while the timing worked in his favor. How opportune to have his father and her father away at the same time. He'll have the bans at the church drawn up before their return."

"You make it sound like a bad thing. I know it's quick, they must hardly know each other, and they are very young."

Emory looked out over the manor's lands. "His family, particularly his father, not to mention the neighboring gentry and friends will cause her hell and she'll be cut off from her own people."

Petra waved at the manor. "The neighbors sound happy – extremely happy."

"I am sure Falstaff uncorked his father's wine cellar in celebration. Be sure, my lady, Anne's days of trial will come."

"Well, if he loves her --"

"He has spent a total of ten minutes of conversation with her, how can he know if he loves her?"

A dead feeling crept over Petra. "He should marry whoever he wants," she said.

"Some matches are impossible." Emory looked bleak, and Petra wondered if he were no longer talking of Anne and Garret.

"Improbable, not impossible," she said, quoting Laurel. She touched his hand. "I'm going to assume they'll be happy. Being happy is a head game."

During her mother's illness, Grammy Jean had taken her to a counselor to "help you make sense of your changing world." Doctor Hartman, a middle-aged motherly sort with a mustache and a fondness for peppermints, liked to speak in platitudes. Petra, though only eleven, had rewritten a few. *She who dares wins* became *she who tries dies*, and *seize the day* turned to *sneeze the day*.

Back then, she had hated visiting Hairy Hartman. She had much better things to do with her after-school hours than chat up with some old, weepy woman. Odd that now, in another time and place, Doctor Hartman would suddenly make sense. She shook herself out of the memory, determined not to give in to *the mopes*—another of Hartman's phrases—or *the dopes*.

She turned to Emory. In the gentle starlight, he was beautiful and he was here. And so was she.

True, she didn't know how long she'd stay. She knew she couldn't take him with her when she left, but according to Hartman, she should be happy right here, right now, doing something she knew was important to the world, not just in her world, but the world in general… meaning everyone.

"What happened at Hampton Court?" she asked.

He moved away from her. She knew he didn't want her involved in his save the Bible crusade. Well, too bad.

"They had trouble getting the kegs in the cellar, but eventually they did."

"You just watched?"

Emory stiffened under her implied criticism. "The King needs to discover the plot and those involved. We have to wait for the right moment."

Petra sniffed.

"Unfortunately, I believe Chambers saw me." Emory shrugged.

"But if he really thought you were a threat, he would have come after you."

Emory took a deep breath. "Not necessarily. It is likely that the Earl will hold Chambers at least partly responsible for Young Falstaff's engagement. I would hazard a guess that at this moment Chambers is furious with Young Falstaff. Of me, he may have suspicions, but of Young Falstaff he has concrete reason for anger."

"We should go to Hampton Court."

Emory shook his head. "My lady, there is no 'we', and I am not in any danger."

"Oh yeah, I forgot. You're Mr. Immunity."

He smiled and borrowed one of her phrases. "Something like that."

"But how are we going to stop Chambers?"

"*You* must watch Chambers and let me know when he leaves again." He pulled her to the side door and lifted her hand. Gently, he kissed the inside of her palm. "*I* will stop Chambers. Until then, goodnight, Petra."

He turned to leave, footsteps scrunching on the pebbles that led down the path. In the dark moonlight, the world seemed quiet and still on this side of the manor, but on the other side of the manor there would be the crowd of villagers. And Chambers.

"Wait, no," she called after him. "How will I let you know?"

"You may send a message through Anne," he said over his shoulder.

Petra scowled. Anne again. Why did Anne get to play go-between? "Where are you going?"

Turning back, he reached around her to push

open the kitchen door and  then he pushed her
inside. "To bed, of course," he said, shutting the
door behind her.

# Chapter Nineteen

*An engagement or betrothal, seventeenth century style:*

*A legally binding contract.*

*Parental permission required for anyone under the age of 21.*

*Penalty, fines and a trip to the church court could result if anyone got cold feet and tried to renege.*
—*Petra's notes*

Mary bustled into her room, and pulled back the drapes with a flourish. If she'd been an actor in a musical she would have burst into song.

"You're happy about the engagement," Petra guessed, watching Mary dance around the room.

Mary shook a yellow dress at Petra, motioning for her to hurry.

"Am I going somewhere?" Petra ran her tongue over her teeth, longing for a toothbrush.

"You have a visitor, my lady." Mary's voice had a new trill. "Tis Mistress Anne."

"Already?" Petra swung her feet to the floor and stretched. Mary came to pull the nightgown over her head. It still felt odd to have Mary dress her, like she was a life-size doll or a store mannequin.

Mary practically threw her clothes on her and then began attacking her hair with a comb. "Do you know why?" Petra asked.

"Well, if I was her, I would use the excuse to spy out my new home." Mary used the comb to pull Petra's hair.

"She's been here before."

"Not as the future mistress," Mary said, smiling, twisting Petra's hair into long coils.

"Mary, do you think Anne and Lord Garret will be happy together?" Petra asked.

"Happy?" Mary poised a pin above Petra's head.

"I know you're happy about Anne, but do you think Anne will be happy?"

Mary looked as if she'd found flowers sprouting from Petra's head. "Why would she not be happy?"

"Will people be nice to her?"

Mary lowered the comb, confusion creasing her forehead. "I thought you disliked Mistress Anne?"

Petra took a deep breath. "Why would you say that?"

"Well, you were not sunshine and happiness when you met. You discouraged Lord Garret from purchasing her tapestry."

The first time she'd met Anne, Anne had

drugged her, poked through her things and had called her stupid.

"And when we went to her cottage, you were..." for once Mary seemed to be considering her words, "telling her what to do."

She'd been bossy. Being bossy in some situations was a good thing. It made her good with animals, it made her a good editor of the Royal Oaks high school newspaper, but probably not a good friend.

"I want people to be nice to Anne. I..." she faltered. "I wish I'd been nicer."

Mary didn't look up from Petra's buttons. "You'll be kind to her, won't you Mary?"

Mary snorted.

"Of course you will. You can't afford to lose your job." How sad if her only "friends" were people who were paid to be kind to her.

"Mary, are you sure Anne is here to visit me? Perhaps she's here to see Lord Garret."

Mary, who'd been bent over the buttons, straightened. "A lady would never presume to call upon a gentleman."

"Even one she's going to marry?"

Mary lifted her eyebrows. "Besides, Lord Garret has gone to London to speak to his father." Mary gave Petra a broad, encouraging smile and pushed her toward the door.

"Well, that'll be interesting." Petra wondered what kind of man he was. He probably wasn't horrible because Garret wasn't horrible.

But he did have a torture chamber in his basement.

And he had hired Chambers. Hadn't he?

\*\*\*

Anne stood in the first parlor, wringing her hands, eyes red. She rushed toward Petra and caught her in a hug.

"Good morning, my Lady Petra," she said loudly enough for the servants to hear.

Then she whispered in Petra's ear, "Friar Rohan has been arrested. I would not have come, because I hate to disturb you, but I cannot find Master Emory."

Petra stepped away, taking Anne's hands in her own, wondering which of the questions flying through her head to ask first. *Where is Rohan? Why was he arrested? Why are you looking for Emory? Where have you looked? Do you often look for Emory?*

Anne moved to the table and placed a hand on Petra's purse. "I've returned your things. I believe you must have left them at my house the other morning."

Petra opened the purse, not expecting to find answers, but for something to do with her hands. When an answer came, it surprised her. The phone, Zoe's Girl Scout Gadget, the lipstick — they reminded her of a faraway world. Her world. In time, would she be more at home in 1610 than 2014? She thought of her family and felt sad. "Would you care to walk in the garden?"

When Anne nodded, Petra took her hand and picked up the purse. "Follow me," she said, drawing her to the French doors.

*Not a great day for walking,* Petra decided when she opened the doors and a bank of fog rolled in. Cold moist air hung between them. When they passed the rose trellis, away from the ears of the servants, Petra asked, "Where have you looked for Emory?"

"Everywhere!"

A twinge of jealousy pricked. It bothered Petra that Anne, engaged to Garret, worried about Emory enough to look *everywhere* for him. She shivered, remembering the torture chamber. "Do you know where Rohan is?"

"In a cell at the edge of town."

Petra relaxed a fraction. A cell at the edge of

town sounded much kinder than the rack and pulleys in the chamber. She reminded herself that Rohan seemed to have amazing healing abilities. "Do you know why?"

Anne shook her head. "I'm sure it has something to do with the trip to Hampton Court yesterday."

Emory had said Chambers had seen him. Had he also seen Rohan? "They can't just throw someone in jail for going to Hampton Court."

Anne looked at her blankly. "Of course they can. My Lord Garret is away, and that leaves Chambers in charge. He can do as he sees fit. He usually does."

Petra thought. Anne had Garret tied around her finger, and Garret had more weight than Chambers. "We just need for Rohan to be safe until Lord Garret returns."

Anne wrung her hands. "We don't know when that will be."

"Not long, though, right? Hampton Court isn't far."

Anne looked bleak. "Perchance 'tis long enough."

Long enough? Court cases in the twenty-first century took eons, but maybe not so in the seventeenth.

"If Emory were here, he could free Rohan." Panic tinged Anne's voice.

Petra wondered exactly how Anne's brother had been killed.

*We don't need Emory*, Petra decided. She took Anne's hand and pulled her back to the manor. "We'll get him out," Petra said. "I've got an idea."

\*\*\*

Raiding Anne's father's chest of clothes gave Petra an odd sense of déjà vu. It reminded her of when she and Robyn had put on their old prom dresses for the Renaissance fair. They'd been dressing up, playacting, then too, although the stakes had dramatically changed. Now, just four days later, it seemed silly that she'd thought a date to the prom had been so all consuming important. Anne's brother had died trying to protect the translators of the Bible. Rohan had gone to jail, and Emory had disappeared. The prom seemed trivial in comparison.

Anne tossed out breeches and shirts. "You cannot guess what has become of Master Emory?"

Petra shook her head, wondering if Anne was in love with Emory. The thought gave her a sick feeling, even though she knew she couldn't have a future with him. Whatever her future was.  A cottage with milk cows? The suburbs with a minivan? A city with a briefcase? Did Emory fit in any scenario other than the one with a cottage and cows? She didn't even like cows, and she really didn't like bulls.

Even though she knew she shouldn't, the thought of Anne's relationship with Emory worried her. If Anne loved Emory, why would she marry Garret?

Petra bolstered up the nerve to ask something she'd wanted to know for a long time. "Anne," she said. "How do you know Rohan and Emory?"

Anne selected a pair of breeches and held them up. "I have always known Rohan," Anne said. "He introduced me to Emory a few years ago." She paused. "I have never shared this, but Emory reminds me of an uncle I had when I was little. But that doesn't make sense, does it? Because Emory, if anything, is younger than me."

Petra reached into her purse and pulled out her panties and bra. They'd been washed and unworn since her arrival at the manor and they reminded her of her other life. She turned her back to Anne, stripped down and put them on. When she turned around, she saw Anne's gaze flinch away, like she didn't want to be caught staring.

"This is what we wear in my village," Petra explained.

Anne blushed and studied her shoes.

Petra looked down at the lacy bra and panties. They were modest by 2014 standards and probably shocking to Anne. To Petra, they felt good, infinitely more comfortable than 1614 underwear. Petra considered a large, ugly jacket made of smelly wool. Maybe smelly could be useful.

"Where did Emory come from?" Petra asked, thinking of the maps in his cottage. She put on a pair of well-worn and loose breeches and tucked them into the baroness' boots she'd borrowed. Then, she rolled the sleeves of the cotton work shirt and shrugged into the wool coat. Tugging at the belt holding up Anne's father's pants, she took a deep breath. It felt so good to move without the weight of skirts, petticoats and stays.

"All I know is he is a friend of Rohan." Anne put on a felt hat and began tucking up her hair. "Are you sure of your plan?"

"Cross dressing always seems to work in Shakespeare's plays," Petra said.

"Shakespeare?" Anne asked. "You know of him? Have you seen his plays?"

Petra started to say she'd read some of them, but then thought better of it. She didn't know if his work had been published in 1614. "A few," she said, squelching the familiar tug of homesickness before it sidetracked her.

*Maybe we should wait for nightfall,* Petra thought, biting her lip because those hips refused to hide even with a long jacket.

"Hold still," Petra said, trying to a wrap a thin blanket around Anne's waist. If she used the quilt to bind Anne's breasts and thicken her waist, maybe it would give her the appearance of a fat man in an oversized coat.

Petra fashioned a scarf about her neck. "Just keep your chin down and your hands in your pockets." Petra gave Anne's figure a doubtful glance, smiled, and nodded.

Petra looked in the mirror. She'd make a good villain in a melodrama. All she needed was a mustache.

"I still don't understand how you're going to cause a distraction," Anne said moments later, as she followed Petra out the door.

"You will," Petra said, considering, for maybe the tenth time, showing Anne the phone. She simply didn't want a long, impossible conversation on how her tiny phone sounded like it had an entire rock band inside. She'd have to explain what a  rock band was, which could possibly lead to a discussion on electric guitars, and techno-pop. And no one could explain techno-pop.

She handed Anne the vial of tincture. "Ready?"

# Chapter Twenty

*The jail, or gaol, was used for detention, not for the punishment of criminals. It held those waiting trial and those found guilty and awaiting punishment. Sentences were usually whipping, flogging, or death. The detention period was short, which, in most cases, was not a good thing. The jail keeper usually kept his keys on his belt, and this was a good thing.*
*—Petra's notes*

The public house sat at the edge of the square. From the woods Petra could just make out the barred windows. Anne drew her to the other side of the building, where a guard sat on a stool in front of the door. He had a brown jug at his feet and a ring of keys on his belt. A dark cloud hovered, threatening rain.

A few villagers walked up the street, on their way to market. No longer breakfast and not quite midday, the inn beside the jailhouse looked empty, although the innkeeper and his wife were probably inside preparing lunch. The bakery across the lane had pies in the window, and a fragrant smoke rose from the chimney stack. From inside came a scolding voice.

A mean wind blew in, tossing leaves and branches. Undoubtedly it would be better to wait for night, but Anne said conviction and sentencing didn't have to wait for a trial. And a storm waited for no one.

What if they were caught? Chambers might want to put Anne behind bars, but would he risk turning Garret against him? Of course, as far as Chambers was considered, Petra was expendable.

Anne lifted her loom mallet and gave Petra a wide eyed look as if to ask *now what*? Petra smiled nervously, and took her phone from her purse. She took a deep breath, trying to calm down. *I'm here to help*, she reminded herself.

Flipping open the phone, she scrolled through the options, and pressed a button. Barking dogs.

The guard, a beefy guy not much taller than Petra but much heavier, looked in their direction, shifted in his chair, pushed back his hat, and closed his eyes. A dog in the street spun in circles, snout lifted for scent.

Anne stared at Petra. Petra flashed her another brief smile and then returned to her phone. Moments later, Breaking Benjamin began to scream. Petra upped the volume and watched the guard dash into the woods.

Anne jumped from behind the log to trip the

charging guard and then hit him over the head with her mallet.

Petra switched off the phone, dropped it and lunged for the keys as Anne whacked the guard again.

"Let's hide him behind that boulder." Petra took one arm. Anne grabbed the other and they dragged him a few feet.

"Hurry," Anne urged, her mallet poised over the guard's head.

Keys in hand, Petra took off for the town square, holding the cloak tight to hide her face. The bakery still rang with scolding. Only a tailor, a round man with a gimpy walk, came to watch Petra throw the keys into the cell window.

"Hey!" the tailor called, but Petra sprinted back into the woods, choosing a path that wouldn't lead to Anne and the guard. Hiding behind a cedar, Petra watched the tailor hesitate at the edge of the woods. He scratched his head, and then, after a few moments, limped back to his shop, wiping his forehead from the exertion.

Petra joined Anne in a thicket of alders. "The guard?" Petra asked.

Anne drew the vial of sleeping potion from her pocket. "He won't be waking soon." She grabbed Petra's hand, and they ran into the woods.

*⁎*

Petra closed the cottage door and leaned against it, breathless. "You were brilliant!"

Anne took off her hat, her hair tumbling around her shoulders. "So were you!"

"Hush," Petra said, listening for something other than the lowing cow and singing birds. She thought she heard snapping twigs and heavy footsteps.

"Quick!" Anne said, who must have heard also. She pushed Petra into her room. "Change your clothes!"

But Petra had never dressed in the Countess' clothes without Mary. "What about you?" she whispered.

Anne threw on an apron over her pants and opened her shirt to unwind the cloths. Moments later someone pounded on the door.

Petra disappeared into the bedroom before she heard the door screech open.

"Rohan!" Anne shouted.

Petra, halfway out of her breeches, called, "Welcome Sir Rohan!" She pulled on the pants.

By the time she'd buttoned her shirt, Anne and Rohan were at the table, clearly plotting. They looked up when she entered, and stopped talking.

Rohan stared, fighting a smile.

"What?" she asked even as she realized her buttons were cattywampus.

Rohan cleared his throat. "I do not think Emory would approve of your involvement, although he may appreciate your revealing attire."

Revealing attire? She wore a pair of pants four sizes too big and a man's cotton shirt. "I don't care what Emory thinks," she lied, cinching the belt of the breeches. "I'm not going to be left out. If it weren't for me and Anne's trusty hammer, you'd be growing mold in the town jail."

Rohan grinned. "I thought you'd say something like that." He cocked his head. "Have you any other tricks?"

A wave of realization hit her. "Plenty, but I'll only share them if you promise we can help."

"Help with what?"

"Don't toy with us, Friar Rohan," Anne shook a finger at him. "Tell us immediately where is Master Emory."

Rohan looked at his toes.

"Has he been captured by Chambers and the Earl?" Anne demanded.

Rohan gave a small shake of his head.

"He's there; isn't he?" Petra guessed. "He's at

Hampton Court." She pulled out a chair and sat at the table, her mind spinning.

Rohan tightened his lips and then spoke slowly, as if unsure of how much to reveal. "Chambers plan begins tonight. Emory is expecting me without a harem."

His implication was clear, but Petra wasn't buying it. She looked at Anne and back at Rohan. "You can't ditch us."

"Yes. You can't leave us in a ditch or in a cottage, for that matter." Anne nodded emphatically. "We are no harem." She took off her apron and showed Rohan her brother's baggy shirt.

"You too, Anne?" Rohan said in mock despair.

"Don't try to leave us," Petra said. "We will just follow."

Wind whistled through the trees, and rain splattered against the shuttered window. Cold seeped through the cracks of the door.

"T'will prove a wild night," Rohan said.

"The storm will be vicious," Anne agreed, but Petra didn't think that that was what Rohan had meant. Anne secured the shutters as rain began to fall

The damp barnyard smell seeped in, giving Petra an idea. "I want to try something," she said.

Anne and Rohan gave her curious looks.

"It might not work, but if it did…I need sugar, no? Well then, honey crystals?"

When Anne nodded, Petra studied the tapestries. "And dye, preferably orange and red." Then she went to the window and looked at the barn. "And whiskey. And cow pies."

Petra dumped the contents of her purse on the table and picked up Zoe's Girl Scout gadget. "And this."

The gadget had a pocket knife, spoon, compass and a tiny pair of scissors, but most importantly, a lighter. Petra flicked it, and a small blue flame shot up.

Rohan and Anne gasped.

"Just wait." Petra sent a silent prayer of gratitude to Bill Nye the Science Guy and Mr. Manning, best chemistry teacher ever.

# Chapter Twenty-One

*Hampton Court Palace sits on 59 acres. King Henry VIII had a court of over one thousand. At the palace he could feed and house them all and still have room for friends. Did King Henry have friends?*
—*Petra's notes*

"It's enormous," Petra breathed, catching sight of Hampton Court. The size of the palace overwhelmed her. "This is never going to work."

Rohan pulled the wagon beneath a thicket of alders as rain streamed through the dark leaves Petra prayed they were sheltered, if not from weather, then from sight. The horse nickered and shook his mane and the harness tinkled, a small sound blending in with the night noises, barely audible above the rain drip-dropping around them. Rohan swung out of the wagon and then held out a hand to help Anne.

"Have faith," Anne whispered to her as she jumped out of the wagon and then tugged her hat over her ears.

"Happy up," Rohan said to Petra as he held a hand to her. "We don't need to ignite the entire palace, only where Chambers is sleeping."

Petra looked at the massive palace. "This place looks like it has hundreds of rooms."

"Thousands, actually," Rohan said casually.

Lightning flashed. Thunder boomed.

"Don't you see?" Petra said, waving her arms at the palace. "This is hopeless. It can't work."

"My dear, heaven is on our side." Rohan sounded as if he'd talked to heaven and personally orchestrated the lightning storm.

Petra rolled her eyes and hunkered beneath the cape, but clothes provided little protection from the weather. How many years until the invention of plastic? No one had an umbrella or even a poncho. No Nyquil or Sudafed. Any of them could catch pneumonia. Or a million other life threatening diseases.

In the coach house, Petra saw Garret's carriage. Her heart twisted with worry. How could Anne marry someone she barely knew? Did she trust him? Did he sympathize with Chambers? Petra nodded at the carriage. "He won't be happy to see you here, Anne" Petra said, pulling her hood so that it covered more of her face.

Anne frowned at the familiar coach. "Emory won't be happy to see you here either. Although," she said with glistening eyes, "it is a very good plan."

Shifting her feet, Petra decided she wouldn't think about Emory. All of her concentration needed to be focused on right here, right now. She contemplated the palace. The windows were shaded, but occasionally she saw silhouettes and shadows moving past like fleeting pantomimes.

Straightening her shoulders, Petra took a deep breath. "Are you ready?"

Anne grabbed one hand, and Petra reached for Rohan with the other so they formed a chain. Petra squeezed Anne's hand and Anne sent her a squeeze in return.

Lightning flashed and lit upon a lone figure running through the courtyard.

"Well done," Rohan breathed. "Well done."

The man had a cape over his head and it flapped around him. He sprinted to the wagon and stopped short. Emory. Disbelief flickered across his face as his gaze traveled from Petra's boots, up her thighs and rested on Anne's father's baggy shirt.

Rohan held up his hands like a cop stopping traffic. "Before you say a word," he said to Emory, "Lady Petra, blow your fire." He handed her the flask of whiskey.

She looked at him questioning and then, after a glimpse at Emory's livid face, she pulled the gadget from her purse, took a mouthful of whiskey, ignited the lighter and spit the whisky. Flames shot five feet into the air.

Rohan looked proud, Emory shocked.

"Just one of many tricks!" Rohan crowed.

"It's actually Mr. Manning's trick," Petra told them, remembering the afternoon in the parking lot when the students had taken turns blowing fire. They'd used corn starch, but whiskey worked even better.

When the blood returned to Emory's face, he said to Rohan, "Despite her parlor trick, she cannot stay."

Rohan flexed his jaw. "She must."

Rain, like tears, trickled down Emory's face. He groaned and flicked his gaze between Petra and Anne. "They have no place here."

"Oh, like this is your place?" Petra took a step forward and brushed the rain from her eyes.

"You, I have no doubt, will prove a distraction." It could have been a compliment, but it wasn't. Emory stood in front of her and lowered his voice. "I cannot worry about your safety."

"Then don't." Petra studied Hampton Court. Moments ago she'd been sure the plan would fail, but with Emory's disapproval egging her on, she itched to set the place on fire. Sort of.

"Did you find Chambers?" Rohan asked Emory.

Emory pointed to a window on the ground floor of the east side. "Unfortunately, the king and his men have left the residence."

Rohan, looked at his boots, his face pained. "We waited in vain."

Emory nodded. "The opportunity to expose the Earl, for the time being, has passed."

"The Earl?" Anne asked, her voice rising an octave.

"The kegs?" Rohan asked.

"In the cellar." Emory spoke confidently. "There's only one guard."

Rohan nodded and reached to the floor of the wagon and then tossed a coil of rope and a strip of cloth to Emory.

"Are those for the guard?" Petra grimaced.

Emory considered his weapons, a smile glinting in his eye, "They are for you, should you refuse to stay in the wagon."

"I'm not staying in the wagon." She laughed and folded her arms across her chest. "You can't do this without me."

Rain dripped off Emory's nose. "We can, and we will."

"I bet you can't do this," Petra flicked the gadget and a small flame flickered.

"And you don't have this," Anne held up her vial of sleeping potion.

"They have proven to be exceptionally resourceful," Rohan said, stepping forward and placing his hand on Emory's shoulder. He cleared his throat. "Perhaps even heaven-sent."

Emory shot Petra a harsh look. "I do not see—" he began.

Rohan laughed. "You will see, you will hear, and you will smell." He gave Anne the whiskey, dye and the basket of cow pies. Anne gave him the vial.

"God speed, my friends," Rohan said, placing his hands on the small of their backs and giving each of them a push forward.

\*\*\*

When Emory tried to follow, a crack of thunder drowned out Rohan's words. Petra knew they weren't words that Emory wanted to hear. Out of the corner of her eye, she watched Emory and Rohan argue as she hurried after Anne.

Sloshing through mud, they crept to one side of the massive hall. Wind pulled at their clothes and spat rain in their faces, but it also masked the sound of their footsteps. Over the noisy storm, she heard her thundering heart.

What was she doing here? When she'd first arrived in 1610 she'd had misgivings about being alone in the dark outdoors. But now, it was after midnight, and she held the makings of a bomb in her hands. A bomb! This wasn't a shoot-em up movie or an episode of CSI where-ever. This bizarre situation was real and she knew the consequences were serious.

Behind her, Anne trembled as they crept alongside the palace. The downstairs rooms had shuttered windows; Petra watched the shadows, hoping to see Chambers' tall frame.

Anne pointed at the doors of a root cellar and a faint glow radiating up the steps. Within a moment Petra heard rustling, a grunt, and then a muffled cry of pain and panic. Who panicked? Was it Rohan or the guard? Anne flashed her a worried look.

Squaring her shoulders against the unknown, Anne set up the explosives. Petra couldn't think why someone would prowl the grounds at midnight in the rain, but still she prayed they wouldn't be caught.

"This plan has holes big enough for a truck to drive through," she said to Anne.

Anne looked up, rain dribbling off her hat. "What is a truck?"

Petra bit back a nervous laugh. If someone had told her a few days ago that she'd be hanging around a palace at midnight in a thunder storm trying to save the King James Bible, she'd have thought they were certifiable. If she ever told anyone that she'd spent an evening setting off smoke bombs in 1614, they would have her committed. Justifiably so. Yet here she was, feeling like her heart would explode, if nothing else. She nervously fingered the powder horn.

Lightning, thunder, the smoke bomb, fire blown outside Chambers' window. *Simple really*, Petra thought. *Easy peas.*

***

Emory crept down the palace halls, mind and heart racing. Candles cast a warm, flickering light down the corridor. He counted doors even as his mind turned with questions. Who was Petra Baron and why had she come? Why did everything about her seem foreign yet familiar? In just days the girl seemed to have affected all she met. How had she persuaded Anne to dress as a boy and storm Hampton Court? What if Young Falstaff learned of the escapade? What was Anne thinking? She wasn't a weak character, easily manipulated or influenced.

And Rohan? What had possessed him to go along with a plan involving maids? Granted, removing Chambers seemed easier than removing nine powder kegs, and with Chambers gone they could empty the kegs at their leisure, one bucket at a time. That made sense.

Petra and Anne did not. Until five minutes ago he would have sworn she and Petra would have rather clawed out each other's eyes than hold hands in the rain.

So engrossed in his thoughts was he that he nearly tripped over a sleeping hound. Stumbling, he caught himself and hid in darkened doorway a black mastiff twitched his tail and repositioned his head on his paws. The dog looked capable of clamping down on a man's head and tearing it from its neck. In fact, beside the dog lay the jawbone of a cow. The dog looked nearly big enough to have killed the cow and eaten all but the largest bones and the few teeth.

Emory leaned against the door as the dog stirred. Only then did he realize he'd lost count of the doors.

\*\*\*

Petra shook from nerves and cold. She flexed

her fingers to keep them warm. The plan depended on thunder. Who depended on thunder? Thunder, like lightning, just happened. It came and went. It wasn't summoned. *This is a very silly and wet plan,* she thought, brushing her sodden hair away from her face.

Anne shivered and tried to keep her hood up over her brown curls. How long would they have to sit in the storm, waiting on something that might not come? Petra curled her hands into balls and blew.

Anne twitched, frowning. "I wish Lord Garret were not here." Her whisper sounded small and uncertain.

"This place is massive," Petra said. "Hopefully, we can distract Chambers and get rid of the powder kegs without anyone, especially Garret, knowing what's up."

"What's up?" Anne murmured. "Moon, stars, owls..."

"Anne," Petra said, "what if he does find out you're here?"

"Perchance he would not recognize me."

"But what if he did? What if he called off your wedding?" *Nosy much?* Petra added, "I know it's none of my business..."

"I have known Lord Garret since birth."

"But a few days ago, it seemed like you didn't even like him."

Anne pushed back her hood, exposing her face. "I thought…I thought he was like Chambers, partially responsible for my brother's death, but as I spend more time with him, I see he is extremely sweet, generous, good-intentioned. True, he's impetuous and impulsive; our hasty engagement reflects that well."

Anne sighed. "I am completely devoted to the efforts of bringing an English bible to the people. If I did not love Garret, chances are that I would marry him anyway. I can accomplish more good as a countess than as an artisan. That I happen to find Lord Garret charming, witty and appealing is my good fortune."

Petra sniffed and wondered how charming or witty he would be if he could see them now, prowling around the palace and firing up smoke bombs.

Lightning lit the garden; Petra's nerves tingled. *Now.* She had to light the bomb to coordinate with the thunder. Petra took a mouthful of whiskey and then snapped the lighter over the makeshift fuse of whiskey soaked linen. Nothing. She struck the lighter again. Whiskey burned in her mouth, stung the back of her throat. In the rain, the tiny flame wavered and then winked away. Ready to burst with frustration and impatience, she struck the lighter again. Orange and yellow methane fueled smoke curled from the cow pie.

Chambers flung open his window at the very moment Petra spit whiskey and blew a flame of fire. Gasping, Chambers stumbled back. Petra tossed the smoke bomb through the window and through a cloud of orange and red haze, she and Anne watched Chambers trip over a chair.

The entire plan depended on Chambers believing that the powder kegs had been set off. He had to run out the door and into Emory, not out the window and into them. Petra held her breath waiting and watching for his next move.

\*\*\*

Thunder shook the palace. Smoke billowed out of the door he leaned against. From its other side came cursing and scrambling. The dog twitched in his sleep. Emory grabbed the jawbone, heavy and slimy in his hand. Its few remaining teeth pointed up. "I'll borrow this," he whispered to the snoring dog. Mallet in one hand and jawbone in the other, Emory braced himself. The door latch clicked.

Chambers burst out of the smoke-filled room,

eyes terror-filled and hair wild. Emory whacked him over the head. The jawbone connected with a sickening crack. Cow teeth flew. Before Chambers crumpled to the floor Emory caught him underneath the arms and dragged his deadweight into the reeking room. The mastiff rose to his legs, shook himself and howled about the theft of his bone. Emory kicked the door closed in the poor dog's face.

Smoke billowed from the cow pie, filling the room with an orange, and red-colored barnyard stench. Keeping hold of Chambers and trying not to gag, Emory dropped the bone and maneuvered Chambers to a chair. Outside the door, he heard footsteps and the mastiff's frantic barking.

Emory slid a bolt through the door and stared at Chambers through the haze, amazed that the plan had, so far, worked. Looking out the window, he saw Petra smiling and pointing her thumb in the air. She looked so beautiful, wet and happy with her thumb protruded he wanted to vault over the sill and swing her in his arms.

For the moment he had a heavier and uglier armful. Not for long, he promised himself, not for long. He dropped Chambers into a chair.

\*\*\*

Although part of her wanted to vault into the room and help Emory with Chambers, Petra knew they had to get back to the wagon. She tugged at Anne's hand. "Anne," Petra whispered, "Come on."

Anne's face was chalk-white. Petra followed her gaze and saw an equally stupefied Garret staring at them through the window that neighbored Chambers.

Rain trickled down Petra's back, sending icy streams along her spine. "It's not what you think," Petra told him, wrapping a protective arm around Anne.

"Pray tell, my lady, what do I think?" Garret said in a strangled voice.

Anne had frozen. She held herself perfectly rigid; she didn't blink and didn't try to speak. Petra took a deep breath and then stuttered, "I…I..I don't know. What do you think?"

Garret's eyes lingered on Anne's breeches. Throwing open the window, he climbed out, exposing long and hairy legs. He wore a cotton button up job that looked like a knee-length pillowcase with sleeves.

Petra rushed over and shut the window, squelching the billowing smoke. Standing in front of the window, trying to block its radiating orange and red haze, she realized that she needn't have bothered. Garret, now outside and striding across the wet grass, had eyes only for Anne.

Garret pulled Anne against his chest and wrapped her in his arms. "By my faith, 'tis heaven to see you." Bending her backward, he kissed her long and deeply. When he lifted his lips from hers, he said, "That you would risk coming here, in the dead of night, in a raging storm, for us to be together." His voice choked with emotion.

Petra stood, rooted at being witness to such an intimate moment.

"My lord, I, I --" Anne stammered.

Garret put a finger to her lips. "Hush. Come away from this charade. Let us go to Scotland and be married immediately." He pulled her toward the carriage house.

"But your father..." Anne seemed to be struggling to bring her truth up to speed with Garret's fiction.

"My father is of no importance." Garret strode away, towing Anne after him, his bare feet splashing through the sodden grass. Rain and mud splattered up his legs.

Anne balked. "Of no importance? Your lands, your title? They matter not to me, but I won't let you give them up!"

"Fear not, t'will all be mine upon his death." He spoke as if that couldn't happen too soon. "I tried reasoning with my father, but he's controlled by greed. Gold dictates all his logic. Fortunately, I'm also heir to my mother's fortune. Until my father asks for forgiveness for his hardness and bigotry or dies, we shall live as man and wife on my mother's Scottish estate. We'll leave now."

"Pray wait, my Lord. This is all new to me. What about my father?"

Garret took off Anne's hat and ran his fingers through her hair. He smiled as the hair tumbled through his fingers. "We'll send word. He may join us, should he choose." He stared into Anne's eyes, and put a hand on her cheek. "Have you not come to be with me? That is why you're here, is it not?"

*Tell him the truth,* Petra mentally urged.

Anne answered him with a soft kiss on his lips.

"How you knew that I would be longing for you, how you knew that I would need you tonight, it astounds me. You amaze me." He caressed her cheek with his thumb.

"My lord, I am not amazing; you must not think of me so." Anne cast Petra a nervous glance. "I would travel anywhere to be with you, but --"

"You are good, kind, and modest." Garret

scooped her into his arms, and headed toward the carriage house. "Nothing matters but our life together."

Anne giggled. "My lord, you're wearing naught but your nightclothes."

*Naught is right.* Petra flushed and looked away. Rain pelted  him and the wet fabric clung. He wore nothing, *naught*, beneath the cotton night shirt.

"I've ample clothes in Yorkshire," Garret said, not breaking stride.

"And I am hardly dressed for a wedding."

"We shall go to your cottage for a trunk, if we must." Garret stopped, as if suddenly remembering Petra. "How now, my lady?" Glancing at Anne's face, for the first time that evening, Garret seemed confused.

Petra looked toward the woods and watched Rohan shepherding a rolling powder keg toward the river.

"Go, Anne," Petra said. "We've… I mean, you have what you came for." She motioned toward Garret.

"Petra must come with us." Anne said. "We cannot leave her here."

Garret nodded at Anne but scowled at Petra. "Come along then." He marched away.

"Umm, I don't think so," Petra said to his

retreating back. "I think I'll go with Rohan."

"The friar?" Garret turned. "What, pray tell, is he doing here?"

What an ego. Did Garret really think that she and Anne would disguise themselves as men and ride to Hampton Court to see him? Petra shifted her feet and felt the cold damp seep through her boots.

"Tis a long tale," Anne said, smiling up into his face. "Best told in a coach, away from the wind and weather."

"Of course, forgive me. You are soaked through." Garret looked down at her, his eyes shining, as if he couldn't wait to have Anne to himself. They disappeared into the carriage house and Petra wondered what the stable hands would think. Could the future Earl ride away in his pajamas? And what about the current Earl? What would he say about his son and an artisan traveling in the dead of night? With *naught* on? Garret definitely didn't seem to care what his dad thought. Was that because his father didn't mind his marrying Anne? No, it was probably the opposite. His father didn't approve, so if Garret wanted to marry Anne they had no choice but to elope.

Petra watched, curious, resisting the urge to get closer for a peek. It took several minutes, but in time, Garret's coach rolled from the carriage house. On the perch, Fritz huddled beneath a large black cape and slapped the reins. The horses looked as sleepy and reluctant.

Petra felt a twinge of sadness knowing that she would probably never see either of them again. Even if she spent the rest of her life in the seventeenth century, she didn't know where she would stay and travel to Scotland seemed unlikely. What would become of her?

Petra shot the dark window a quick glance, but Emory had gone, presumably taking Chambers with him. Smoke milled about the empty room, the bomb remnants fading to a small golden glow.

A second explosion ripped through the air. Petra covered her ears with her hands and closed her eyes. When she opened them she was dangling two feet off the ground.

Hands like a vice clamped around her waist. Petra screamed and flailed. She hadn't seen or heard anyone, which wasn't surprising. Her ears still rang, and everything sounded underwater. She couldn't hear above the ringing in her ears or see through the rain pelting her face, but she could fight.

Although not from midair.

She kicked, squirmed, and tried to reach behind

her to stop the chuckling. She didn't like being abducted, but she hated being abducted and mocked. Waving her powder horn, she tried to connect with any of her assailant's body parts, but every bit of him seemed out of reach.

"Put. Me. Down." She swung the leather strap that held her powder horn and it whistled through the air, smacking something hard. The impact sent reverberations down her arm. "Ow," she muttered as leaves, twigs and seed pods rained down on her head. She spit and increased her thrashing.

"I knew you'd put up a good fight," said a voice, frustratingly calm and steady.

Her energy flagged even as her temper flared. This guy seemed to be enjoying himself. He also sounded familiar. When she caught a glimpse of his massive forearm, her hopes for escape waned. This vaguely familiar man easily outweighed her by more than a hundred pounds, maybe two hundred pounds.

"I like a fighter," he said.

Petra willed herself still and tried to go limp with a vague idea of slipping through his hands, but her captor tossed her over his shoulder, holding the right wrist while pinning the left ankle. Petra felt like a calf being carted to the slaughter. The powder horn swung from her neck.

A calf that blew fire!  She twisted and aimed her lighter for his head, but her captor only chuckled, grabbed the powder horn and tossed it to the ground before depositing her in the back of a hay-filled wagon.

# Chapter Twenty-Two

*How to blow fire:*
*You need fuel (ale) and flame (Girl Scout Gadget)*
*Step 1: Take as much ale in your mouth as you can hold.*
*Step 2: Take a deep breath, inhale through your nose.*
*Step 3: Light the flame source and hold it close to your mouth.*
*Step 4: Spit.*
*—Petra's notes*

He'd need to wait. Petra and Anne might be able to glide through the smoky confusion without notice, but Emory doubted he'd be able to sling Chambers through the palace without gaining unwanted attention.

The wait in the dark hall amidst vaporous reek of smoldering cow pies may have only been a few minutes, but it seemed an eternity. He easily carried the inert Chambers down the hall, more afraid of asphyxiation than exertion. Finally, Emory pushed open a door and took a deep breath of clean air. Although Chambers' room had pulsed red and orange, it appeared the rest of the palace's occupants had contributed the explosion to thunder. To Emory's relief, not even a dog was in sight.

As he'd hoped, the courtyard was also deserted. Then he noticed a bright flame shoot out of the back of a wagon. The flame died as his heart leapt. Was he mistaken? No, Petra sat up just as lightning brightened the sky and glistened off her round shoulders.

Emory swallowed fear mingling with rage. What was she doing in the back of hay-filled wagon? Where were Anne and Rohan? The wagon lurched over the bridge, sending Petra down again behind the slats holding the straw.

The wagon turned, and light played on the massive forearms of the driver.

Marshall.

\*\*\*

While Emory's heart thundered in his ears and adrenaline surged, it seemed wrong for Centaur to stand so nonchalantly munching on grass in the thicket of alders where he'd been tied. Emory swung Chambers across the horse's back. Centaur shifted under the unexpected weight and turned to Emory with large, questioning eyes.

Chambers' tied hands and boots pointed to the

ground on either side of the horse; he would have a raging headache and a stiff back by morning.

Emory took a last look at the palace as he bound Chambers to the horn of his saddle. Hampton Court looked asleep until Rohan emerged from the root cellar trap door rolling the last powder keg. Emory sprinted to him. "Any sign of Anne?"

Rohan shook his head and then pointed at Centaur's burden. "What you got?"

"Rubbish. I was hoping you might deposit it for me." After a quick explanation to Rohan and transferring Chambers to Rohan's wagon, Emory was off. He knew Centaur could overtake Marshall, who was still in view.

Marshall could have killed Petra—why take her? In any other circumstance it might have been amusing to watch Petra bobble in the wagon. Several times she attempted to stand, or even come to her knees, but the lurching wagon pitched her up, down, and sideways. She appeared unhurt, but that could change in an instant. A well placed bullet or a blow to the head would silence Petra forever, and from his current vantage point, all he'd be able to do was watch. He tried to imagine his long bleak life without her, and disliking the thought, pushed Centaur harder and faster.

Did Marshall know they'd destroyed the powder kegs? Had the kidnapping been random? It couldn't have been directed by the inert and unconscious Chambers. Marshall was a ruffian, hired by who? The Earl? Did the Earl know Petra had staged the explosions?

Emory dodged a low branch. As of yet, neither Petra nor Marshall had noticed him. He prayed that the rattle of the wagon and clip clop of the nag would overpower the rumble of Centaur's hooves.

No such luck.

Marshall slipped a gun out of his holster. The gun barrel gleamed in the moonlight. Marshall glanced at Petra and then turned to Emory's direction, aimed and fired.

***

Petra lay on the wagon floor and gathered the hay in a pile. Then, using the lighter, she set it on fire. Bracing herself, she jumped from the wagon seconds before the horses started screaming. The horses smelled the fire before Marshall and bolted. Marshall fought to control the careening horses, but they clattered away as the wagon burned, Marshall hanging onto the reins.

Stunned, Petra lay on the ground trying to catch

her breath. A voice in her head urged her to get up. *Emory,* the voice said. Struggling to her feet, she lurched toward the palace, searching the dark for him. She found Emory leaning against a tree.

He tried to smile, but she crouched beside him and touched his lips with a finger. "Shh, don't speak," she said.

She had never seen so much blood. She pulled him to her. His labored breath blew hot across her neck, and his blood soaked the front of her shirt. She rolled Emory so that his head nestled onto her lap. Beneath her bare skin the ground felt cold and gritty. She tried to inspect the bullet wound, but blood gushed beneath her shaking fingers and the charred and ragged edges of his shirt. Emory's ashen faced stared up at her, his eyes begging questions she didn't know how to answer.

His life slipped away with his spilling blood. She pinched a strip of her shirt. The cotton tore easily and she took a wad of fabric and held it against Emory's red stain with shaking hands.

"Petra?" Emory's voice sounded something between a moan and a rasp. His lips were chapped, bloody, and soot smeared his face. Violent red streaks crisscrossed his chest and arms, and the wound in his shoulder pumped out blood.

Despite the gore, despite her fatigue, Petra

wanted to kiss him. Instead, she brushed the hair off Emory's face. He shifted and attempted to sit up.

"Stay still," Petra whispered, running her fingers through his hair.

"Bossy," Emory croaked, settling against her. "Will you always be so?"

"Forever," Petra promised.

"Forever," he murmured. "There is something you should know about forever."

"Don't speak, Emory, just stay still." Petra tried to hold him

Emory pushed up so that he sat directly in front of her. She watched, mesmerized, as the bleeding staunched, then stopped as if a spigot had been turned off.

Emory took her hand. With his other hand he pulled back his shirt.

Petra stared as the wound healed, the skin turned pink and completely closed around what had been a gaping hole. "Forever, for me, is a very long time," Emory whispered huskily.

# Chapter Twenty-Three

*Thunderstorms are caused by atmospheric instability and not by an angry heaven or a vengeful hell.*
*—Petra's notes*

"I don't understand." Petra slowly shook her head. True, Emory's healing from that sword wound had been miraculous. She didn't know how that had happened. She guessed it had something to do with Rohan and the faith healing, or whatever it was, that she'd seen him do for the gypsy. It was one thing to know someone had healed way too quickly and another to see it happen right before her eyes, like a trick of television editing or computer animation.

"Come," he said. "It isn't safe here." He uncurled away from her, standing slowly, but clearly without pain. Upright, not favoring the side where he'd been shot. She let him pull her to him, feeling that perhaps she shouldn't, that maybe she should scream. Her mind reeled. She touched his bloody, tattered shirt, and smooth, unblemished chest. At her feet, a metal gun-ball covered in gore lay in a puddle of blood. *The bullet,* her mind reasoned the unreasonable.

Emory held her elbow with a vice-like grip, and she staggered in his wake.

At the edge of town, Emory put his fingers in his mouth and blew out a long whistle. A big Arabian horse trotted toward them from a thicket of alders. Moments earlier she'd worried that Emory would die in her arms, and now he easily swung her in his arms and placed her on top of the horse. When he tossed her the reins she considered, for only a moment, riding away and leaving him. She'd ride and ride until she found her home—and her own century.

She couldn't let Emory just carry her away. Not without explanations. With her arms around his waist, she jostled against him the way her thoughts jostled and bounced as the horse carried them further and further from the town's sights and sounds. Every lurch should have caused Emory great pain. She touched where he'd been shot and he stiffened beneath her hand.

"You must wonder…" he said over his shoulder.

"And you have to tell me." Petra leaned against his back and spoke into his ear.

"In time." He kept his face turned toward the road.

Petra knew she shouldn't allow herself to be

swept away, yet she couldn't muster the nerve to slide off the horse and demand answers. She didn't know what else to say or ask, so she kept quiet, thinking.

"It will not be long before they regroup and come after us," Emory said.

"Why?"

"Because we thwarted their plan. Dorrington won't be safe for us for a long time."

"Time." That word again.

The horse slowed, picking his way along the narrow dirt track that skirted around rocks, stumps and trees until it came to a stream.

The storm had blown itself out, leaving only gray clouds and a cold morning drizzle. The horse flicked its tail at the flies that swarmed along the marshy banks.

Maybe the guy who didn't die belonged with the girl who time traveled, because a more unusual pair couldn't exist. They were meant to be together. Obviously.

"Tell me your secret," she said, wishing she could see his face.

He shook his head. "I want to see you when I tell you. I...want to watch you hear what I'm going to say."

She considered this. "Fair enough, but—"

"Yes?"

"What if after I learn your secrets, I don't want to go away with you?"

He laughed softly.

"Tell me now." A realization made her voice hard, and she pulled away from him, which wasn't easy while riding a horse bareback. To keep from falling, Petra had to hold onto Emory and hug the horse with her thighs. Her legs bumped and rubbed against Emory's. "Stop this horse. I need to know right now."

Emory chuckled and clicked the horse into a gallop. Petra's frustration rose with every clip-clop as sweat formed on the horse's bridle and the animal's heat radiated through her. The faster Emory rode, the tighter Petra held on. She told herself she didn't want to cling to him, but as they flew across the meadow, destination unknown, she decided holding on was the smartest thing to do.

When the late afternoon sun glinted off the distant hills, Emory pulled the horse alongside the river. Boulders lined the bank, stacked like a giant game of Jenga. Emory reined the horse to a walk before sliding off.

"My lady." He held out a hand. Again she had the chance—she could take the reins and ride far, far away, but where would she go?

"My lady?"

"Where are we?" Petra looked at the wild and craggy landscape.

"Half a day's journey from London."

"Where are we going?"

"We have arrived. Further decisions can be made in the morning."

"We're going to stay here?" Her voice broke. "Like camping? But we don't have..."

"We are safe." He continued to hold out his hand. "What more do we need?"

Petra hadn't spent a lot of time camping, but she remembered going with her cousins and a truck full of stuff. "How about sleeping bags, a propane stove, freeze-dried food, insect repellent, a tent, a flashlight for starters."

"I'm sure those items, whatever they may be, would be nice to have, but they are not necessary."

*Necessary?* She looked around. Of course, there wasn't a restroom or even a port-a-potty. Necessary suddenly seemed relative.

Emory dropped his hand and turned away.

"Where are you going?" she called after his back.

Slowly he pulled his shirt over his head and continued toward the river. Petra slid off the horse, following. Emory sat on a rock and tugged off his boots. Standing a few feet away, Petra's heart began to hammer as Emory stood and undid his belt buckle. She let out a small sigh when she saw he left his pants on. He dove into the river, and the water swirled red and brown around him. Seconds later he surfaced. His chest that been torn and bloody, looked clean and new.

Petra closed her mouth and turned away so that Emory wouldn't catch her staring.

"Join me?"

Dying sun sparkled on the current pulling the water to the sea. Petra hung back.  In 2014 her bra and panties would be considered modest on most beaches, but what did women wear swimming in 1614? Bloomers? Or maybe Elizabethan women didn't swim. Undressing in front of Emory was nothing like undressing in front of Mary. Turning her back to him, she unbuttoned the blood crusted shirt and hung it on a low branch. Sitting on a rock, she pulled off her boots. Then she slipped off the pants that reeked of horse sweat and worse.

Emory had his back turned as she waded into the water. The rocks were slippery and she had to catch herself a number of times as the river's current pushed at her legs. She waded out to where the water covered her shoulders, pulled out what remained of her hairpins, lowered her head into the water and let her hair fan out around her. The river washed away the stench of horse, sweat, smoke and ash, and the knot between her shoulders loosened a bit. She rose from the water and saw Emory watching.

"In truth, who are you?" His voice carried over the water.

She'd been waiting for this. What if he didn't believe her? Yet his own story had to be so incredible; hers would probably seem boring in comparison—what's time travel compared to the ability to miraculously heal from lethal bullet and sword wounds? She trusted him enough to know he wouldn't abandon her in the middle of nowhere, even if he didn't believe her.

"I'm Petra Baron from Royal Oaks, California," she began. "About five days ago I went into a fortuneteller's tent at a Renaissance fair. The year was 2014." She took a deep breath, watching his impassive face for a reaction. "When I left the tent, I found myself in Dorrington, England year 1610."

He stood three feet away, not close enough to touch. She thought about wading over to him and taking his hand. Instead, she added quietly, "I don't blame you for not believing me, but it's the truth."

The sun dimmed quickly, slipping behind a

cloud in a pink haze. Trees overhanging the creek cast short shadows on Emory. Standing in the sun and water, Petra didn't feel cold, but she wondered if Emory was cold in the shade. She wondered if he *felt* cold, if he ever felt tired or hungry. She wondered what he felt about her.

Emory gave a small nod, as if he understood the illogical and impossible. How could anyone buy her story? She didn't understand and it had happened to her. "Who are you?" Petra asked. "Or, maybe I should ask, *what* are you?"

"I'm Emory Ravenswood. In the fourteenth century, when I entered my eighteenth year, my life...changed. Forever."

Petra let out a small gasp and a wave of relief washed over her. "You're like me. We're both time travelers!"

Emory went forward and she went backwards. How amazing that they met in the middle, that they shared this rare and phenomenal experience together, that she didn't have to be alone, that she'd been given someone to share her life with.

"I'm not like you." Emory interrupted her thoughts. "I did not travel through time like you. I am like most men."

"Like most men?" Petra slipped on the rocks. She treaded water until her feet hit sand which shifted as she wrestled with what Emory had told her. "Most men don't live for hundreds of years. Are you saying you're two hundred years old?"

A cold wind picked up, shaking the trees. Leaves danced from the branches and landed in the water. Petra shivered.

Emory, taking note, waded toward her and took her hand. "I've been on this earth since the fourteen hundreds, but my body is eighteen years old. In that, we are the same."

Petra's arms and legs were growing stiff in the cold water. She wanted to drown in disappointment. "We're not the same."

He pulled her to him and held her. She felt lulled by his warmth; she wanted to lean into him, let him take her, but she felt wooden and hollow.

"I've been alone a very long time. It's very difficult to watch the people I love grow old and die." He brushed the wet strands of hair off her face. "Until you, I've managed to keep my distance."

"But Anne? Rohan?"

"I've known Anne since she was a babe. She's the last of my family, the daughter of my brother's grandchild. I could not stay away."

"And Rohan?"

Emory laughed. "Rohan is different. I'm afraid

he will always be a part of my existence."

"Why would you say that? Eventually--"

Emory reached one finger out to tilt her chin so that their eyes met. "For Rohan and for myself, there is no eventually."

"What do you mean?"

He stepped away. "It's a very long story best told over a camp fire."

"I've had enough of fires." She didn't want to be led away or distracted from his story. "I want to hear about you and Rohan."

"Come, Petra. It's getting cold." He pulled her toward the riverbank and she followed relunctantly while the river's gentle current pulsed around her legs. He retrieved her shirt and wrapped it over her shoulders. She shrugged into it, despite its smell and filth. It hung past her thighs.

"I'll make a fire and then I'll tell you all you want to know," he said, buttoning a few of her buttons. "And much more that you probably do not."

# Chapter Twenty-Four

*The thin place:*
*Where the veil between this world and the*
*Otherworld is thin.*
*To some it is heaven, the kingdom, or paradise.*
*To others it may be hell or an abyss.*
*Maybe the hell is not knowing which.*
—*Petra's note*

Emory disappeared behind an outcrop of rocks and returned moments later with a blanket and a small box. He smiled at her surprise. "I have been here many times before." He cleared his throat. "It is a second residence to me."

She looked around at the small clearing in the grove. "It's nice," she said, sarcasm touching her voice. "It's a wonder you ever leave."

He smiled as he shook out the blanket and wrapped it around her. "I'll have the fire going soon."

She grabbed at his hand. "No, don't do that now. I want to hear—"

He shook his head. "You had a long, sleepless night. You must be hungry and tired."

"But not you, right? You won't be hungry and

tired, because you don't need to eat or sleep?"

He tucked the edges of the blanket around her and then pushed her onto a log. She sat with a disgruntled huff.

"Mere moments," he promised.

She called after his back, "In a lifetime of moments that, for you, never end?"

He shook his head as he disappeared into a thicket of aspens. "Wrong," he said, when he reappeared carrying an armful of gathered wood and a leather flask. "My life ended more than two hundred years ago."

Despite the warmth of the blanket, a chill passed up Petra's back. "You're dead?"

"Not exactly." Emory set aside the flask and used a log to clear a circle where he piled his logs and then broke twigs into kindling.

"You're either alive or your dead. There's not an in-between."

"And you know this how?" He arranged the fallen wood into a teepee and placed twigs beneath. Petra wondered how it would start after the drenching rain, but then he uncorked the flask and poured ale on the wood. "There is an in between. The old people call it the thin place."

"The old people? Being two hundred years isn't old?" Petra shivered in the blanket. She'd thought it creepy when Auntie Dee had dated a man twenty years older, even creepier when her forty-something neighbor Mrs. Duncan married her twenty-something gardener. Compared to two hundred, twenty was nothing.

"I'm not so old." He cleared his throat. "Look at me, Petra. I am the same age as you, stuck in the thin place, between the living and the dead."

"Not a ghost?" Even in front of the fire, wrapped in a blanket, she shivered with cold and something else. Not dread, not disappointment, more than disbelief—she couldn't categorize her feelings.

"I cannot die because I have already done so." Using flint and tinder, Emory lit the wood.

Petra watched the pile of wood burst into flames.

Emory leaned back on his heels, studying the smoke that curled into the sky. "It's something that can only be done once."

"How? What was it like?" She wrapped the blanket around her a smidge tighter, her shivering increased. "Maybe I've died, too. Maybe that's why I'm here. This is my in-between."

Emory sat beside Petra. Wrapping his arm around her, he pulled her against his chest. "No, you are very much alive. There is no mistaking death."

Pressed against Emory, Petra's shivering eased slightly. "Are there others like you, trapped in the thin place?"

"Not many." He held her tight, resting his chin on the top of her head.

She breathed out a sigh. He didn't feel dead. He felt warm and alive. "Why are you here? Why am I here with you?"

"Those are two different questions."

"Then I want two answers."

"Do you know what happens when we die?"

Of course not. No one living did. She wanted to believe that her mother lived on, somewhere, somehow, and that she'd see her again. In her imagination she'd pictured a reunion with her mother and her father in a heaven of sorts, a place without cancer or accidents. She looked at Emory, confused, fearful and hopeful.

"It is one of life's grand secrets, one all who pass are instructed to keep."

She smiled. "And you're going to tell me?"

He nodded. "Heaven is already angry with me." He turned his lips toward hers and gently kissed her. "Are you willing to be with someone who's on the wrong side of heaven?"

Petra shivered again. The fire and blanket

didn't help. If she'd been home and someone had told her he was caught in a thin place, on the wrong side of heaven, it wouldn't matter how hot he was, or how attracted to him she felt, she would have said goodbye and gone on with the rest of her life. But she didn't have a life here. She had no one, nowhere to go and nothing to do. Turning her back on the one person she knew wasn't an option.

"Do not worry. I'm not in league with hell, although they have done their best to recruit me." He kissed her deeply and the earth shook beneath her.

*No, really, the earth is shaking.* A dark cloud billowed overhead and a mean wind whipped through the trees.

Lifting his lips from hers, he said, "See, they are angry already. Both of them."

"Them who?"

Lightning crackled, thunder rumbled and Emory laughed. "Heaven and hell. I must keep their secrets although they promise me nothing in return."

Scattered rain drops, heavy and stinging, fell. The fire quivered and sizzled. "Will they put out your fire?" Petra didn't know what she believed of heaven or hell, but making either of them angry seemed stupid. She readjusted the blanket. "You shouldn't tell me, then."

"Is that what you want?" he asked, his face inches from hers. He pulled the blanket so that it protected her head from the rain. "Moments ago you were willing to stand in the river until your legs turned to ice if I did not tell you my truth."

Thunder boomed and the rain turned from a few desolate drops to a driving deluge. The fire lost its roar and flames and began to smoke.

"I don't think you should make heaven or hell angry!" Petra said, raising her voice above the escalating storm's noise.

"I thought you didn't believe?"

"Do my beliefs matter?"

He laughed. "Absolutely." He leaned his forehead against hers. "Your belief is the only thing that matters." Standing, he drew her up and led her to an outcropping of rocks.

She trailed after him, tripping over sticks and fallen branches. "I don't even know what that means."

Emory stopped to grab his clothes off the branches where they'd been hung, and then he led her into a cave so deep and dark that she couldn't see the end. She blinked in the gloom. Emory lit torches that hung from the wall and the cave sprung to light. An animal fur rug sat on a dirt packed floor. A stack of wooden crates held a variety of supplies including a jug, a bucket, and a knife.

*The ultimate man cave.*

As if he could read her thoughts, Emory looked sheepish. "I wasn't expecting company." He sat down on the bear skin and pulled her beside him.

"In the year 1414, I was...foolish."

Outside the cave, the wind howled. The tree branches whipped against each other and moaned in their movement. Looking at the raging storm, Petra said, "I think maybe having this conversation is foolish. I really don't want to make heaven or hell mad." She paused. "Would it help to whisper? Can they hear us?"

He smiled and shook his head. "Heaven and hell aren't easily thwarted."

"And yet, you did it when you were...foolish."

"I was more foolish than most at seventeen. My friends and I were setting a fire. My family died in the fire. And the entire village."

Petra gasped and reached out to touch his arm. "I'm sure it was an accident."

"I'm still responsible. Everyone I knew died, except for my brother who happened to be away. I watched him return," Emory's voice choked. "I saw him realize that he had no one and nothing left."

"But you?"

Emory shook his head and leaned against the stone wall. He pulled her so that she lay against his chest. "Not even me. You see, I had also died." He took a deep breath. "When you die, you're gathered up to your people. Do you know what that means?"

A chill shook her and her body turned cold everywhere except for where she and Emory touched.

"When we die we're gathered to our people," he repeated. Lifting his face toward the roof of the cave, he addressed it. "I've shared nothing that she can't read in the Bible for herself." He smiled. "If you can find the King James version, there'll be no need to learn Latin."

The storm raging beyond the cave's opening seemed to subside. The wind stopped howling and the rain slacked off.

He turned back to her. "There are numerous references on the subject. Genesis gives an account of Jacob dying and being gathered to his people, for example. Should you like more, there are many. I'll admit that at one time I became something of an expert on the subject."

Petra shrugged. She wanted to say *I believe you* but she wasn't sure if that was true.

Emory's voice turned fierce. "I don't want to be gathered to my people. And as for the judgment bar of God —"

A laugh rang through the cave, echoing off the walls. Emory bolted upright and Petra struggled to her feet. She imagined the arrival of a host of winged avenging angels, carrying bows, swords and righteous indignation.

"You think you can escape the judgments of God?" a voice boomed.

Whirling, Petra breathed a sigh of relief when she saw Chambers standing at the opening of the cave. At least he was human. Although frightening in the flickering torch light, his shadow, long and lean, across the floor.

After Emory's conversation, Petra had half expected an angel or a demon from hell. Although,

Chambers didn't possess unearthly powers, but he did look scary. The wind, whistling through the cave lifted his hair so that it flew about his face. His cloak swirled around him as he lifted his arm, pointed his gun and fired a shot into Emory's chest.

The cave exploded in a haze of smoke and blood.

## Chapter Twenty-Five

*In Elizabethan times, the church went to great lengths to root out the influences of Satan and his servants. They used torture, such as hot pincers, the thumbscrew, and the 'swimming' of suspects, to force confessions of witchcraft.*
—Petra's notes

Petra huddled in the corner of the carriage in a fog of pain. The wheels churning through the mud and the steady clomping of the horses did nothing to ease the driving rain's sting. Above her, the heavens churned in revolt, the clouds heaved, lightning sparked and thunder shook the ground. The horses pulling the coach strained against the bits, pushing toward Dorrington, to find shelter from the storm, food and comfort. Petra knew she wouldn't be so lucky. Where would Chambers take her?

Chambers rode ahead, astride a white stallion, while one henchman drove the coach. Another guy carrying a pistol rode behind. In the scuffle, someone had hit her over the head and she felt the pain with every wagon jolt. Occasionally, as she bounced along the muddy and jutted roads, Petra considered escape. The ropes around her hands and ankles wouldn't prevent her from flinging herself out the carriage door, but then what? The henchmen would most likely pick her back up and toss her back in like a wayward sack of potatoes. She wasn't thinking clearly. Everything jumbled together.

Closing her eyes, Petra replayed a memory in her mind: Emory falling, blood draining from his face and staining his shirt. Petra had to keep reminding herself that he couldn't die. Probably. Yes, she'd seen him heal in minutes from a bullet wound not too many hours ago, but what if it only worked so many times? He hadn't really explained the rules of his existence.

Where was he now? When a henchman had banged her head, she'd lost focus. Maybe just for a moment, or maybe for hours, she didn't know. By the time her vision cleared, all she saw was the sky swimming in rain. *Heaven's rage*, she thought. It was her last conscious thought for a long time.

***

Petra woke in the dark. As she pushed herself to her elbow, away from the hard, cold ground, her head thundered, though the whistling wind and beating rain had stopped. When her eyes adjusted to the dark she realized that she was no longer in the coach, but inside somewhere. Sitting up, she tried to register her surroundings. Dark, damp, stone walls and floors. She was in a cell identical to the one where she'd seen the gypsy. Maybe close to the torture chamber. She bit back a swell of panic, which seemed to be her go-to emotion whenever Emory wasn't around.

Scooting across the floor so her back rested on a stone wall, Petra took stock. She felt every stone and pebble through the thin fabric of her panties, but that was the least of her pain. Her head, her arm, her belly—she ached everywhere. Pulling her knees to her chest, she rested her forehead on her knees and closed her eyes. Somewhere along the way she'd lost the blanket. Emory. She shivered violently in her filthy shirt, bra and panties.

If Emory couldn't die, why hadn't he rescued her? Where was he? What had happened to him?

When the cell door swung open with a screech, and Petra looked up, hopes raised.

Fritz stood inside the cell bearing a tray of food. *Breakfast in bed,* she thought. The sight and smell made her stomach roll. She wondered if Chambers had ordered the meal or if Fritz had brought it on his own. Because of his nervous twitching, she guessed the latter. Fritz kept his gaze focused on the ground; he wouldn't look at her. He set the tray on the ground and undid a satchel he had slung over his shoulder.

"Fritz, thank you. Tell Mary thank you too," Petra said, suspecting that Mary had made the tray. Petra braced herself against the wall so she could stand. "How did you know I was here?"

He reached into the satchel and shook out her dress. Wrinkled and dirt smudged, it was better than nudity. "Tis common knowledge." Fritz kept his gaze over her shoulder and made the sign of the cross over his heart with one hand and handed her the dress with the other.

With a sinking feeling, Petra took the dress. "Is *why* I'm here common knowledge?"

"They be saying you a witch, mistress." Fritz edged toward the door. "They've sent for the examiners."

*Examiners?* Petra pictured the man at the DMV who gave her the driver's test. She hugged the dress to her body.

Fritz nodded. "The ecclesiastic examiners. They'll be bringing a witch-pricker."

*Witch-pricker?*

"They'll test my blood?"

"If ye have blood." He looked at her then and

focused on her wound. The tightness in his shoulders seemed to ease when he saw that she definitely had blood.

She touched her head and felt the dried blood in her hair. "Who sent for the examiners? Chambers?" Fritz didn't deny it, so she continued. "But Lord Garret, he won't let me be pricked."

"My Lord Garret has eloped with Mistress Anne."

The previous night swam into focus.

"They're saying you be responsible for his enchantment." Fritz continued, looking somber. "His marriage so shortly after his father's death is highly irregular."

"The Earl is dead? How?" Petra rubbed her head.

"He died in the storm at Hampton Court."

Petra considered the news. She wanted to ask more about his death—was it an accident, did anyone suspect foul play—because she did. What if the law, whoever *that* was, suspected Garret, Rohan or Emory? And what if the law was Chambers until Garret returned? A chill crept through Petra. "Lord Garret falls in love and I'm to blame?"

"Yes, bewitched, miss, so it seems." He gave her an apologetic smile and turned away, locking the door behind him.

\*\*\*

One or maybe five hours later, a figure in a black robe and hood opened the cell door. For a wild moment, Petra had a flash of hope that the man, the same size and shape as Rohan, had come to rescue her. When the man roughly yanked her to her feet, hope died. He wasn't Rohan in disguise. He was Chambers' henchman.

She understood why Chambers was angry. She'd helped spoil the plot to prevent the distribution of the Bible. Maybe he held her responsible for the death of the Earl. Not that she'd pulled the actual pistol triggers or brandished swords, but she'd been there spitting fire and throwing smoke bombs.

Chambers no doubt would say Petra was on the other side of God. He believed in his cause. With the Earl gone and Garret sitting in his place, what would become of Chambers? Garret seemed to tolerated him, but with Anne whispering in his ear, how long would Chambers have a place in the manor?

The henchman drew her through the catacombs. Petra let loose a sigh of relief when they passed the torture chamber. Pushing open a heavy wooden door, the henchman strong-armed her across the courtyard and up a wooden stairway to an elevated platform.

A noisy, restless crowd milled around the square. Dimly, she recognized a few faces: Mary, red eyed and blotchy skinned, and Muffin Face and her perpetual scowl, Fritz staring straight ahead. Another hooded henchman stepped forward so that the two men flanked her.

Father Knightly slowly climbed the stairs, his face grim. He took center stage and addressed the crowd.

"The judgment of God has fallen on our fair village. Satan has come upon us in great wrath. God, for a wise yet unfathomable reason has left us vulnerable. God's will, in time will be manifest, but only if we repent and purge ourselves of all ungodliness. We must not fall prey to the lion who seeks to destroy us."

*Is he seriously comparing me to a lion?* Petra's mind reeled.

Father Knightly faced the crowd with outstretched arms. "We must guard ourselves against the wiles of Satan!" His voice boomed, face red, eyes wild. "We must watch, pray and humble ourselves before God!" Spit flew from his mouth.

*Good heaven*, Petra thought, *he really believes what*

*he's saying. He honestly thinks I'm an instrument of Satan.* Looking over the crowd, she searched for Emory and Rohan. They had to be nearby. They wouldn't let Chambers win. They would save her. *Now is the perfect time for a hero to show up.*

"True piety toward God is our only safeguard from the ills of life, our only hope for the life to come. Our village can only be saved through sacrifice and extermination!"

*Extermination?*

He pointed. "What say ye?"

Petra swallowed. "What charges do you have against me? Why do you think I'm a witch… or a lion?"

Father Knightly circled her, still pointing at her chest. "Do you have a supreme respect for the laws and authority of Gods?"

She shook her head, swiveling to watch his slow rotation of her. "Of course, I --"

"Are you disposed to resist His will and gratify your own?"

*This is a good time to lie,* she decided, although lying while defending her adherence to God's laws seemed wrong and counterproductive.

"Do you surrender yourself, body and soul, to my service to be employed in whatever way I may judge conducive to the progress of God's kingdom among men?"

"Absolutely not," Petra said, standing straighter. "I don't know who made you judge of this kingdom."

The crowd roared.

Father Knightly took a step closer, dropped his outstretched arm and pulled her cell phone from his robes. He pressed a button and Breaking Benjamin screamed. The jeers, the catcalls and the whistling went silent. Father Knightly spoke quietly, "Can you deny this is an instrument of the devil?"

Petra wanted to laugh. The two men with vice-like grips on her arms were proof that this wasn't funny, yet a nervous giggle bubbled inside of her. "It's an instrument from Apple."

The crowd jeered and cat-called, reminding Petra of the angry crowd in the old Frankenstein movie. They even waved the same pitchforks and clubs. Father Knightly raised his hands for silence. "She admits it!" he screamed over the crowd's roar. "She admits that Satan, who tempted Mother Eve with the first apple, has sent another."

"That's not what I meant!" Petra said as the henchmen tightened their grips and led her to the edge of the stage.

A pole stuck from the middle of a heap of

wood. As true realization hit, Petra kicked and
screamed. Twisting her legs, she aimed high. *Hit
'em where it hurts*, she coached herself, but she
couldn't seem to hurt them at all. Henchmen
secured her arms with leather straps.

"Burn her! Burn her!" the crowd chanted in
time.

Panic. Petra writhed as the henchmen lifted her
to the pole. *Where's Emory? This can't be happening*.
She took a breath, swallowed her fear, and opened
her lungs to yell again, but she could hardly hear
her own shrieks over the tumult of the crowd. They
tied her to the pole and a man in a dark hooded
robe lit the pyre with a flaming torch.

Smoke, heat, and crackling flames. Fire flickered
toward her dangling feet.

She heard another roar and another name, her
own. She saw Emory shoving through the crowd,
tossing aside grown men, women and small
children. Insults and fists didn't slow him. The
taunts shifted as he shouldered toward the growing
fire.

"The witch's lad!" someone shouted.

Another called, "Burn him too. Burn 'em all!"

The fire, many inches below her feet, suddenly
rushed toward her. Dimly, she realized that the fire
had burnt the pole supporting her. She crashed.

Something hit her head. Pain shot through her body and then, suddenly, nothing.

# Chapter Twenty-Six

*Dreams are:*
*Images, sounds, or emotions that pass through the*
*mind during sleep.*
*A response to neural processes.*
*Reflections of the subconscious.*
*Predictions.*
*Messages from gods, the deceased, or from the soul.*
*Not really understood.*
*—Petra's notes*

Her eyelids felt heavy, as if weighted and yet unsubstantial against the white, unnatural glare. She licked her lips; they were cracked, dry and tasted of blood and ash. Her head pounded. Someone touched her hand and whispered what sounded like an apology. "Petra Pooh?"

"Daddy?" Her eyes flickered open and his face swam into focus. Immediately, she began to cry hot tears that made her cheeks sting. She remembered being tied to a stake and falling into the flames. There had been horrific pain and then nothing. Had she died in the fire? *After this life we're gathered back to our people,* Emory had said. *Her dad, her mom, her people.* She tried to swallow and her throat felt raw.

"Where's Mom?" she asked.

"Oh, baby," her father said, and his voice cracked. He pressed her against him in a fierce hug, but when she winced in pain he gently let go and settled her against the pillows. She saw his tired, lined face, the gray sprinkling in his hair, and his blue, worried eyes. He was alive and so was she. Her mother was still dead.

Petra slipped a hand into his and looked beyond him to the sterile, white hospital walls. Outside, the distant lights of Santa Maria Boulevard sparkled in the twilight. Cars rushed up and down the parkway; street signals flashed yellow, green and red; a blinking airplane headed for the airport.

*I didn't die in 1610. Did I live in 1610?* She touched her head where it was tender, she felt the bump beneath her fingers, so she understood the pain, but that didn't explain everything.

Not at all.

She still wore Emory's ring. She closed her eyes and opened them again. Her father was still there. "I missed you," she whispered.

"I've missed you too. After losing your mother..." his voice broke. "I don't know how I would have survived losing you too."

She let her heavy eyes close, trying to make

sense of her new world. Her old world. This different world. A world without Emory.

*** 

A battery of tests and doctors filled the next day. During the poking, prodding, and bandage-changing Petra learned a few things: An earthquake during the Renaissance fair had sparked a fire; she'd been lost beneath the tangle of the fortuneteller's tent for a day. She'd been in the hospital, unconscious, for four.

Petra closed her eyes against all this information. She tried to process the hospital truth with her time in 1610. Intellectually, she lined up coming to the hospital with her arrival at the manor, her swim at the river with Emory with a bed bath given by a nurse, and her phone playing Breaking Benjamin. But while her mind told her one thing and her heart said something else entirely.

"It's common for a patient suffering severe physical and emotional distress to have delusional episodes," Doctor Graham, a mental health counselor told her. "It's your mind trying to escape the horror of your reality." The doctor, a petite blond in an oversized lab coat had purple spotted fingernail polish. She looked a lot like Mary.

"But wouldn't I go to some happy place?" Petra asked through cracked lips. It hurt to speak, her throat dry and scratchy, but she had to try. Worrying that she'd lost her mind was making her crazy.

"Not necessarily," Doctor Graham shifted in the chair beside her and settled a clipboard in her lap, "just as your nightly dreams aren't always happy. There's a great deal of research and controversy concerning the workings of our subconscious. Some say dreams are a random firing of neutrons and have no meaning. Spiritualists believe they are messages from God."

"It seemed so real," Petra muttered, staring past the doctor and out the window, beyond the bustling city to the green hills where the canyon began. "And there are so many things I didn't know, that I couldn't have imagined...like cockfights."

Doctor Graham smiled. "Our subconscious minds are incredibly powerful. We know many things that we've never given much thought, yet our brains have filed away the information." She patted Petra's hand. "You can't believe the nightmare. You can't argue with it, or challenge it. Your only option is to destroy it."

"Destroy it?" Petra thought of Emory, his face, his smile. How could she destroy someone she loved? Because she did love him, even if, or maybe even especially because, he was the work of her imagination.

Doctor Graham gave her a kind and sympathetic look. "It's not real, so it can't be destroyed literally. The only way to defuse its power is to shine your light of reason upon it. There's no other option. You can't believe the lie, but you might find it helpful to write it down. It will help you clarify your feelings. Journaling about such a traumatic experience will let you explore, process and release your emotions."

*Now would be a good time to mention the ring.* But Petra remained silent. She wasn't ready to try and prove or disprove Emory.

Giggles and voices from down the hall caught Petra's attention. She turned to watch Robyn, Kyle and a giant pink and purple pony approaching. The trio stood hesitantly outside the door.

"Your friends are eager to see you. They've been by many times," the doctor said, gathering her things and rising to her feet. "You're lucky that you have so many people who love you. If you're interested in journaling, I'll get you a pad of paper and a pen."

"Thank you," Petra lisped, wetting her lips and tasting ash. "I'd like that."

Doctor Graham patted Petra's hand and beckoned for the trio to come in. Robyn, Kyle and the pony trooped through the door. Behind the pony, Zoe. Petra's heart leapt and she suddenly realized how grateful she was to see her sister. She desperately needed to apologize.

Kyle and Robyn began talking at the same time. They looked at each other and laughed. *They're nervous,* Petra thought. She imagined an electrical current running between them. They talked too fast and laughed too much; she barely understood them.

Pushing herself up on the bed, Petra saw her reflection in the window. With her singed hair, chapped, red skin, and the swollen lips, she looked like someone else. She was ugly. She was ugly and she didn't care.

Zoe plopped the pony at the foot of the hospital bed. "This is supposed to be your stallion, and Kyle's supposedly your knight in shining armor."

Robyn rolled her eyes and pushed Zoe into the chair where moments earlier Doctor Graham had sat. "Zoe! You're totally ruining it!"

Zoe rolled her eyes. "As if she cares about prom. Look at her! She can barely sit, let alone dance!"

Petra laughed and it sounded wheezy and it hurt, but she couldn't help it.

Kyle stepped in front of Zoe, and cleared his throat. He shifted from foot to foot, and a pink stain flushed his cheeks. He began.

*"When the moon first shines pale in evening's light,*
*At the senior prom we'll discover delight --"*

"Did you write that?" Petra interrupted.

"Wait, there's more," Robyn said, waving her hands and shushing her.

Kyle looked uncomfortable but started again.
*"Your beauty --"*

"Please stop!" Petra held up her hand. Robyn pinched her lips closed and looked cross. Petra smiled and said, "Thanks, Robyn, Kyle, that was great. You guys are great, but I really, really need to speak to Zoe."

"Zoe?" Robyn and Kyle asked simultaneously.

Petra smiled at Kyle and then with a hand that felt like it weighed a hundred pounds she moved Kyle so that she could see Zoe. "Zoe, I'm so incredibly sorry I lost you at the fair. I worried and worried. I'm so glad you are safe." She took a deep breath. "And you're right. I don't want to go to prom." She turned to Kyle. "I'm sorry. I don't want to go. I don't think I could even if I wanted to. Which I don't."

Zoe beamed and shot Robyn and Kyle I-told-you-so looks.

Petra studied Robyn and Kyle. They looked so much like Garret and Anne, she decided that as soon as possible she'd learn about their ancestry to see if they were distantly related. Oh, after she found out if Anne and Garret Falstaff had even existed anywhere other than in her imagination.

A flash of pain and loss zipped through her that had nothing to do her injuries. She settled against her pillows. "I think that you two should go to the prom together," Petra said.

Robyn's mouth dropped open, and Kyle flushed red and looked out the window.

"But I'm going with Zack Pepper!" Robyn said.

Petra watched her friend, her tele-buddy. They'd always prided themselves on being able to read each other's thoughts. How had she been so clueless? *How could anyone know what someone else thinks?*

Petra realized she'd probably been projecting what she wanted Robyn to think, which, when she thought about it, really wasn't very nice because it made Robyn less of her own person. "Do you want to go with Zack?" Petra asked, even though she was pretty sure she knew the answer.

Robyn looked at her shoes.

"You guys should be together," Petra said, her gaze going from Robyn to Kyle.

"What?" Kyle said at the same time Robyn said, "You don't mean that!"

Laurel pushed through the door, carrying an enormous basket of fruit. She also had Trader Joe's grocery bags tucked under each arm, most likely filled with whole grain crackers, cartons of hummus, and loaves of gluten-free bread. Petra knew Laurel would turn up her pointy nose at hospital food. Petra smiled watching her tiny stepmother wrangle the groceries. *Everyone shows love in their own way.*

"You should help her," Petra said to Kyle.

"Robyn doesn't need my help." Kyle looked unhappy.

"Not Robyn." Petra shook her head. "Help Laurel. With the groceries."

Laurel sighed a thank you as Kyle took the basket and set it on the wide window ledge. Laurel settled the Trader Joe's bags on the counter. "Now, you probably won't need all of this since hopefully." She crossed her fingers, "Your dad will get his way and have you out of here tomorrow, but you never know."

Laurel rummaged through a bag and pulled out a bottle of Vitamin E. "To facilitate healing," she said, holding it up. Then she returned to her bags, still talking. "I talked to the nurse about what they've been feeding you through that IV, and it's a wonder you're still alive. And do you know what they were going to give you tonight? Clear chicken broth! Nothing but flavored salt water!" The thought of all that sodium made her shudder.

Petra caught Kyle and Robyn's glances and smiled. "You guys should go before she tries to tofu you."

"Are you sure?" Kyle asked, and Petra knew the question was loaded.

"Yeah."

Robyn turned to Kyle. "Is she breaking up with you?"

"I'm right here, guys," Petra said.

"I think so," Kyle said, not looking hurt but confused.

"Why are you doing this? I don't think you're thinking straight," Robyn said, turning to her and taking her hand.

"I'm still me. I'm still your best friend. Only now I'm Kyle's friend, too." She swallowed. "You know, I don't think I was before and I should have been."

Kyle looked at Robyn and shrugged. He turned to Petra. "I always thought of you as my friend."

He flushed. "And more, of course."

"I just want the friend part, now," Petra said. "I can't handle any more. I'm sorry if that hurts you…but I don't think it does."

Kyle bit his lip, and Robyn put her hand on his arm.

Laurel, oblivious as usual, held up a carton. "I bought this Greek yogurt. It'll help your GI tract, which is really important because after so many days in bed you must be constipated."

"Seriously," Petra told her friends. "You should go. This might get ugly."

"Oh, it's already ugly," Zoe said, touching Petra's foot that had escaped the bed sheet.

Petra hadn't noticed that her feet were wrapped in bandages. One black and charred-looking toenail had torn through. She stared at the foot as if it belonged to someone else. An alien perhaps.

"Your feet are the worst." Laurel took a seat on a chair beside Petra's bed.

"No dancing." Zoe gave Robyn and Kyle now-get-out-of- here-looks.

"Well, I guess we'll go then," Kyle said, shuffling.

"See you soon," Robyn said, stooping to kiss Petra.

Laurel stopped her, shaking her head.

"Infection," she warned.

Robyn blew a kiss. Kyle picked up Petra's hand and kissed the tip of her pinky finger. She waited for the rush she felt with Emory's touch but felt nothing other than overwhelming relief when they walked out. In the hall, Robyn reached out and took Kyle's hand.

Petra closed her eyes and lay against the pillows, thinking about what she'd do when she got home, when she was well. She opened her eyes and saw her little sister watching her intently. "I want to know everything that happened to you, Zoe. How did you get home from the fair? What was the fire like? How did it start?" Petra had heard the story from doctors, nurses and her parents, but she wanted to hear her sister's version.

Zoe leaned forward, her elbows propped on her knees. "Well, the whole ground shook and the animals went absolutely crazy. People were screaming and running around. The horses were screaming too. Chickens and goats from the petting zoo escaped. There was this pig – E-nor-mous – just running loose, well, almost all the animals were loose. And the Horse Guy, remember the Horse Guy?"

Emory, images of him floated through her. *A figment of my imagination,* she thought, remembering Doctor Graham. *A random firing of neutrons, whatever that means.*

"He saved me. He took me home."

"Wait, what?"

"Yeah. They didn't want to let him through the guard gate, so we just rode around and JUMPED THE FENCE!"

"You jumped the fence? The fence to Bear Ranch?" Eight feet high, wrought iron, topped with spikes and monitored by security cameras.

"On his horse!" Zoe bounced on her chair. "Remember his horse!"

"Zoe, you know better than to go with a stranger," Petra said, sounding like Laurel and not caring.

Zoe put her hands on her hips. "What was I supposed to do? The funnel cake stand tipped over. The glass blowers oven literally exploded. Everything was on fire. *And no one could find you.*"

Petra looked away, fighting back a wave of guilt. The guilt for leaving Zoe alone on a stump while she waited for Kyle made her sick.

Laurel pushed to the bed waving a glass of a green liquid. "How are you feeling?"

Petra shook her head, blinking back hot tears. "Zoe, I'm so, so, so sorry I lost you that day."

"You already said that." Zoe looked confused.

After an awkward moment she shrugged. "It's okay."

"It's not okay," Petra said, trying to stop her tears. "It'll never happen again. I promise."

"If you hadn't gotten lost, I wouldn't have gotten to jump the fence."

*And I wouldn't have met Emory.* Sobs welled in Petra's chest.

# Chapter Twenty-Seven

*Once upon a time and happily ever after are stock
phrases common in fairy tales, but what is the definition
of "time" and "ever after?" How does time work? Is it
linear, or does it fold and overlap like a Chinese fan?
How can you have an after if the ever doesn't exist?*
*—Petra's notes*

Petra spent the next two weeks in bed looking at
the wallpaper and reading books from the library
and researching on her laptop. Frosty and Zoe kept
her company. Frosty wanted to walk. Zoe wanted
to go to the stables. Petra could do neither.

She made lists of books for Laurel to pick up,
anything on time travel and anything on the
England's 17th century. Laurel happily obliged, and
books grew like small teetering towers on Petra's
bed.

One morning Petra's dad stuck his head in her
room to deliver a lecture on a pursuit in history or
literature versus the practicality of a business
degree. "In today's world, a woman needs to be
able to stand on her own financial feet. An intellect
like yours shouldn't be wasted on yesterdays'
mistakes and—"

"I'm not picking out a career, Dad," she said, not looking at him, her nose buried between the cover of H.G. Wells' *The Time Machine.* Beside her, her laptop had the flickering image of King James.

"Well then, what are you doing?" he asked, hanging in the doorway and waving at the books.

"I'm just..." She didn't know how to explain it. "Other kids play video games. Laurel reads romances. Zoe rides horses. This is how I waste time. You should be happy I'm not reading gossip magazines."

Her dad didn't look happy or convinced, but Petra had at least another week before she could go back to school, so he said goodbye, shrugged and walked away with his shoulders set, as if he bore the world's financial weight.

Petra put down her book and pulled her laptop closer. There were so many things that she hadn't known; how had she imagined them? Hampton Court was a real place, a huge place. And hell hounds: there were innumerable accounts of hell hounds, including the English legend of Black Shuck. The chained oak, gypsy hunts, ecclesiastical examiners, witch prickers. They had all once existed beyond her imagination. She hadn't known about a controversy surrounding the publication of the King James Bible, so how had she become involved?

*At a conference held in 1604 in Hampton Court Palace, a few miles from London, King James I appointed a committee to make a new translation of the Bible. The result, published in 1611, drew heavily on the works of Tyndale and Coverdale, martyrs who had dedicated and sacrificed their lives to bring the word of God to mankind. It is impossible to overestimate its beauty, power and influence. As Galileo's work opened the door allowing science to freely discover God's universe, so did The King James Bible set mankind free to discover God and man's place in His universe. Science and the Bible coexisted in relative comfort alongside each other for the next 200 years.*

Two hundred years. She'd read in one of her books that the original translation of "once upon a time" was two hundred years. Curious, she typed 'once upon a time' on her computer's search.

*"Once upon a time" is a stock phrase that has been used in some form since at least 1380 (according to the Oxford English Dictionary) in storytelling in the English language, and seems to have become a widely accepted convention for opening oral narratives by around 1600.*

*The phrase also is frequently used in oral storytelling such as retellings of myths, fables, and folklore. These stories often end with "... and they all lived happily ever after", or, originally, "happily until their deaths".*

But what if no one dies? Can there be a happily ever after? Petra lay back against her pillows, suddenly tired of research, tired even of the wallpaper.

Zoe popped her head in. "Can you take me to the stables?"

Petra opened one eye. Zoe had on her riding boots and breeches. She carried a helmet under one arm and a whip in her hand. Petra smiled, wondering if Zoe would turn the whip on her if she said no. "Why aren't you in school?" she asked.

Zoe rolled her eyes. "It's Saturday, dummy."

"Hmm." She'd lost all sense of time since she'd been home. The days and nights melded into each other, and she realized with a start that today must be the prom. She wondered if Robyn was at that moment having her nails done, or her hair, or her make-up. She wondered in a detached other-worldly way where her friends had bought their dresses, where they were going to dinner, who'd they'd hired to take their pictures. It seemed amazing that just a few weeks earlier it'd all seemed so important to her. The clothes, the hair, who was seen with whom. She'd been a part of it. She'd *lived* in the walking, talking fashion drama.

Soon she'd have to go back to school and make

up all the work she'd missed. She didn't care. She supposed she'd have to go to summer school and maybe take classes at the junior college. She'd overheard her parents arguing over hiring a tutor, yet she still didn't care. She'd get into a good university eventually. If that was something she still  wanted.

It wasn't that she didn't know what, or who, she wanted. She just didn't know how to get him.

"Stables?" Zoe flicked the whip in her direction.

Petra bit her lip. "You know I can't risk infection."

Zoe sighed. "You didn't use to be all obey-the-rules-or-hell-breaks-loose."

Bored to distraction and tempted, Petra sat up and moved the laptop off her bed. Zoe broke into a happy jig when Petra swung her legs from between the bed sheets. Frosty, who'd been lying nearby, jumped up, as if something momentous was about to happen and he didn't want to get left behind.

Zoe stopped dancing and frowned. "I'll wait for you to shower."

Petra touched her frizzled hair. "Shower?"

"You know, stand under a stream of water so that you don't smell like poop."

"I don't smell like poop!"

Zoe raised her eyebrows. Frosty sat and cocked

his head, as if he agreed with Zoe.

"Fine." Petra limped toward the bathroom. Frosty followed, nails clicking on the tile. "Where's Laurel and Hardy?" Petra asked over her shoulder.

"They've gone to the car show, so we've got loads of time."

*Loads of time. Two hundred years. Once upon a time. There's no such thing as happily ever after.* Petra locked the bathroom door and turned on the shower full blast.

A few minutes later she found Zoe watching TV in the family room. Zoe clicked off the TV and looked her up and down. "Is that what you're going to wear?"

Petra looked at her black toenails sticking out of her flip flops, the jeans that hung on her hip bones like a saggy gray flag below her Blue Man Group t-shirt. "What?"

"At least let me do your hair." Zoe grabbed a hairbrush and elastic from off the table as if she'd been expecting to do Petra's hair.

"Zoe, why am I getting dressed up to watch you ride horses?"

"It's not like you're getting an up-do. I'm just combing it. For once." Zoe twisted an elastic band around Petra's hair.

Looking in the glass doors at her scrubbed clean

face and pulled-back hair, Petra decided she looked better than she had since the accident. Frosty even wagged his tail at her.

"You'll do," Zoe said, gathering her whip and helmet.

***

"This is as far as I go," Petra said, staring at the stone-and-timber building across the muddy parking lot.

"Come on," Zoe whined, her hand on the door handle. She gave the stables a mournful look before turning her large green eyes to Petra. "You've come this far. You *showered.*"

Petra laughed. "I know. It's all remarkable and amazing, but I can't ride, and watching someone else ride is boring. Besides, the stable is a pretty infectious place." Leaning over Zoe, she pushed open the passenger door. "You have your phone. Just call when you're done."

Zoe leaned her head against the seat and wailed. "You promised you'd never leave me again!"

Stunned, Petra said, "I'm not leaving you alone. Pete, Rose and probably half a dozen of your friends, human and equine, are just through that gate."

"Come and make sure," Zoe wheedled.

"You know I can't."

"What if someone abducts me?"

"It's ten yards! But if by some random chance someone tries to carry you away, scream and I'll come to your rescue."

"Triple-dog-dare promise." Zoe's mouth was a grim straight line. "Say it."

Petra pushed Zoe's shoulders. "Get out of the car."

Zoe said, "Repeat after me. I, Petra --"

"Fine. I promise that if anything happens to you I have to do triple dog dare."

Zoe beamed. "Then you have to stay. You can't hear me scream from home."

Petra leaned against the seat. At least looking at the canyon was different from looking at wallpaper. "I'll stay within screaming distance."

"Here?"

Petra shook her head and pointed to the trail on the other side of Bear Ranch's gates. A small bench sat beside a water fountain. It looked peaceful and germ-free. Petra picked up her journal and a pen. "I'll be over there."

Zoe looked like she wanted to argue, but suddenly her expression lightened, as if a light went off in her head. "'kay, bye." Zoe slammed out the door and bounced away.

Petra climbed from the car. From the other side of the stable wall she heard Zoe greeting friends, human and animal. Clutching her notebook to her side, Petra put her pen in her pocket and hobbled the short distance to the gate.

Fitz the guard, who looked suspiciously like Fritz from 1610, waved and buzzed open the gate. Smiling, she remembered the time Kyle had tried to break through the gates. He'd been captured on camera climbing the fence and had to spend an hour waiting in the guard house for her to finish her swim meet and rescue him.

Petra took the sidewalk to the trailhead and then sat down on the bench. Flipping open her notebook, she wrote down the Fritz/Fitz similarity. She looked over her weeks of writing. Emory, Rohan, Anne, Robyn, and Kyle. In her head, it was beginning to make some sense, but that didn't make her happy.

Next on her agenda was to do genealogical research on Garret, Earl of Dorrington and Kyle to see if they correlated at all. A long shot, she knew, but she was curious. As a wedding present, a friend of Laurel's had done family history search on Petra's father to see if Laurel's family lines had ever "entwined," her word. Petra had thought it a lame word and an even lamer gift, but now, she wanted to know.

A scream tore the air. Petra bolted up from her bench, heart thumping. Open-mouthed, she watched Emory and Zoe on a giant stallion sail through the air and clear the gate. *Horse Guy*, the rational part of her brain told her, but her heart was telling her another story, an irrational, emotionally charged story of another time and place.

The stallion and his riders landed on the grass with a rumble of hooves. Zoe laughed while Fitz catapulted from the guard gate, waving his arms and yelling threats laced with obscenities at Emory and Zoe.

Horse Guy swung to the ground and slapped the horse's flanks. The animal took off, carrying Zoe away. Petra stared as Emory/Horse Guy walked toward her.

Logic caught up with her. "Zoe! No!" Petra called after her sister, limping after the horse thundering down the trail. "No! You can't!" She hobbled for a few yards and then stood, horrified, as Zoe and the horse disappeared around a corner. "Fitz, stop her!"

The guard gave Emory a scowl, then took off after Zoe, running, his walkie-talkie pressed against his lips.

Arms from behind wrapped around Petra's waist; lips touched her neck and the familiar zing tingled up her spine. She stiffened in the embrace. Turning, ready to attack, she stopped when he caught her chin. Tipping her head back, he softly lowered his lips to hers and gave her a gentle kiss. All Petra's fight drained away. *Once upon a time, happily ever after, happily until death.* Her head and emotions sang with questions.

"I've been waiting two hundred years to do that," he said.

Two hundred years. No, four hundred. She didn't say it out loud, because it sounded crazy, but he read her expression.

"Ah, I see you've forgotten Sleepy Hollow." He laughed softly, cradling her face in his hands. "Tis of no matter. This, perhaps, will remind you."

And he kissed her again.

# Excerpt: Beyond the Sleepy Hollow

Petra Baron couldn't sleep.

The Santa Ana winds whistled through the canyon, spat dust and tossed the branches of trees. The wind seemed to be laughing at her. Not a hahaha aren't we clever laughter, nor a teehee jokes on you giggle, but a cruel, moaning laughter that whistled through the stable, toyed at the window jambs and rattled the doors.

Petra fluffed her pillow, and adjusted it so that she could see through the French doors without lifting her head. Out of the suburbs, away from streetlights, cars and the blue glare of neighboring TVs, the moon and stars carried more light. The late autumn moon, as big and as round as the pumpkins in the field, shone through the window and cast the room in a silver glow. Sleeping at the Jenson's farm didn't frighten her, even though she could see the golden eyes of the mountain lion pacing at the fringe of the property, looking for a hole in the fence and access to the animals safely tucked in the barn.

Since her return from England, she'd been training at the rifle range. She could shoot (gun shooting lingo) pistols as well as rifles. Determined to never again feel at any one's mercy, she'd also enrolled in a martial arts program at the gym. Not that she'd try to Ninja kick a mountain lion, but should a horse scream or a sheep bleat she planned on shouldering the shotgun and scaring away the big cat.

But little cats were a different story.

Petra shifted and tried to pull the quilt around her shoulders, but Magpie wouldn't budge. Large, heavy, a glob of fur and drool, Magpie was a bed-hog. Magpie's counterpart, Rudy, preferred to sleep under the slipper chair. As was the case with so many couples, Magpie was emotionally needy and Rudy was emotionally distant. Petra had tried locking the cats out of the bedroom. After all, they had a five thousand square foot hacienda at their disposal. Six unoccupied bedrooms, a den, a living room, a billiard room—they had free range. Petra only asked for one room. In fact, she'd have settle for one bed, but Magpie, as noisy as her name implied, refused to be shut out. And it didn't really make sense to allow Magpie to share her space and not Rudy. Who, by the way, snored. A malady typical of Persians.

Persians or mountain lions, which cat species did she prefer? Given a choice, she'd choose to be at home in her own bed, Frosty, her standard poodle asleep, sans snoring, at the foot of her bed. But the house-sitting gig at the Jensen's paid well. She needed all the money she could lay her hands on if she wanted to attend Hudson River Academy, a small liberal arts college where Dr. Finch, the world's leading professor of Elizabethan England. Her dad would pony up for a state university, but he wasn't interested in paying for 'liberal farts.' Petra began to mentally recalculate her finances and because money bored her she fell asleep listening to the wind's laughter and Rudy's snore.

***

*The wind whispers the prayers*
*Of all who live there*
*And carries them to heaven.*
*And the rain beats a time,*
*For those caught in rhyme,*
*For any who've lost life's reason.*

Petra bolted up, and Magpie flew off the bed with a meow, her cry barely audible above the music. Pushing hair out of her eyes, Petra tried to wake from the deafening dream. She swung her legs over the side of the bed, and felt the cold tile floor beneath her feet. Music still played. Electric guitars. A keyboard. Drums. Seventies sound.

She oriented herself. *Who's here? The Jensons? No, they had just posted pictures of the Vatican online less than two hours ago. Garret? He attended UCSB. A three hour drive. It must be Garret,* she thought.

She looked out the window for a car in the driveway. No car. He would have put it in the garage. He'd have the remote. The wind had quieted, and the trees had stopped dancing. Steam from the horse's warm breath rose from the stable. On the side of the hill, on the far side of the fence, gold eyes watched her window. The mountain lion, threatening, but incapable of manning sound systems.

She took a deep calming breath. It had to be Garret. She waited for the music to die.

*If there are stories in your stream,*
*Don't let them stop you mid- dream,*
*They're just pebbles for the tossing.*
*They're just mountains for the climbing.*

She caught sight of herself in the mirror. Wild hair, smeared mascara, long arms and legs poking out of her Domo-Kun pajamas. She considered slipping into her clothes, but she didn't want to fumble in the dark, making noise, and maybe alerting the intruder. If there was an intruder. No, it had to be Garret, returning home, unexpectedly for the weekend. Why would anyone else break into a house and turn on a stereo? Who would do that?

Petra shuffled to the door, and plucked the shotgun off the wall. She slipped a cartridge in the barrel and cocked the gun, just in case it was a Seventies-sounds-loving-lunatic and not Garret.

Rudy squalled when she stepped on him. *So much for not alerting the intruder,* she thought as she righted herself and brought the rifle to ready position. Pushing through the door, Petra crept through the dark house until she found the source of the noise.

> *Your head is singing with the whispering,*
> *So many voices, so many choices,*
> *Which roads to take.*

The stereo, an old fashioned tape player, six feet tall, flashing lights and thrumming bass, boomed in the billiards room. Petra stared at it and then shouted above the music, "Garret?" When no one answered, she called, "Who's there?"

Only the music replied. Magpie curled around her ankles. Her pajama topp slipped off her shoulder as she slowly circled the room, gun raised. Outside, beyond the fence, the mountain lion blinked at her.

Petra turned on the light just as the music ended. The tape sputtered at the end and clicked. She walked to the elaborate sound system, a relic of some distant time, and stared at it. Tiny flashing lights, a series of buttons and switches, it looked as complicated as an airplane cockpit. She didn't even know how it worked. *Maybe* she'd walked in her sleep, but turning on the stereo?

The tape clicked out its questions, spinning round and round. Click. Click. Click. She found a switch, flipped it, and the system died. In the sudden quiet, she heard her heart's rapid beats and her accelerated breath.

"Not exactly a lullaby," she said to Magpie, her voice nearly as loud as her thrumming blood.

"Garret?" she called out again. Maybe he was in the shower, or in the garage, or asleep.

She shouldered the gun again. Every bathroom and bed empty. The garage dark, and the cars vacant. She checked the windows and doors of each room. Securely locked. All of them. She flung open closet doors, and used her shotgun to poke through the wardrobes. The alarm system in the front hall blinked its tiny red light. No one had broken in, at least, no one who didn't know their way around the security system.

Petra sat down on the sofa in the living room and laid the gun across her lap. Magpie jumped up beside her, while Rudy watched from underneath the grand piano. She absently stroked the cat and felt a smidge less panicked. What should she do? Her cell didn't get reception in the canyon, so she padded to the phone in the office and picked up the line.

Nothing. She looked at the receiver. The wind *could* have knocked down the line. *Maybe* she'd walked in her sleep and turned on the stereo. Since her return from Elizabethan England five months ago, she'd realized that life doesn't always make sense. Sometimes random, inexplicable, even crazy things happened. And crazy things don't have to make sense. Maybe the craziness makes sense to someone else, because everyone has a skewed sense of reason, and as mortals, mere humans, we can't know everything. Sometimes, really truly, only heaven knows. Or hell.

The obvious answer would be to go home, crawl into her own bed, listen to her father's snores rumbling the house. His snores were so much more reassuring than Rudy's. But, looking out the window, she could see the mountain lion pacing. She couldn't leave the animals. Shoot the mountain lion and then go home, a voice whispered in her head.

Petra shivered and pulled the quilt lying on the back of the sofa around her shoulders. Sleep had eluded her earlier and now it was nothing more than a happy idea, as realistic or likely as chasing the mountain lion and making it her playmate. The grandfather clock in the hall boomed four times. Four a.m., California time, seven a.m. in New York. Maybe her Aunt Dee was awake and online. Petra plucked her laptop off the coffee table and turned it on. She'd much rather talk to Aunt Dee than try and shoot a mountain lion.

She kept the gun on her lap and positioned the laptop on her knees. Her panic, so overwhelming just minutes ago, had nearly subsided by the time the computer powered on. Aunt Dee's profile picture flashed on the screen. Seeing her aunt, her mom's sister, always hurt a little, because the sisters with their siren red hair and clear blue eyes, looked so much alike, despite the fifteen year age difference. Petra realized with a jolt that Aunt Dee was the same age her mother had been when she'd died. The thought depressed Petra because Dee was so young, only thirty-two, beautiful and full of life.

A screen popped up. *"Hey, sweetie, why're you up?"*

It took Petra a moment to rearrange her thoughts. She'd learned to keep her time traveling a secret from everyone but Emory, of course, because since her release from the hospital, she'd done her time with Dr. Harmon and she didn't want to revisit crazy town.

*"Couldn't sleep,"* she typed.

*"Poor Petra. Are you still coming to my opening?"*

Petra nodded, although she knew her aunt couldn't see her. *"Wouldn't miss it."*

*"You'll be working up a sweat."*

Petra looked at the muscles in her arms she'd developed while playing Ninja. *"How much sweat does it take to serve cheese and wine?"*

*"You'll be hanging paintings."*

*"That's Vince's job,"* Petra said. When her aunt didn't reply right away, Petra swallowed a small lump of fear for long suffering Vince. He'd been trying to wheedle Dee to the alter almost all of Petra's life. When she was little, Petra had hoped to be her aunt's flower girl. Now she wanted to be her aunt's bridesmaid. She did *not* want to be a matron of honor when her aunt finally married long

suffering Vince.

"Wine and cheese?" The deep voice, silky and smooth, lilted, like a question or an offering.

The laptop clattered to the floor as Petra scrambled for the gun and pointed it at the intruder. Black hair, blue eyes, red lips, other than an athletic build, he looked nothing like beach blond Garret.

He sauntered to the counter and picked up a bottle of wine. "After all, this long last reunion deserves a celebration."

Petra jumped to her feet, stepping on first the laptop and then a cat. She cocked the gun and pointed at the guy's chest. *Always aim for the heart, her instructor had said.*

"Who are you?" she wanted to sound intimidating, but Petra's voice came out barely louder than a whisper.

"Sweetling, have you forgotten?" His eyes swept over her and goose-pimples rose on her bare arms and legs. *Sweetling?* So close to her aunt's endearment, and yet, somehow he'd corrupted it by just adding the letter L. "I much prefer twenty-first century fashion to the maid get up you used to wear."

Petra looked down at her pajamas. Dumo had his teeth bared in an I-want-to-eat-you expression, but no one took him seriously. Petra felt a strange kinship with Dumo -- she had gun, her teeth bared, but this guy didn't look threatened. At all. With his eyebrows lifted and a smile flirting on his lips, he looked *amused*. She tightened her grip on the gun as he stepped closer. He had her pinned between the sofa, the laptop and the coffee-table. She bit her lip and put her finger on the trigger.

He laughed, watching. "You know that won't work on me."

"Don't come any closer," Petra said, finding her voice.

"We were close at one time," he murmured. His black jeans matched the color of his hair; his shirt, blue but nearly black, matched his eyes. He wore boots -- could she outrun him outside, barefoot?

He laughed louder and it sounded familiar. She recognized the laugh from another time and place. "You've forgotten." He cocked his head at her and looked hurt. "How could you?"

She opened her mouth and wondered if they'd met in Sleepy Hollow. Her memory had been blocked, although Emory assured her she'd been there. He'd told her bits and pieces, but he'd also told her it was something he wished he could forget. She kept her gaze on her uninvited guest and a name came to her memory. Something that sounded like Cain… Dane.

He leaned forward, his eyes focused on her lips. "We were lovers."

"No," Petra breathed, inching around the sofa and coffee table, no longer caring about fallen cats or laptops. She would have remembered *that*. Her first time, that wouldn't be so easily forgotten. "You're lying," she said, but she didn't sound convincing, even to herself. She had known this person; something told her that she'd known him well. She shivered.

He smiled and looked wicked. "You know angels can't lie."

She choked and then spat out, "You're not an angel." This time her voice carried more certainty.

"Who says?" Two wine goblets appeared on the counter and he filled them with golden liquid. "Champaign?"

Petra stared at the goblets and managed to shake her head.

He studied her. "No?" He sipped from his goblet. "Pity. It's sad to drink alone and I've missed you, these past two hundred years."

"Once upon a time," she said, quietly, remembering that the original translation of 'once upon a time' was two hundred years.

"It was not unlike a fairy tale," he told her,

setting down his goblet. A heartbeat later, he stood beside her, placed his hand on her cheek, and the hacienda disappeared. They stood in a meadow of buttercups and dandelions. Puffy clouds filled the sky. Birds sang. He kissed her and the world went dark.

# A Note from the Author

Thank you for reading Beyond the Fortuneteller's Tent.

If you enjoyed it, I would appreciate it if you'd help other readers enjoy it too.

**Recommend the book**. Please help other readers find this book by recommending it to friends, readers' groups, and discussion boards.

**Review the book**. Please tell other readers why you liked this book by reviewing it on any of the ebook retailers, Goodreads or your blog.

If you write a review on the Amazon book page, please notify me at <u>kristyswords@yahoo.com</u> and I will send you a copy of one of my other books as a gift. Thank you!

# Other Books by Kristy Tate

The Highwayman Incident: Celia and Jason must tread carefully, as what happens in the past can reverberate through the ages. Their lives, hearts and futures are caught in time's slippery hands. (Witching Well, book 1)

Ghost of a Second Chance: With the help of her grandmother's ghost, Laine Collins unravels the mystery of her grandparents' marriage and is forced to face a question of the heart—Can love live even after it has died? (Rose Arbor, book 1)

The Rhyme's Library: Blair Rhyme discovers crazy Aunt Charlotte's dead body amongst the boxes of want-nots and what-evers in the library's basement. Unfortunately, when she returns to the library with the police Charlotte is gone. Desperate to prove that she doesn't share her aunt's mental illness and that Charlotte really has been murdered, Blair tangles with a former lover, a disturbingly handsome stranger and a wacky cast of Rose Arbor characters. (Rose Arbor, book 2)

Losing Penny: A cooking show diva in hiding. A literature professor writing genre fiction. An admirer who wants more than the tasty morsels a cooking hostess is willing to share. A dangerous recipe for romance in the town of Rose Arbor. (Rose Arbor, book 3)

Stuck With You: Andie, real estate photographer, wanna-be philanthropist and blogger, is saving her pennies and dimes until she can afford to travel and shine a bright light on the world's poor and needy. Whit, an investment banker and adventure travel magazine writer, wants nothing more than to escape his mother's match-making schemes. So how do the end up stuck together?

Beyond the Fortuneteller's Tent: When Petra Baron goes into the fortuneteller's tent at a Renaissance fair, she expects to leave with a date to prom. Instead, she walks out into Elizabethan England, where she meets gypsies, a demon dog and a kindred spirit in Emory Ravenswood. Can Petra and Emory have a future while trapped in the past? Or is anything possible Beyond the Fortuneteller's Tent? (Beyond, book 1)

Beyond the Sleepy Hollow: With a collection of the writings of Washington Irving in her hand and a prayer that the same nine-pin playing ghosts that gave carried away Rip Van Winkle will give her drink of their ale, Petra Baron heads into another time defying adventure Beyond the Hollow. This is the second book in the Beyond series, where Petra is reminded that love is always timeless.

Hailey's Comments: A sassy but shy advice columnist flees to a sparsely populated island in the Puget Sound seeking peace and refuge, but instead finds mystery and romance.

A Light in the Christmas Café: In LA, Deirdre's perfectly constructed life made sense—a lucrative, albeit boring, career and an adoring boyfriend. But when her beloved grandmother tumbles down the stairs, Deirdre returns to Lake Vista and picks up the apron strings at Rosie's café. She believes her old, safe life can still be salvaged. Until she sees a mysterious light in the café's attic. A light that like her, doesn't belong. Or does it?

Stealing Mercy: The night before the Great Seattle Fire of 1889, flames spark between Mercy Faye and Trent Michaels, leaving the life they know and the city they love in ashes.

Rescuing Rita: When Christian rescues the kidnapped Rita and witnesses a triple murder, he realizes that it's a lot more interesting to hold a feisty actress than a hand of cards. But is she worth joining the cast until the ultimate final curtain? (Seattle Fire, book 2)

75004548R00215

Made in the USA
San Bernardino, CA
24 April 2018